GANG

Graham Johnson is an investigative reporter and crime writer.
This is his first novel.

Also by Graham Johnson:

Powder Wars
Football and Gangsters
Druglord
The Devil
Darkness Descending

GANG WAR

GRAHAM JOHNSON

MAINSTREAM
PUBLISHING

EDINBURGH AND LONDON

This edition, 2011

Copyright © Graham Johnson, 2010
All rights reserved
The moral right of the author has been asserted

First published (under the title *Soljas*) in Great Britain in 2010 by
MAINSTREAM PUBLISHING COMPANY
(EDINBURGH) LTD
7 Albany Street
Edinburgh EH1 3UG

ISBN 9781845966997

No part of this book may be reproduced or transmitted
in any form or by any other means without permission
in writing from the publisher, except by a reviewer
who wishes to quote brief passages in connection
with a review written for insertion in
a magazine, newspaper or broadcast

This book is a work of fiction. It is inspired by real events but all
characters are fictitious and any resemblance to actual persons is
entirely coincidental. Names of real well-known people appear in
the story, but the events surrounding those individuals and quotes
given are entirely the work of the author's imagination

A catalogue record for this book is available
from the British Library

Typeset in Downcome and Sabon

Printed in Great Britain by
CPI Cox & Wyman, Reading RG1 8EX

1 3 5 7 9 10 8 6 4 2

To Emma, Sonny, Raya,
Connie and Clara

ACKNOWLEDGEMENTS

I would like to thank everyone at Mainstream Publishing, and I am grateful to Tom Williams and Annabel Merullo at Peters Fraser & Dunlop. Thank you to G.W. for his advice and support. In addition, I would like to thank Marcella Edwards for her support and Tony Mitchell for his detailed information about the Mac-10 sub-machine gun.

ACKNOWLEDGMENTS

CONTENTS

PART THREE: ON CAMPAIGN

PART ONE

BUILD-UP

CHAPTER 1

AGGRAVATED BURGLARY

Bang! Door goes in, kicked through. White plastic UPVC, double-glazed, brass handle. It's hanging off at an angle by the lower hinge. Tax raid. Burg. The lads run in, Lowied up, head to toe in black. Black Berghaus trapper hats, black North Face jackets, ski masks, black Reebok Classic trainies, Lowe Alpine leather gloves.

Jay, 14, runs into the front room with a golf club, a sand iron. The dealer's bird's sat off on the couch, her baby in front of the plasma. Jay swings. Wallops the bird on the side of the arm. 'Fuuuuck Offf!' he shouts, like he's just scored a goal, concentrating on the contact at the same time. He gives a little Stevie G goal celebration, finger pointed lazily to the non-existent crowd. 'See that arm go, lad,' he says, as one of the others bails past the living room door, heading upstairs. The girl goes down. Screams. Urine.

New Loon, hooded up, is right up the stairs into the front bedroom. Knows where he's going. The dealer's in his pit. Smell of green and a few stripes chopped out on a CD box. Knocker has his nine millie out, held ghetto-style, turned anticlockwise so that it's on the horizontal. He's buzzing off the sight of the Lowie glove gripping the nine. 'Where's the gear, lad?'

Nogger flies through the bedroom door behind him. No messing about. Shiv out. Quilt off. One up the arse. Stab. Stab. Stab. 'Where's the parcel, lad?' Anal prolapse. Shit and blood all over the sheets. New Loon laughs, pure hyena, snorts the lines off the CD case. Nogger, again: 'Where's the gear, lad?'

Bloot goes through the bathroom door. Granma on the bog. She's only thirty-odd. Bang! Alehouse haymaker right to the side of her head. 'Fuuuuck Offf!' She's banged out straight away. Right into the bath she goes, leg sticking out. KO'd. Looks like she's still sobbing, but she's gently convulsing, spittle bubbling off her gob, sighing like a dog.

'Girl, girl? Be quiet, girl,' says Bloot, convinced she can still hear him. 'We'll be gone in a minute.' Just in case she's blagging, he tries to give her the chance to save herself from further torture. 'Where's y'lad's parcel, girl? Give it up and we'll get off.' Bloot looks side-on and sees one of the lads, Iggo, bounding up the stairs.

'See that, lad?' asks Bloot, visibly proud of his punch on the auld one, grinning under his Lowies, eyes dancing with fire. 'Into the bath, lad. One dig. Right into the bath.'

Iggo stands at the top of the stairs, leaning on his putter, laughing. 'Go 'ead, lad. She's a fucking snitch anyway. Remember that, lad.' The woman registers the statement. Slightly louder moaning sounds. She sighs a denial.

Iggo gently lifts his club, swings it slightly, taking aim. Carefully to and fro like a pro, aiming for the ball of the ankle that's sticking out of the bath. 'Move back, lad,' he tells Bloot. He nods for Bloot to step back against the tiled wall as he gently moves his feet up and down, wiggling his toes. He loosens his swing, flapping his arms up and down in a gentle, slo-mo version of 'The Birdie Song'.

Crack! The putter smashes into the woman's ankle. The foot dislocates from the leg, and, for a split second, shoots off into the air, before it is pulled back sharp by the bag of skin it is in. It then rotates, *Misery*-style.

Iggo: 'Fuuuuck Offf!' Stretching the words out slowly, as though tracking a ball flying to his satisfaction over the green. Granma lets out a mad howl. 'See that go, lad,' says Iggo. 'See her ankle just . . . go.' Iggo, made up with his shot, swaps the putter into his left hand and clacks his fingers, ghetto-stylie, but there's no sound because of his gloves.

He turns left into the bedroom where New Loon and Nogger are terroring the dealer. Blood's still pouring out of his arse but he's not yet shitting out the goods. 'Is this prick said nothing yet?' he asks, speed-growling through his teeth, emphasising the sound 'ick' with genuine anger, emitting a gurgling sound at the same time. Feeling confident after his boss bit of green work in the bathroom. 'Fucking little prick,' he repeats, his accent so thick you could wring it out, cracking the putter across the dealer's back, the word prick bringing him some stress relief.

He's still coming down off the rush of smashing the woman's ankle, but frustrated that the dealer hasn't yet collapsed.

Nogger turns to Iggo: 'Where's the iron, lad?'

'Here y'are, lad. Here's an iron, lad,' he says, proffering his golf club, laughing at his 19th-hole joke.

'That's a putter, you soft cunt.' They're all grinning under their hoods now, knowing full well what type of iron is being referred to. 'I mean the Tefal, lad. Or the Rowenta. A red-hot one, if you please.' Nogger using the banter for effect, casually warning the dealer that proceedings are about to be upscaled considerably – unless he tells them where his stash is. No response.

New Loon bails out of the room to look for the iron. Down the stairs nearly in one go, then back up, more slowly this time, Morphy Richards 40311 in one hand, the baby, in bits, in the other.

Downstairs, the younger lads have been in by now – and out. Plasma gone, Xbox gone, Wii gone, Virgin V+ box and all that gone. The dealer's car – a boss little blue Vectra – is off the drive now, on the main road, ready to go. The young ones are revving it, scanning for po-po. Later, this one's good for a show, flooring it round the estate in front of the lads, on video.

New Loon plugs the iron in, Nogger holding it. Bloot leaves the ma in the bath, comes into the bedroom to watch the money shot. 'Red hot, lad,' he says. 'Turn it right up, lad.'

Nogger: 'One louder, lad.' Iggo cranks up the thermostatic dial.

Word goes round that Dylan's here now, on the premises, Lowied up, but no black – he's wearing dark, inky blue instead, and clean, lime-green Adidas John Waynies, fresh from Amsterdam. Unarmed, no shottie, nothing. Just his calm, relaxed self. He climbs the stairs slowly, head down, like he's at home. He can hear the steam jets from the iron in the bedroom and it bubbling too hot, the baby crying hysterically in the same room, a dry, manic scream.

He hears Nogger's voice: 'Tell us where the gear is, lad. Don't make me do it, lad. I'll burn the baby.' Through the banisters, Dylan sees Nogger dangling the baby Michael Jackson-style with one arm, holding the hot iron in front of its face, slowly, intermittently squeezing the steam out. Finger on the trigger.

Nogger doesn't *really* want to do it, but he will. Everyone knows that. Nogger isn't bothered too much. He'll be arsed for a bit, later, pretend to display the right emotions – pity, half-regrets. But he's a good mimic, is Nogger, an expert at imitating human emotions, the feelings he doesn't have. Not everyone knows that. Not everyone knows that that's how he gets through the day. But Dylan does. Nogger pushes the iron a touch nearer the baby. The skin is actually reddening up now. Baby goes skew-whiff, wriggles its body with shocking force, trying to grab hold of someone, despite being upside down. Its cry is grating and repetitive, unnerves the lads. The mother has to be restrained by Jay downstairs. Arses of the lads a bit gone now. They're in the gone-too-far zone. 'This is bad, to be fair,' half of them are thinking. 'How did we get to here? We only came out for a bit of graft.' Their thoughts are coming through clearer now that the green is wearing off.

Nogger orders New Loon to take off the kid's jim-jams. New Loon rags them down straight away, tears off the shitty Pamper underneath. Nogger moves the red-hot iron closer to the baby's pink and flabby arse.

Dylan bounces into the room just in time. 'What's going on, lad?'

'Where you been, lad?' asks New Loon, trying to ignore Dylan's implicit condemnation of the situation, trying to hide his shame.

'What d'you mean, Dylan?' asks Nogger, feeling a bit bad about the baby scenario but not giving ground to Dylan.

Dylan nods towards the kid, staring at the iron. 'The baby, lad. What are you doing to the baby?' But he knows that he's got to be a bit careful here. Be on top with Nogger at your peril. Go about this the wrong way and he'll pay the price, heavily, later. *Sick waters here, lad. Need to be navigated with care.*

All of them are full of the stripes and ready to go. What Dylan half-said was half a slight, stung Nogger, for sure. But the situation, however delicate, is still recoverable. Dylan knows the key is not to make Nogger feel any more embarrassed over the baby. Otherwise he'll turn the iron on him. *Don't cross the line, lad. No telling him off. Just keep it neutral.* Dylan thinks the situation through methodically, even while the baby is dangling and crying before him.

Eventually, he speaks again. 'The baby doesn't know where the gear is, does it?' Nogger nods slightly in agreement, not knowing where Dylan is going but wanting to go with it all the same, as he can't think of a solution himself. Dylan nods towards the dealer on the bed. 'He does, though. So put the iron on *him*, lad.'

Good win-win outro to be had here: Nogger can save face with a practical, no-nonsense course of action. Dylan asks Nogger for the iron – asks, doesn't tell. Once he's in possession of it, Dylan quickly presses it down onto the dealer's cock, ragging the lad's trackies off in the same motion. As the scalding plate touches the tip of his bell, the dealer is already shitting out the goods. 'It's in the loft, lad! Fuck off! It's in the tank!'

'You fucking little prick,' Dylan shouts at the dealer, agitated that he's been forced to burn him. *Greed, that's all it is.* Not giving up the goods even when they were going to iron his baby. Growling, he punches the dealer in the head with the iron, ripping the cord from the socket as he does it.

Job done. Dylan gets off, picking up the baby and carrying her downstairs to her ma in the front room. Clegsy's up through the hatch already, no ladder, up the sides of the wall. New Loon's stood off below, staring up into the darkness, arms dropped to his sides, machete in one hand, nine in the other, half covering the stairs in case anyone comes through the front door.

'Have you found it, lad?' he asks Clegsy, up there with a halogen Maglite, all over the gaff now. Iggo kills time by wiping the shoeprints from Clegsy's black-and-white Nike Air Max Torch 5 trainies off the walls and the frame underneath the loft hatch. The prints are bland anyway because the grip is made up of blocks and horizontal lines. Iggo plays off some small talk with New Loon. 'Air Force 1, for instance. They've got 11 concentric circles on them. You may as well leave a fingerprint.' Showing off that he is forensically aware. New Loon checks the soles of his black Nike Air Zoom Vapor V1 Tours. They're a zig-zag repeat with a small circle in the middle. Iggo's Zoom SPARQs are the same.

New Loon nods, but he's not arsed. Still staring up into the void above, waiting for dollars from heaven.

Downstairs, Dylan shushes the baby, pulls his fleece neckwarmer down so it can see his face. The baby stops screaming. Dylan wipes the tears and snot away with the soft fleece. The ma is sat on the edge of the couch, holding her broken arm. She can see Dylan's face, but he's willing to take the risk. Rather that than have a hysterical baby.

Jay's guarding her. Now he's sunk into an armchair, playing a DS he's found, elbows resting on his sand iron, which is laid across the arms of the chair. Before the off, he tries to get his grabs off the woman. He throws her a little twenty bag of cocaine he found in an ashtray to null her pain. 'There you go, you dirty baghead,' he says as he throws the little plastic wrap to her. Jay never takes Class A drugs himself. After she's rubbed it on her gums and bugled it up her nose, Jay walks past her and grabs her tits, knowing that she can't stop him because of her broken arm, that she's momentarily indebted to him for the gear. Dylan calls Jay a sick little twat. But Jay's just laughing, buzzing with some of the younger ones, until the DS catches his eye again.

Activity upstairs. Clegsy shouting down from the loft, 'Got it.' Nogger steps aside as a heavy, wet kitbag comes flying down the hatch followed by Clegsy, buzzing. 'Come 'ead. Let's get off.'

Dylan carries the baby into the living room and puts it in its mum's OK arm. He tells Jay to get off and on the way out drops the ma a tenner for some nappies or for some credit on her phone. Dylan's made Jay give her back her Samsung. Life'll be hard for her in the next few days. They bail into the Vec and offski. Behind them, one of the younger ones is trying to keep up on a Whizzer, a motorised scooter darting through the traffic, another one on a little motorbike.

CHAPTER 2

PHONES

Back on the Boot Estate, everybody's buzzing. True Nogzy Soljas. Got away with a quarter of green, one corner white and six ton in notes. The younger lads have shot off to the chippy and Mackie D's. Bubble's gone the Armenian shop for 24 cans. 'Only a tenner,' he says.

The older lads are sat off in someone's pad. Some rip off a nearby estate, Danielle, is putting on a floor show, squatting on a half-full bottle of Hennessy on the kitchen floor by the back door. All hands have got their phones out, getting on it. Up and down, up and down, slowly, her hands on her thick thighs, the muscles and tendons in her legs visibly tensed. She's balanced like a Russian dancer. Pacer's checking intently. He can see, ever so slightly, her lips, her inner labial folds, sucking on the bottleneck during the upstroke.

New Loon, top off, skinny twat, wearing just a pair of mountain-gear bottoms and his neckwarmer, covering his grid for the cameras, the toggle tied tight at the back so it won't fall down. He's behind her now, one finger up her arse, John Gotti in the other hand. The long feller. All the lads buzzing, Danielle just smiling. Daft, silly *Zoo* bird. She'll do as her told. She'll be getting a good drink for her dirty efforts and all the gear she can snort, up her nose, up her twat, blown up her arse. Danielle: scowly grid, pure tan, blonde bob, boss tits, full tackle from Ann Summers on – white stockings, lacy bra. She'll be getting walloped all over the gaff in a minute. Tomorrow, all the lads'll be in the local, the Canada Dock, with their phones out on the bar, Bluetoothing the new Danielle vid to all hands. The match lads will love that.

She gets on the mattress, which has been pulled off the bed especially and onto the floor. On all fours now, New Loon walloping her from behind while Clegsy's getting half a blowie up the front, still fully Lowied

19

up, but with his trackies and the Everton shorts underneath pulled down a bit, at least until the cameras go off in a minute. *Can't have your ma seeing this, can you?*

Dylan's just sat off on a chair in the corner, building up. He's got a twenty bag of green. Gone in three joints, that. He likes watching the party girls. Feels half a lob-on pushing up on his trackies, a taut bit of composite fabric pulled tight when he sat down. He fucking loves these dirty young Scouse princesses, has half a dozen vids on his phone. Some of them getting ragged in their cosy teddy-beared bedrooms by the local fucking gangster, while their dickhead dads who've spent a life spoiling them are downstairs half-crashed in front of *Granada Reports*. Another shows a pinched-nosed beauty getting ragged over a bog in a nightclub, being filmed over a low partition wall by the doormen. He'll have a tug over Danielle later, but first there's business to be taken care of. After this joint.

No one can think. Brains wiped clean by the green. 'Good gear, that, lad,' says Lupus. 'Sandstorm blowin' in me head.'

Nogger appears at the window at the back door. Tall and broad, even in his Lowies. Behind him a young girl, no more than a shadow of a bird, shuffling nervously. Dylan sees her put down a bottle – probably cider by the glint of brown plastic – on the doorstep, embarrassed at her teenage vice.

Nogger comes in, head down in his chippy, booting fuck out of curry, rice and chips. At first, he pretends to ignore the floor show, protecting his position, acting as if he's above it. But then he nods towards Clegsy, who's sperming over Danielle's face. 'Go 'ead, lad.' He stops to stab a fork into a hot chip and dip it in the curry. 'Next on that, lad,' he says, buzzing, pointing the chip at Danielle. But everyone knows Nogger can't be arsed with the older girls.

He's got the little bird with him. A little rip off the shops. She hangs round outside the offie. About 13, her perm cheap and wet, stuck to her head. Little jacket. Poor. Just got changed from school and ran out to see her mates, full of Friday-night anticipation. Ran into Nogger.

'Fucking lovely, that curry from there, innit?' he says to the girl, flicking a hot chip around his mouth to cool it down and so he can speak at the same time.

'Fucking sound, that chippy, isn't it, Nogger?' the girl replies, trying to sound grown-up. Her ma has remarked similarly on the quality of that chippy before. She's a bit wasted off the cider and a bit nervous in front of a room full of older lads, legendary lads off the estate.

Nogger has her watch the floor show, letting her know what will be required. The girl looks at Danielle, half stunned, half intrigued. Puts her hand over her face, pretends to look away. 'Feel ashamed.' Danielle doesn't even notice her. The stripes have sent her sex haywire by now. Won't be long before a three-piper is on the cards. Pacer's giving it loads up Danielle, the sensation making him serious. 'The birds and the coke, mate. Ruthless.'

Nogger scans the room to root out Dylan. Nogger to Dylan: 'All right, lad?'

Dylan's keen not to show too much respect, in protest at the underage bint. 'Sound, lad,' he replies, looking at the little girl to show Nogger that he doesn't approve.

'What are you up to, lad?' asks Nogger.

'Gonna take this' – holding up the taxed parcel of heroin – 'over the other place, lad, to get rid.'

'Sound. Catch up with you, later.'

Nogger takes his bit of a bird up to a bedroom. It's one of the younger lad's houses. Everton FC quilt on the bed. He lashes his chippy on the floor, over a pile of ironing. Manoeuvres the bird on the bed, rags her little Asda skirt up (George, kids' section). Dylan recognised it before because his ten-year-old sister has the same one. He ruffles his trackies down to his knees, violently yanking the mass of elastic cords, toggles and ties to get them untangled. Bums her from behind. The bird trying to look serious, copying the dirty enthusiasm of Danielle.

Halfway through, Nogger pulls out his phone and videos the spectacle. She's excited but tries to appear cool and controlled for the footage. Downstairs, the lads whack the Tupac up one louder to drown out Nogger's virgin child.

Dylan ponders Nogger's curry rape. He looks round the room. Jay is back from Mackie D's, manoeuvring himself under Danielle so he can get into her fanny. Fishing and finishing off the three-piper, Iggo getting a blowie, New Loon still up her arse.

Bloot and Lupus are having a wank, Bloot gripping her hair with one hand as he does, moving it down now and again to grab her swinging, lacied-up taigs. 'Go 'ead, Danielle,' he says. 'Boss, you, girl.'

Dylan observes the scene through a cloud of green. Not one of these lads has ever chatted up a bird. Not one has ever picked one up in the alehouse, or done a bit of romancing at the pictures or over a Chinese. Raised on a diet of Internet porn, Bluetooth blueys and instant gratification, brasses like Danielle. Even the little meffs off the shops have to pretend to be porn stars to please the lads nowadays. Dylan gets off into the night.

CHAPTER 3

BLACK HAWK DOWN

Bleeker's funeral on Monday. RIP Bleeker. Tension all over the estate. There's a fleet of ships sat off up and down The Strand, yellow riot vans slashed with the Vaderis police unit insignia. They're expecting a revenge shooting.

The po-po are getting very heavy over Bleeker's floral tribute. 'Bout four grand's worth of flowers there now,' one of the lads says. Two grand's worth are from the lads alone. Even the bizzies have sent a wreath. *The pricks.* And now they're turning Turk on it. There's a big 'RIP Bleeker' a foot high in red roses. 'True Nogzy Solja' spelled out in mad black flowers, specially dyed. 'Mates 4 Ever'. 'Happy Death from the Troops'. A Lowe Alpine badge, black background, the name spelled out in white flowers, with half an orange sun rising above a snow-capped peak. From the younger lads.

'Sick, that, lad,' says Pacer proudly, nodding in admiration at it. Then there's just loads of little bunches tied to the railings, loads of cards from everyone saying what a great feller he was. Bleeker: rapist, drug dealer, urban terrorist.

Tommy from the flower shop is chokka with it. Started crying the other day after the lads sent him and his wife a card to say nice one for all his hard work with the flowers, for lining himself up with the lads. The top bizzy gets out of his command shipper, a battered yellow base, and goes over to Tommy, rather than going straight to the lads, who never speak to the bizzies on no account – except Dylan, who can give as good as he gets and never loses his temper. 'The floral tribute, Tommy. We're going to have to take it down.'

Tommy knows that'll cause murder. 'You'll have a riot on your hands. You know that, don't you?'

The bizzy can't back down, but he can't lose face by giving in either. Tommy says he'll bring one of the lads over to negotiate. Dylan moseys over, puts his hood down as a sign of peace but keeps his Berghaus sun hat on because the bizzy keeps his hat on. Dylan gets him to agree that the flowers can stay, but the top bizzy insists that the graffiti all over the shutters has to be cleaned off. 'RIP Bleeker' has been sprayed on each shop. The top bizzy radios in for the council's anti-graffiti clean-up team to be brought in under police escort. No one has ever seen council workers work so fast.

That night, the crew that killed Bleeker, Crocky Young Guns, robs his body from the Connor and Co. Chapel of Rest. They put a robbed Focus through the big metal shutters at the back and put Bleeker in the boot. When they're safely away, the body is tied to the back of the car and ragged around the estate, General Aidid-style.

Nogger gets the video sent to his phone the next day. All the lads are watching it. Dylan thinks it's boss, but he doesn't say nothing. It shows them tipping the body from the coffin into the open boot, the car revving loudly round the back of the funeral parlour, waiting to get off.

'Fucking shitbags,' says Dylan. 'Look. They're too fucking scared to touch the body, lad.' But within a few seconds, the video shows them booting fuck out of it. While they're preparing to tie it to the towbar, one of them runs up and wellies the head repeatedly. Dylan knows what's going on here, but he doesn't say nothing except to murmur, 'Vietnam, lad,' vaguely remembering a magazine he'd read, US Marines dehumanising the enemy by kicking fuck out of dead prisoners.

Another Crocky rat pokes a stick into Bleeker's cheek. The bullet hole – from the shot that killed the poor cunt – has been covered by death make-up. But the lad with the stick clearly knows where the entry wound is. 'Cos he fucking done it,' says Iggo, without taking his eyes off the phone's LED screen. Dylan and Bloot nod an acknowledgement, in agreement with Iggo's sharp detective work. He pokes around until he's picked away the thick specialist foundation. When the concave film of powder caves in, he shoves the stick a little further through the bullet hole and into the taut flesh of the cheek.

The rat with the stick talks to the camera: 'Look at Bleeker. He's got two fucking mouths now. To chat twice as much shit.' Another one – a faint, hooded black silhouette against the night sky – goes: 'Bleeker, you grassing twat. Tell the bizzies twice as fucking much now.' All the rats are buzzing. Another is bending down, putting a noose around Bleeker's neck and tying it to the towie. He pulls the noose up, lifting Bleeker's upper torso off the ground with the rope, saying, 'Told yer not to hang around by our shops, Bleeker.' One-liners coming thick and fast now. *They're a top act. No denying.*

Bloot's like that: 'Check that fucking tow rope, lad – cheap one out of the 24-hour.' No one in Bleeker's crew feels sorry for their mate's body watching the video. They're mainly curious.

'Watch this,' says Nogger, revelling in his expertise having watched the vid many times. 'They drag Bleeker along the tarmac. Poor cunt.' He's trying to sound sympathetic and shocked, barely containing his excitement. The robbed Focus races past the camera with the body bumping behind, like an overloaded plane trying to take off. 'Get on this bit,' says Nogger. 'Sick, lad.' The car does a handbrake turn and the body flies fast through the air until the rope becomes taut. Snap! The force separates Bleeker's head from the body and it flies off across the road. The car stops and all the rats crowd around looking for the head. 'It's over there, lad,' says one, pointing. 'There, lad,' he repeats impatiently to another rat who's searching in the dark.

Bleeker had a skinhead, so no cunt can pick his head up when it's finally found. No one wants his fingers coming into direct contact with dead flesh. It's worse cos his scalp was peeled back during the post-mortem and reconstituted afterwards. Their gloved hands keep slipping off his scalp. One of them tries to pick the head up by the ear, but he freaks out and drops it almost immediately, hopping away, laughing. Eventually, one of them wraps a car-seat cover from the old Ford around the head. He holds it up for an ICF-style group shot, all of them yelling and shouting abuse, making gang signs.

When the video stops, everyone's head is wrecked. Nogger is the first to speak: 'Let's walk over there now and shoot every fucking one of the little cunts.' Amongst the others, anger hasn't properly set in yet. Most of the lads simply feel an overwhelming urge to watch the video again. Dylan feels edgy, his soul uneasy and blackened. He always feels a bit mad after watching a happy slap. And he's seen some fucking bad ones. But Bleeker's one was in a different fucking league.

'No,' he says to Nogger. 'We can't do that. Not the day before the funeral.'

'Why not, lad?'

Dylan sues for temporary peace using false sentiment. 'Cos his ma's in bits already. Po-po all over the show. We can't even let her find out. Tell her that her son's body's been swiped from the funeral parlour? And then dragged through the road like fucking Somali? Are youse mad?' He makes sure to use the plural, not singling Nogger out. 'No way, lad. Never mind start a fucking wagar over it, as well.'

'So we gonna do fuck all then? That it?' asks Nogger.

Bloot, stirring now, adds, 'Fucking humiliating, lad. Doing that to one of us.'

Dylan, the voice of reason again: 'Wait till it cools down, lad. Then you can do what you want. What *we* want.' Dylan knows that he has to distract the lads quickly from the subject of revenge if he wants to stop the idea dead. 'Anyway,' he says, 'we've got to get Bleeker's body back.' Good move, he thinks. Action. Practical. Something to do. 'Just for his ma's sake,' he goes on. 'If the bizzies get to it before us, there'll be untold. Nother fucking autopsy, not releasing the body for another fucking three months, no fucking funeral at all.'

Dylan has a couple of aces up his sleeve. He knows that the lads are actually looking forward to the funeral – and the party afterwards. And he knows that the little snides have already bought their coke for the wake. Bits and bobs have been ordered or paid for, so to call off Bleeker's big day now would only cause personal loss to them. Bubble has already had all the T-shirts made up: 'RIP Bleeker' on the front, 'Anthony Mulhearn Is A Grass' on the back. Cars have been booked and all that carry-on, the lads chipping in a tenner each. Lots of talk about the cortège already. 'Should see the main funeral car. It's fucking boss.' They've got a blacked-out stretch Humvee with Dutch plates on it. 'How shady is that?' one of them says.

'Total slim shady, if you ask me,' says Iggo.

'Too much. Roasting,' says Clegsy. 'Bleeker'll get five years mandatory for just being near it – and the cunt's dead.' Gets a laugh off the lads.

All the lads behind are gonna be cortèged up in Lexuses and four-by-fours, some rented, some lent by the older ones, the bigger dealers, out of respect. The lads are seeing this in their minds' eyes now. Weighing it up, heads ticking, coming round.

Clegsy, adept at political manoeuvrings and riding the wave of his quips, says, 'And you know what? Think about Bleeker's ma.'

Dylan's thinking that was a boss move, bringing Bleeker's ma back into play. 'What a beauty,' Clegsy's thinking. Always loyal to D. Always Dylan's number two.

Clegsy carries on: 'She's paid for the funeral. Two grand, lad. She'll be paying that off for two years. Twenty-five quid a week for two years.' The final remark wins the argument. The funeral is now most definitely on. *For Bleeker's ma's sake.* No one wants it postponed. Dylan carries the day. Nogger gives him a bad stare.

CHAPTER 4

BODY RETRIEVAL

From the Black Hawk Down video, as it's already being called, Dylan gets onto where the Crocky Young Guns have dumped Bleeker's body. The final scene shows them throwing Bleeker's headless corpse down a sewer bank next to a run-down Evangelical church near the boundary between old Crocky and new Crocky. Odds are, Dylan figures, it's still there.

Dylan asks – asks, not tells – Nogger to take Jay and a few of the younger ones up to get the body back. At the same time, he'll go up to Connor and Co. to have a word with the funeral director. 'If he's called the bizzies about Bleeker's body already then we're fucked, lad,' he says. 'But if he hasn't, I'll try and get him to hold off. I'll tell him we can get Bleeker back, no one will ever know and we can get on the funeral tomorrow.'

'What d'you mean, *ask* him, lad?' says Nogger. 'Tell the twat if he phones the bizzies, he'll be burying himself.'

At the funeral parlour, proceedings are active already. There's a beige Lexus on the forecourt; Dylan's onto it straight away: 'community leader' in the building. Paul McQuillum, 'the Imperator'. Former world-champion kickboxer, heroin/cocaine financier/importer, famous, well loved – dollars.

Dylan moseys into the office, hood down, trapper hat off. The bird on reception is half-tasty: slim, boss tan, swingy ponytail.

'What d'you want, lad?' she asks. 'One of yer big mad gangsters been shot?'

Dylan, looking up at the speakers, says: 'All right, that music, girl.'

The girl sits back: boss tits, lovely tight jumper; short black skirt, thick black tights; ponytail swinging with the movement of the sprung office chair; little smile. *Bend you over that coffin, y'li'l rip, skirt riding up your arse, girl.*

'Boss in, girl?' he asks. The bird gets a bit excited and Dylan knows she's heard the jangle from the back room. Why else would Dylan Olsen want to see the MD? *Other than Bleeker's body and that?* Dylan is relaxed. He already knows the funeral man has done the right thing. Why else would Paul McQuillum's car be here? He's not phoned the bizzies. Instead, he's called a 'well-known community leader' for help to get the body back. What other option did he have?

Dylan's shown into the office by the boss little bird. *Top little arse, there, girl.* Paul's standing there, dark-blue crew-neck on, smart, half-Chinese with an urchin crop of black hair, precisely shaped and at odds with his slack middle-aged face. The funeral director, looking nervous, is stood behind his desk. *Fuck him, the little prick. No let-on for him. He'll do what he's told, the fucking beaut. But Paul. Different story, lad. Fucking love him. Everyone, fucking loves him.*

Dylan gives Paul a big smile. Warm greetings, big mad gangster hugs. Paul goes a bit over the top, giving him a full body embrace *Goodfellas*-style, like the doormen do in town outside the clubs.

'You all right, lad?' asks Paul. 'Good to see you.'

Paul turns to the funeral man. *Here comes the big-up. I love this. I fucking love these big-ups from Paul.*

Paul and Dylan are facing Andy Holden, the managing director of the funeral parlour. McQuillum has his left arm around Dylan's shoulder, his right hand pointing to Dylan's face. Paul's finding his footing on the carpet, ready for the speech.

'Andy, I'd like to introduce you to Dylan. He's a good friend of mine. He's a friend of *ours*.' A little smile passes between Paul and Dylan, both getting onto the *Godfather* reference. Everyone loves buzzing off the filmies. 'He's one of the most respected young men around here and he's a nice man. All the young lads around here look up to Dylan and he's got a lot of respect.'

The underlying message to Andy is clear: 'Dylan is the up-and-coming gangster in Norris Green. He's the new kid around the area, so he's got to be shown respect – and fear. Even though he may look like a rag-arsed kid to you and me, he'll kill you as soon as look at you.' Andy acknowledges receipt of the message with a slight nod.

Dylan blushes inside, barely understanding what this feeling is. Embarrassment? Confusion? No one ever says stuff like that to him.

Everyone likes that about Paul – he never stands on the up-and-coming lads, the street dealers, the robbers, the pistoleros. He shows them *all* respect. Here he is – Paul with his banks in the Far East, mines in the Baltic, building his motorways in Mexico – stood here, on these premises in his nice new crew-neck sorting out a problem with Dylan. Dylan in his Lowies, with three pounds in his pocket and no credit on his phone.

After the big-up, Paul walks around the desk and stands next to Andy, both of them facing Dylan, like businessmen posing for a photograph in the *Echo*, Paul introduces Andy, stretching his mouth and licking his lips. 'Dylan, this is Andy. As you know, he's the boss of this place. He's also one of the most respected businessmen in the city and he's been a great friend of mine for nearly twenty years.'

Dylan keeps his eyes on Paul, listening carefully to the speech, full of admiration for Paul's rich language and sense of drama, at least compared to anyone he knows. *How can someone just praise someone else like that?*

Paul turns away from Andy and speaks directly to Dylan. 'Got something to talk to you about. That OK?'

'Yeah.'

'It's a bit of a mad one. Andy phoned me this morning . . . And please don't take it as a sign of disrespect that I'm asking you this.'

'Yeah.'

'One of the things from around the back went missing last night.'

'Mad, innit?'

'Now, it goes without saying that he [looks at Andy] didn't tell them [points out the window, meaning the bizzies].'

'Course, yeah.'

'He phoned me to help him get it back, before there's a problem. D'you know what I'm saying?'

'Yeah.'

'You don't want everyone knowing that a corpse has gone missing, do you? Could be your little daughter, couldn't it?'

Andy is clearly shocked and embarrassed about the theft of the body, but he also understands local sensibilities. He's frightened it could get him dragged into a gang war.

'So, Dylan,' Paul continues, 'it goes without saying that we want to get the thing back, without any harrishment.'

'Yeah. Sound.'

Dylan's made up. Can't fucking believe it. Paul is asking him to do *him* a favour, which he's *already onto*. And can sort. *Good graft or what?* Paul will be made up with him. And he'll probably get a little drink out the funeral man. For real.

'All right, Paul. I'll sort that,' he says, hoping Paul will admire his no-fuss, no-frills approach.

'You all right with that, lad?'

'Yeah. Sound. And if we get the thing back, can we just carry on with the funeral tomorrow as normal?'

Andy looks at Paul and nods slightly, as though that's what he's wanted all along.

'OK, Dylan. If you get it back, Andy will just crack on, you know what I'm saying.'

'Nice one, Paul.' For the first time in the conversation, Dylan turns to the funeral director, although he still speaks to Paul. 'Only one problem, though, mate. We can get it back, but the jangle is that his head's been chopped off, you know.'

Paul looked at him, serious, sucking his teeth for a second: 'Go way. You messing?'

'No, it's . . .' shrugging his shoulders, not knowing what more to say.

'Mad, innit?' says Paul, but he's not too fazed and too busy to be too arsed.

'I know, yeah. Mad, aren't they? Fucking rats, you know what I'm saying, mate? You know what it's like.'

'I know, yeah.'

'I'll send the lads out now to get it back. And I'll tell them to grab both bits. That be all right?'

'Make life easier, wouldn't it, lad?'

'I was just thinking, though, if we do get it back, can the head be stitched back on? Just for his ma and that. At the funeral . . .'

'Work wonders him, mate,' says Paul, nodding at Andy, looking at his watch, Dylan clocking the Rolex. 'He's a flippin' master.'

Andy looks horrified.

'As long as it can just be made to look all right, d'you know worramean?' says Dylan. 'It's just his ma, so she doesn't have to see it.'

Paul's a bit fazed, but only a bit. Weary of a 1,000 street mini-crises. He looks to Andy for guidance on the technicalities of stitching a head back on, but Andy is still reeling, too stunned to talk. Paul turns back to Dylan. 'If you get the thing back, I'm sure it can be sorted, lad,' he says, not wanting to get bogged down in the details.

Andy clearly doesn't want to get involved in any compromising conversations with the rag-arse stood in front of him, so he just stares back at Paul. Paul and Dylan take his silence as agreement.

'OK, lad. Just get it all dropped off around the back and Andy will do his best to sort it. That OK, lad? C'mon, best be off, hadn't we.'

Dylan walks with Paul back to the beige Lexus. He knows he's going to get the pep talk that always comes sometime after the big-up, as night follows day. He's not liking these as much, though.

Paul breathes a sigh of mock perplexity: 'Why do youse all do it, lad? Behaving like this. All this gang stuff. I mean, there's no graft in you shooting him and him shooting you, is there?'

'Just the way it is, isn't it, though, Paul?'

'But you can't be making much dough, booting in his door and him booting in your door. And arguing with this feller and that feller. And him saying he's robbed an ounce off you, and you saying he's robbed a motorbike off him. It's mad, isn't it, mate?'

Dylan feels chastened, a bit embarrassed, like a kid. 'Just a bit of drama to get through the day, Paul.'

'It's like these flippin' bouncers, isn't it, Dylan? Him shooting his house up, then him putting a call out on this feller. Made up cos the takings have gone up a fiver. I mean, it's beyond belief. But there's no quality, is there, lad? I mean, far be it from me to say something disrespectful, but youse are just hanging around the shops and in McDonald's. I mean, youse might as well be working in McDonald's, cos you'd be better off. You're hanging around in there to get a warm. At least the girls who're working in there are getting paid to. Know where I'm going? And the minute you step outside, you're getting nicked. Mad, isn't it, lad? I mean, where's the sense in that?'

'I don't know, Paul. It just makes the lads feel a little bit important, having all those bizzies come after them. Big convoy of ships and that. Lights on. *Star Wars* on Earth, d'you get me? Anyway, fuck all better to do on Friday night, is there?'

Paul feigns bemusement, looking up into the sky for the spaceships. 'Get into some proper graft, lad. Put your Lowies in your back bin. Got a bit of work for you, any road. Get you over the other place, if you fancy it,' he says, nodding in the general direction of Amsterdam, Spain and Portugal.

CHAPTER 5

THE FUNERAL

Everyone in T-shirts. White ones with a head shot of Bleeker at 16: blond skinhead, Prada shirt on. Black ones for the hardcore mourners. Those are printed with a picture of Bleeker sitting in a pub, smoking a joint, showing his own T-shirt with 'Anthony Mulhearn Is A Grass' on it, all the younger lads hanging off him, buzzing off Bleeker's T-shirt. The T-shirts for the funeral were Dylan's idea. He didn't want anyone to feel last about not having a suit.

Some of the people lining the streets are ghouls, busybodies who hardly knew him but whose cries are loudest, whose calls for revenge are the most passionate. A lot of the mourners are young lads and washed-out mas. Most of the dads are long gone off the estate. They start off at Bleeker's ma's, Julie. She's hysterical. One of the lads shoots off to Julie's mate's house to get her to come round and help, to dress her – she's been in her pyjamas for days – to stop her wailing. 'Have you heard her, lad?' asks Clegsy. 'She's like a fucking Muslim.'

The house is getting chokka. Bleeker's auld feller Laurence turns up. Red alky face, skinny as fuck, wearing their Bleeker's old black Berghaus. That's what Bleeker left him. Their kid Jimmy got his motorbike (a robbed one). His cousin Marie – who he was shagging – got his stash: £2,500 in cash, 2 oz beak and 23 £10 bags of brown. Dylan's got his Gotti. That was the entirety of Bleeker's estate. Laurence goes outside. Can't smoke inside cos of the babies. He's at the door having a ciggie, already snided a can out of the fridge, baseball cap on, hooded up in the drizzle. He looks like one of the lads. He's 67.

There are three couches in the living room, all skewed at mad angles. Their Jimmy's sat in the back room, hidden in the corner, on the PlayStation 3. Premier League Stars.

'Fuckin' 'ell, lad,' says New Loon, 'half of fucking Milan are playing for Everton there.'

'I know, yeah,' says Jimmy, thumbs going mad on the gamepad, taking blasts on a joint when new Everton signing Kaká gets the ball. Jimmy's bird, Keeley, is lying on the couch in the front room, with the baby under a coat to keep it warm.

Marie's there, with the confidence of a newly wealthy woman. Wagged up in a new Cavalli basque. It cost £600 of Bleeker's £2,500 'bequest'. Nogger's sat next to her, chatting shit, half trying to find out where she's stashed the rest of Bleeker's white and brown, half thinking of bursting her ken while the funeral's on. Tax her, tax dead Bleeker, then slip quietly back to the wake. But Marie's half onto him and fucking him off, the shady twat, telling him that she's sold the lot wholesale to a firm from Anfield who came down last night. She says it's all gone, even Bleeker's side-by-side shottie, which she gave to Dylan, out of respect, in a tearful ceremony in the Canada Dock. Nogger's angered by this detail – by Dylan's popularity. But he starts blimping her sussies instead, makes a mental note to try for blowie off her in the bogs at the wake later, after she's full of the stripes.

Whizzer arrives with the coke, a plentiful bag of squidgy soft powder. Just weighed it on his new electronic scales. Usually, he'd bag it up in little knotted squares of carrier bag, not the smooth plastic type you get from Tesco's, but the crinkly, rustly kind you get from the corner shop. That way, people snort it all in one go, cos they can't be arsed tying it up again. A trick of the trade. But because it's a funeral, he's put it in a few resealables out of respect. He dishes them out to the lads.

Bloot and Whizzer disappear into the upstairs bog to rack up in private. Got to show respect – it's a funeral, and there's bin lids about. The toilet's yellowed and shit-stained, the lino ripped, the sink caked with dirt. Blobs of dried toilet paper are stuck to the wall just above the outflow. They chop out two fat stripes on the cistern.

Clegsy does his downstairs in the kitchen. Not so arsed about respecting the dead. Just wants to get charged up for the funeral. He clears a bit of space on a dirty worktop, chops out a few lines. He shouts in to Bleeker's auntie Carmen, 'Carmen, look, come 'ere. This bottle of milk is leaking.'

'Our Peter must have dropped it off his bike coming back from the shop. Didn't say nothing, though,' Carmen shouts in the general direction of her son Peter, who is perched on the edge of their Jimmy's armchair, watching him on the PlayStation. 'Peter, you little twat. Did you drop this milk and not say nothing?'

'No, it wasn't me.'

'Fucking hell,' says Carmen, looking at Clegsy. 'What are they like?'

'I know, yeah,' replies Clegsy, pretending to be grown up. 'They won't admit to anything will they? 'Ere y'are, girl. Stand it in one of these pans 'ere,' he says, but he can't be arsed looking for a clean one.

Clegsy snorts his line, tells her, 'Carmen, there's a line there for you, girl. Have that,' and takes the opportunity to get off into the crowd.

The kitchen is a tip: sink full of dishes; chip pan on the side, half full of solidified fat; three half-full plazzie bottles of orange, big size; two polystyrene trays from the Chinese, sides shrivelled and brown from reheating in the oven, bit of fish in one, half a chicken fried rice in the other with a portion of curry, two days old, a skin on the curry sauce.

Bleeker's ma comes in, half ashamed of her midden kitchen. She has a fat, squashed face, a bulbous veiny nose. She's an alky, too. In a vain effort to appear house-proud, she says, 'Got some nice bowls under there. Pour the milk in there, Carmen.' But there's too much shite all over the place to get in any of the cupboards. She wanders off, stressed by the thought of digging out some clean bowls.

Bleeker's coffin's upstairs. He's been laid to rest in his Lowies, hood up, jacket collar zipped right up to the top, forming a perfect cylinder around his neck, hermetically sealed, hooligan-style, by the toggles, to cover his garrotted nape. Everyone's telling his ma that this is what he would have liked, to be buried in his uniform. Solja and all that. But everybody's buzzing because they know the real reason.

All the lads are in there now, stripes racked out on the coffin lid, which has been taken off and set across two chairs, a makeshift table. When that becomes sticky with spilled ale and broken ciggies, some of the lads balance their lines of coke on the thin rim of the open casket, wafting plumes of excess powder over the corpse. Some of the lads are building ceremonial joints. Spark it up, have a few pulls, put it out, then throw it in for Bleeker to get high in the afterlife. Lupus pulls out an old .38. It's a bit fucked, rusty with bits of soil on it. He's just dug it up from a stash, a disused garden on The Boot. He puts it in the coffin at Bleeker's side, then changes his mind. Joint in mouth, eyes smarting from the back smoke, he hides it down the front of Bleeker's trackies, where he used to carry it. He half shudders at the thought of touching Bleeker's cold, dead cock, but notices Bleeker is wearing a new pair of Everton shorts.

'What are you putting that in for, lad?' asks Nogger, bullying.

'For Bleeker, lad,' says Lupus. 'Full solja honours and that.'

'What the fuck does he need an auld .38 like that for in his state?'

Bloot, laughing, pointing his joint at the body, says, 'Bleeker's going straight to hell. There'll be Mac-10s and all sorts down there. Doesn't need an auld banger like that.'

'Well, it's better than nothing, lad,' says Lupus. 'And there's fuck all else that can be done with it. It's too on top anyway.'

'What d'you mean, lad?' asks Bloot.

'Roasting, lad. It's the one I used to shoot thingio. Remember? That prick?'

'Fool, wasn't he, lad? Smoked him, didn't you?'

'I remember, lad,' says Clegsy. 'Shot him in his Audi, lad, parked up by the shops.'

'One right in the head,' says Lupus.

'Is right, lad,' nods Bloot.

'Didn't mean to do it properly, lad. But it was just one of them, a fluke.'

'I see, lad.'

'So the police know the gun. So Bleeker's better off having it in his box, rather than me.'

Nogger: 'But what if Crocky rob the grave? Bound to happen, lad. Have you thought about that?'

'What d'you mean?' asks Lupus.

'Are you mad? The cunts have already had the body off once from the fucking funeral home. The jangle is now that they're gonna dig the poor cunt up tonight and drag him down the street again. And when the bizzies find the gun, it's all gonna come back to us, isn't it?'

'Not so bad, is it, lad? Cos Bleeker'll get the blame, won't he? And he's dead, lad.'

'Suppose so,' concedes Bloot.

'Can't arrest a body, can you, lad?'

Just then, Dylan bounces in. He's not in Lowies. Black trousers, shoes, white Marksies shirt on, a bit see-through, and a tie. He's in a bit of a fluster, his speech scribbled down on the back of a betting slip. He looks at Bleeker in his coffin, says no to a line but opens a green can of Carlsberg. 'Got to stay straight to make sure this goes off half all right,' he explains, looking around.

'Is right,' says Lupus.

'Heard the funeral man had done a boss job on Bleeker's head,' says Dylan. 'Looks good, dunnit?'

The funeral director had tried hard to reattach Bleeker's head to the body but failed. The side of Bleeker's head was caved in and there were lacerations on his forehead and across most of the body. There was no way he could have sewn the head back on – with clearly visible, Frankenstein-style thread – and covered up the other horrific injuries with make-up. He concluded that the only solution was to physically cover up most of the face and body somehow. At first, he thought of using silk and lace and various tricks of undertaker's upholstery, like he did with crushed car-crash victims. He'd phoned Paul to ask him to phone Dylan and run it past him. It was then that Dylan had come up with the genius idea of burying Bleeker's body in his Lowies. His black Sprayway had a full peaked hood and the six-inch-high, cylindrical collar easily covered the area of severance. They put a grey Berghaus baseball cap on the head and covered the whole lot with the oversized Sprayway hood, toggled tight so that only a disc of face around his nose could be seen.

Dylan checks out the coffin. 'Mad, isn't it? Look how thin the wood is, lad. It's plywood.'

'Nice though, isn't it?' says Lupus. 'Got a nice finish on it.'

Clegsy uses the technical term: 'Veneer, it is. Veneer.'

'OK, fucking veneer, then,' says Lupus, still stung by Nogger bullying him over the gun.

Dylan tries to calm it all down: 'I know, lad. Thought they were solid oak. But it's just a *wood effect*. Can you believe that, lad? Reminds me of that auld plastic wooden wallpaper me nan used to have.'

'I know, yeah,' Lupus agrees. 'It's like the wooden floor in ours – shit. And look at the handles. They're plazzie brass as well. Weird, innit?'

Bizzies line the whole route of the funeral cortège. A police helicopter hovers at low altitude, the noise enveloping the whole estate. Everyone's buzzing with it. Old women standing at the front gates of their houses are forced to talk in higher voices.

What they can't see or hear is the unmanned surveillance drone that the police have launched, flying high above the chopper, spying on them from just under 20,000 ft. It's their latest weapon in the War on Gangs, or so said the police propaganda in the *Echo* a few weeks earlier. A Watchkeeper Tactical Unmanned Air Vehicle, the article called it, next to a picture of a remote-controlled plane about the size of a car and the chief con, his silver buttons and medals gleaming, showing it off. Clegsy says it's the same as the ones the army use in Afghanistan. But Clegsy, who reads all the technical sites on the Internet to keep up on latest police kit, says the bizzies bought it because similar ones had been used to good effect by the Israelis in the Gaza Strip. He says it sends back its video feed to a specially built suite on a secret industrial unit – disguised as a civilian business – on the dock road.

Yellow Vaderis bases – heavily armoured, computerised Mercedes Sprinter vans – are sat off in side streets. The Vaderis Disruption Corps is Merseyside Police's semi-militarised anti-gang unit, set up to 'tackle gun crime and faction-based disorder'. The corps' motto – 'Speed. Aggression. Mobility.' – is stencilled underneath the Vaderis logo – a hooded criminal in the crosshairs of an electronic target designator – on the sides of the vans. The corps is fully independent with its own armed response units, incident response vehicles and rope access teams.

A battle group of 20 vans had descended from the dawn horizon at 4 a.m., come in low out of the rising sun. The plan is to contain the funeral with a two-pronged manoeuvre, an urban warfare Schlieffen Plan. One arm is Operation Sphere (objective: show of force). The second, lighter arm is Operation Neon (objective: rapid deployment/ operational flexibility). The convoy of ships peeled off into a two-line formation at the roundabout at the entrance to the estate, cruising through like a fleet of spaceships, their state-of-the-art emergency lights strobing and randomising in the Vaderis Corps' colours, lighting up the sky. *Star Wars on Earth*.

Vaderis disruption reconnaissance teams are already plotted up secretly on the estate, Waffen SS camouflaged up, buried SAS-style in holes and in dugouts in derelict houses, infrared sights on, safety catches off their sniper rifles. They're waiting for the high-impact players to come onto the battlefield, into the crosshairs. They've got standing orders to take them out if they threaten public safety.

As soon as the cortège leaves The Strand, council workers move in to remove the flowers. Riot bizzies stand to, the back doors of their ships open, their shields – giant Perspex rectangles – stacked purposefully but untidily against the roll-bar cage in which they are stored. Armed response vehicles are parked nearby to protect the flanks of the stationary Vaderis columns. A detachment of StreetSafe vans has been drafted in, small Peugeot Expert vans known as 'bugs' because of their bulbous shape. Two of the yellow bugs have got their periscope cameras high in the air.

Bleeker's coffin is in the back of a blacked-out Humvee. Behind, there's a big crew of mourners. They look like a football crew being escorted to a moody away, all in black and masked up. A few high kicks are aimed at the camera crews and snappers at the side of the road. Two photographers get had off. A backpack full of equipment is ragged off one, a £4,000 Apple Mac G4 is swallowed up by the crowd. 'Victim. Bringing that to this. Imagine that, lad.' The tail end – a crew of about 20 lads – start rioting with the bizzies. The route of the cortège was deliberately planned by some of the older lads so that it cut right through The Boot. That way there'd be lots of urban-disturbance ammo to hand. Vaderis vans are getting twatted by concrete and metal bars now. Chants of 'RIP Bleeker' and 'Dead Crocky Rats'.

A few of the lads are carrying. Some are not. Five years mandatory, and there'll be a load of arrests today. Mostly the ones that are owe money to someone or other. The best place to cop for someone you're after is at a funeral. Everyone knows that.

Into Norris Green cemetery and gravestones are being booted over, others hid behind to stop the bizzy surveillance photographers getting shots. Big stone crosses are being toppled from plinths, clay pots being booted to fuck, tagged, sprayed up. The priest and the gravediggers have been ran and are stood by the wall of the cemetery under police protection. Two gravediggers were chased with a samurai sword. The lads are arming themselves with the spades and pickaxes they left behind.

Dylan takes charge of the funeral, trying to restore order, trying to get Bleeker buried before the Vaderis pile in. 'Come 'ead get Bleeker's coffin,' he tells the lads. It's ragged out the back of the Humvee and Bloot jumps down the hole so that he can help lower it in. ''Ere y'are, let me get this end.' The coffin's manhandled into the hole. All hands have got mobiles out filming it for the video DJ tribute later. Lupus jumps in the Humvee. The drivers have cleared the scene. He puts on a show for the

TV cameras, flooring it up and down the cemetery – handbrake turns, doughnuts, double-clutching it, smoke, burning rubber.

Dylan makes his speech: 'We're gathered here today to remember a true Nogzy solja. What people forget is that Bleeker had never had fuck all. He never had a chance. His ma was a scag and an alky. His auld feller was a baghead.' He looks at Laurence in the crowd, thinking, 'No disrespect, Laurence, but you were bang into the rocks for time when Bleeker was a kid.'

He continues, 'It's mainly down to that he turned out the way he did. Who wouldn't, sat in front of the vid watching *Scarface* all day? Poor cunt. Ashes to ashes, lad. God bless.'

The finale. An IRA-style honour guard appears out of the chaos, and quickly takes up position near the grave. Two lads, Lowied up, stand on the muddy edges. One lad with a long feller jumps into the grave to hide the length of the shottie, stands on top of the coffin.

Nogger gives the orders: 'Present arms.' The lad in the grave with the shottie puts the stock into his shoulder and raises the barrel like a lord on a grouse shoot, squints his eyes. One of the other lads at the side of the grave raises a nine millie, held horizontally. The other raises a Magnum revolver, frailly, heavily, with both hands, like the kid in *Once Upon a Time in America* who shoots little Dominic. 'Take aim.' Everyone's cocked and ready to go. Extraction teams discreetly take up position ready to get the lads out ASAP. 'Fire.' Bang! Bang! Bang!

Nogger, head bowed: 'Is right.'

CHAPTER 6

THE WAKE

Back to the Station House for the wake. Running battles with the bizzies all the way, them trying to snatch the honour guard, the lads trying to rag the camera crews. One bird TV reporter – thin, petite, smart, in a tight-fitting, satin shirt from Pink, an elegant stripe running through the dark, well-cut pinstripe trousers, a glossy black belt with matching practical heels – has blood matting her severe, shiny bob. She's winded, holding her chest, been booted in the tit, a flying cage-fighter kick. A dark-red stain is spreading like a blood blister through her shirt from under her bra. Her cameraman, a war reporter, is panic-sobbing now, running into his outside-broadcast vehicle to hide inside. His mobile, lappy, video camera are gone, smashed and scattered on the floor. He's covering his arse, on the phone to his bosses already, telling them that it wasn't his fault.

Pacer's terroring the bystanders lining the route. He lets off a CS canister then follows through with a squirty full of acid. 'You fucking ghouls! Bleeker was our Lady Dee,' he buzzes, pronouncing it wrong on purpose, French-wise, like he's seen on the telly.

On the steps of the pub, no one's happy. The manager, Roberto Griffin, has come out to the door to see what's going on. By day, he's the estate crank; by night, a mercenary. He shot Bleeker's bird once, way back, after she aborted his kid. Nogger pulls out a .38 to do him. Dylan steps in to negotiate with the head doorman, who's standing shakily behind Roberto.

The head doorman's a big roid head, but all right, old school: 'Look, lad,' he says, beginning his talk-round. But he's put under manners straight away.

'Never mind the "look, lad" and "we're only doing a job" and all that carry on,' Nogger tells him. The head doorman shuts the fuck up.

Lupus is arsing about in the background, howling, 'We're only out for a bevvy,' mimicking the knocked-back Friday-night revellers.

'I know where you're coming from, Dylan,' says the head doorman, 'but youse can't be causing any trouble here tonight.'

'It's up to you, lad,' Dylan tells him. 'That's all I'm saying. But mark my words, lad,' he says, pointing at Roberto, 'big mad mercenary or not, if he doesn't let us in, he will be fucking smoked.'

They're surrounded by little skinny kids armed to the teeth. Everyone's a bit panicky now, even Roberto Griffin. He's wanted in the Balkans for torching villages, was leader of a Croatian fascist HOS unit during the war there, 20-odd women and children to his name, he says, triangulation of fire, textbook IRA, no DNA. But even he's a bit 'What's going on?' now, looking around him, arse gone. He's naked – no gun. He knows there's nothing he can do to the rats. He'll stew in private later, shout at his sister, say that he's gonna put their heads on sticks, all the Rhodesian Army dogs-of-war stuff. But he can do fuck all for now.

'Listen, you fucking crank,' says Nogger. 'I'll put one in you now the same way you dropped those refugees, you fucking maggot. Now fuck off.'

Roberto, the regional ju-jitsu champion in his £900 military-strength bulletproof jacket, is impotent.

'Big fucking gangster? Fuck off!' Clegsy tells him. 'You fucking prick. Big-time Charlie fucking atrocities. Still live with your biff fucking sister, you prick. I'll set the fucking scrubber on fire if you don't fuck off now.' Roberto's sister has multiple sclerosis. She works for the council. Everyone thinks she's a grass.

'Think of your little sister, lad,' says Pacer. 'I'll rape her arse, lad. Anally rape the fucking mong slag. I'll ram that fucking pole up her baggy, red arse, lad. At the bingo, lad.'

Roberto Griffin, kidnapper, torturer, player of Romanian fascist marching songs, reckons he was asked to 'stay behind' by NATO after the Russian invasion, is humiliated now.

'No need for this, lads,' says the head doorman. 'Youse are only out for a bevvy.'

'Shut up, prick,' says Nogger, his .38 palmed at 90 degrees to the vertical, quick off the draw. He has it pointed at Roberto's skinny neck. Code Red now. Lupus and Dylan are wincing backwards slightly. New Loon has his fingers in his ears, waiting for the bang. They're all getting out the way of the blood spray, the forensics, Dylan not wanting to get his new shirt bukkaked up with claret and sulphur on the day of Bleeker's funeral.

Roberto breaks the deadlock, agrees to stand down, giving 'out of respect for Bleeker's family' as his outro. 'Fuck off, you big lanky ming,' Nogger tells him, wiping a bead of sweat off Roberto's wobbly neck with the barrel of the snub-nose.

Dylan, trying not to laugh, shakes Roberto's hands, big mad bear hugs, little pats on the back. 'Nice one, Roberto,' he says. 'Sorry about all that carry-on. Lads are bit tense and that, cos of the funeral.'

'It's all right, mate. I understand. It's just the shock and that, when you lose one of your crew. I know . . .' Dylan has to try not to burst out laughing at the word 'mate'.

Into the function room. Nogger and Dylan have a little livener off the table. Iggo tries to cop for the till behind the bar.

There's a little group of lads in the corner left over from the previous do, squaddies having a last drink for their mate killed abroad somewhere in the War on Terror. Dylan sends over three pints. Jay starts asking them about 'dropping niggers', before robbing one of their mobile phones and laughing at them for fighting for someone else.

Bleeker's bird's playing the grieving widow, holding court, loving the attention. Nogger cops for her as she's coming out of a cubicle in the birds' bogs, pushes her back in. Stinks. She's just had a shit. There's baby laxative in the charlie. *Bogs'll be pebble-dashed up in half an hour. Anyway, this'll take the smell away.* He chops out a line for her on the cistern. He's got half-decent gear, cut with the beno. She's crying. *Weeping widow, lad.* She won't give him a blowie 'out of respect' for Bleeker, but settles on a wank for him instead. Nogger roughly uncups her big puppy tits. He's soft off the stripes, soft because she's not young enough but dying to come off the stripes as well. He finally spurts over her falsies, bought in the boom by a local baron but balloony and droopy now.

Then he tries his luck over Bleeker's stash again as she's cleaning herself up with some bog roll. *You fucking animal.* He despises her. Desperate to get away from her within seconds of coming, but having to be nice to her, his eyes on the prize now. 'So what about this parcel, girl? That Bleeker got before . . . he got walloped.'

Marie's adjusting her Just Cavalli top from the wank and her hotpants from her shit. 'Told you, lad,' she says. 'It's gone. Told you. Couple of lads from Anfield came down last night.'

'Why didn't you bell me, girl? I would have sorted that,' he asks, pride dented cos he should be able to sort the graft on his own patch.

'Fuck off, Nogger, lad. Sorted? Snorted, more like. Or fucking had it off.'

Nogger bangs her right on the nose, a heavy, precise boxing-club jab. Bang! Fuck Off! Her septum spreads across her face, splits like a ripe fruit on concrete flags, blood all over the show. 'You dirty fucking animal,' he says.

Nogger grabs hold of her extensions at the back of her head, wallops her face against the cistern. 'Anfield? Fucking Anfield. Beef down there, girl. Take the little cunts to an abode.' Garbled rage.

Nogger pulls the extensions out, a fistful of hair coming away at the wax-adhesive joins. Then he rips her earring out of the fleshy lobe. It's gold, bejewelled, so it goes into his vertical side pocket, no messing about. One of her false lashes is hanging off by a string of lash gel, dried residue like flakes of dandruff on her eyebrow and lids.

'Can't believe you'd do that!' he rants. 'Offload Bleeker's graft to someone you don't even know. While I'm being nice to you. Fucking cocaine? 'Ere y'are. Here's some fucking cocaine.' Nogger pushes her bladdered nose into the small heaps of cocaine racked out on the cistern. Some of the blood dissolves the powder, the liquid sucking it up. Viscous suspension.

Nogger peels her head back with his arm and smashes it into the cistern again, her teeth cracking against the rounded ceramic edges. She's had SuperSmiles Mobile Teeth Whitening. Seen it in *Grazia*. Now they're smashed and her mouth is full of blood. He follows through by ragging her eyes downwards across the broken flush handle. Marie howls, hysterical.

'Take away the pain, girl?' Nogger asks, taking out an ounce bag of white powder from his pocket. He grabs a fistful and sprinkles it over her bubbling mouth, her hair, her smudgy, bloody ear. 'Don't need Bleeker's bits, girl. Got me own. And it's not shit either. No fucking mannitol in this. Bashed up with the beno. From a Paki in Nottingham.'

Nogger rags up her skirt, draws her down and rapes her arse, his herpes sores grating against her tight, hairy rectum and the rib of her stretched knickers. She's sobbing. Nogger's pushing in and out, no hands, just vibrating his hips. In and out. Kerfuffling about in his jacket pockets for his phone. Finds it. Menu. Applications. Camera. Flicks through it to get the video on and starts filming it, pulling his neckwarmer up over his grid just in case. *Could be reflections in the tiles.*

In the quiet, concentrating hard to come, Nogger can hear a few girls snorting in the next cubicle. One shouts over, 'You all right, Marie?'

Nogger answers for her. 'She's just having a little cry over Bleeker and that, girl. No sweat. Just sorting her out,' he says, knowing they'll think he means he's giving her a line to help with the grief.

'Aarh! You'll be all right, girl. Have a little line and you'll feel better.' The girls go back to snorting their own off their fellas.

Marie sobs a bit louder and turns her head towards Nogger, bent over the bog, her face covered in blood, congealing now and shiny with surface tension. Black blood is bubbling up from her gums. She's flicking her tongue in and out like a lizard, trying to lick a few specs of powder off the coagulating film of blood and powder, her face a grotesque mask. Money shot. Nogger splurges. Can't help it. Right up her arse. Tight and silent. Keeps his dick in there, balling her deep down with his hips, even during the flourish of his orgasm, but doesn't make a sound. He's used to keeping his rapes under wraps. 'RIP Bleeker,' he whispers finally.

Back in the function room, everyone's charlied up to death, drinking loads. Three-day bender on the cards, for sure. A few of the girls, just arrived, are in new pyjamas and Ugg boots, standard daytime wear for flitting between their mates' houses and nipping to the shop for a pint of milk. Tupac and Biggie Smalls on the disco. But everything's turned off when Bleeker's nan turns up. She's very old, 90-odd, in a wheelchair, no teeth. Laurence gets out his mobile phone, plays 'You'll Never Walk Alone'. Puts it through the MC's mike. Everyone joins in for the street hymn. Loads of crying. The room is smashed up, petrolised, then set on fire.

The lads head down to the ePod, a concrete and sheet-metal box on an industrial estate. It was originally built as a giant logistics complex but was turned into a club after the local factories were pushed out by the new light industry – mass drug-dealing. DJs from the Pleasure Rooms are on. All the lads bail in. Everyone gets a walkover, so they don't have to pay, but the doormen make Lupus and Clegsy, who are carrying the guns, leave them in the car.

Pauline's over there, Pauline MacInerney, the girlfriend of Everton's new wonderkid Rocky O'Rourke. *Heat/Closer/Grazia* are calling her the new Coleen. She was a sixth-former at Holly Lodge last week; this week she's a multimillionaire WAG.

She's reverting to type now. Her phoney smile has started slipping into a crooked snarl as she argues with some girls off her old estate who've come over to wish her well. She's wearing tight jeans, heels, dark, oversized sunglasses, a tight, white body, fastened at the gusset. Looks half-decent over her bumps. Her hair's done in a mad WAG style, kind of a rockabilly bun, with a big hairsprayed quiff.

New Loon shouts over, 'Tell your Rocky I'm gonna burst his ball, girl. Then I'm gonna burst him – from the stands with a sight-mounted SA80.' He grins. Pauline can't hear him because of the music, so he brings his arms up to shoulder height, as though he's holding a sniper rifle, Lee Harvey Oswald-style.

'Bang. I'm going to 'plode his grid. Ugly twat.'

Pauline's ex-SAS bodyguards close ranks around her. Doormen, plated up in body armour, move in. To ease the tension, a trayful of whiskies is brought for the lads. Appeasement.

The lads are taking Magic, powdered Ecstasy. None of them dance. They line up, shadow boxing on the spot in time to the music.

Dylan's mobile goes off. Caller ID shows a code name he's keyed in for Paul McQuillum.

'How you doing, my mate?' asks Paul.

'Sound.'

'What are you up to?'

'Just at the ePod. At the wake and that.'

'Was all right, that, wasn't it?' Paul says, obliquely referring to the successful body retrieval and the execution of the burial.

'No sweat, lad.'

Paul makes a mad, strangulated sound, like a coughing animal, the automatic, ingrained behaviour of a drug dealer used to covering up his phone conversations with random noises in order to prevent being taped. It's a cue to move on and say little else over the phone.

'Pop into the hotel, if you're around, for a cup of tea,' says Paul.

'OK.'

'We can have a walk around the town, bowl of soup in the Chinese, whatever you're up to.'

'Nice one.'

'Whenever you're ready. Any time when you've got five minutes.'

'OK.'

'By the way, the other feller [Peter] got a little thing for you there for helping him out there.'

'You don't have to do that, mate.'

'Listen, mate, we've all got to live. We've all got mobile bills to sort. We've all got families and sisters and that.' Paul's letting Dylan know he understands his situation.

Dylan wants the dough badly. It's much needed. He divvies it up quickly in his mind, guessing it'll be about a grand: £500 to his nan for looking after his two younger brothers and his sister; £100 to his sister for some new gear; £100 to his ma for a day's brown and white; £150 for some new gear for himself; £150 for the night out tonight. But he has to pretend to Paul that he isn't arsed about the money, that he's mysteriously doing all right from his gang graft.

'Listen, mate, that was a present from me. A gift on the day of my daughter's wedding, mate,' says Dylan, both of them buzzing off the in-joke off of *The Godfather*.

'No, no, no. Listen, mate, behave yourself.'

'Sound, mate,' says Dylan, massively relieved about the money, buzzing.

'And I've sorted you out at that Sacchanalia bar for a little drink and that. Take your bird or one of your mates if you want.'

So Dylan and Nogger got off in a Joe into town.

CHAPTER 7

WAG PARTY

Dylan, Nogger. Graft-reward meeting for getting the body back, a little sweetener off Paul McQuillum. Outside the bar, the roid-head doormen – shaved heads, black coats, ID passes in white plastic holders on silver-ball chains – are serious but a bit too undisciplined and not arsed to be professional. Regional. Dylan and Nogger are not arsed either. No let-ons, no shaking hands, no 'all right, mate', no big mad doorman hugs, no Scouse *Sopranos* stuff – just right up to the door.

The door team stand back in deference to Dylan and Nogger. For the first time tonight they're cowed. They've been rock hard all night to bits of birds and office workers, bullying daft waglets, *civilians*. But not any more. The doormen are suddenly aware of their mortality.

They're impotent. Any gyp, and Nogger will do one of them. Nine out. Bang! Bang! Bang! Or tomorrow he'll find one of the two-up, two-downs where they live. And before the roid head even has a call-out, before he's even started his morning ablutions – shitting out the smelly weight-gain powder, the runny raw eggs by the glass, the chemically steds – Nogger'll nail the windows shut, seal the door shut, petrol-bomb the place. Industrial fireworks through the windows, kids' bedroom as well. Stick a nail bomb in there. Everyone understands this. *In an instant.* The roid-head doormen pricks are seeing images of their toddlers burning, Peppa Pig PJs melting like a plastic bag.

Dylan and Nogger bounce through, expressionless but buzzing off facing down the doormen, egos pumped up off the serious gangster flex. Pianoey house music drifts over them in waves, getting louder, pumping them further. *Scarface*.

A row of ten tellies is stuck to the right-hand wall above head height, showing Nogger and Dylan walking through the atrium. Live. Liverpool

Fashion Week TV. Nogger instinctively covers his face with his right arm, flicks his hood up with a slight bow. Inside, the place is full of waglets in short, floaty dresses with patchy orange tans and straightened, shoulder-length blonde hair. Dylan knows he should feel aroused, but an image of their waxed, red-raw-round-the-edges fannies flashes into his mind and he feels deadened.

Dylan and Nogger head into a VIP booth off to the left. The table's dirty and wet with spilled drinks. Dylan gets onto a waglet: silky empire-line dress, two strips of fabric covering her false tits, hard, angular face, funny, scowly grid. She's dancing a bit, serious, pretending she doesn't notice she's desired. But she soon loses her on-top-ness when the Queen WAG waltzes in and steals the show. Pauline MacInerney's out to celebrate her feller being picked to play for England.

Everyone's looking. All the girls want to talk to her, talk shit to her about a shared experience in Cricket. She gives a random waglet the nod of approval: 'You're lovely.' Tells her her dress/handbag/shoes are gorgeous. The random waglet has got her hair seriously wrong. Even Dylan can see that. Peaches Geldof messy bob crossed with a retro beehive. *You're not Amy Winehouse, girl,* Dylan thinks to himself. How can that dirty rip Pauline think that that's a good hairdo? Dylan cannot believe it.

Nogger, oblivious to the gone-wrong hair and a bit confused that he's no longer the centre of, starts shouting over, 'Pauline, you fucking smelly ming, your Rocky's a tit.' A few of the older gangsters look over. The ones who like kissing Rocky's arse, the match-heads who look after Pauline when she goes around the town and that. The ones who keep away the beauts who dance too close, stop anyone with a moody camera phone getting on her case. But then try and shag her on the way home, try and cop for her in Rocky's Rangey, to viciously, jealously put one up him while he's playing away. None of them wants to say nothing to Nogger and Dylan.

Rows of low-status WAGs are lined up at the bar gawping at Pauline, wanting to talk to her. Dylan feels deadened by the shallowness. Nogger can't chat up birds: no socialisation process. He just goes to brass-houses and shags schoolies. Instant gratification. But Dylan has a go. He moseys over to the waglet he spied before, not the rough Peaches Geldof one but the scowly silk-dress one, hard-faced, pursing her lips and flicking her hair dramatically.

'D'you wanna drink?' he asks, shy. He's seen this on the telly, on *Corrie* or *Easties*. The waglet fucks him off immediately, because he looks like a scruff. She looks into the distance, into the green dance-floor LEDs, not blinking. She's wearing True Sapphire blue contact lenses. Her face is taut, tough. Waxen cheekbones. Her dream is to marry a cage fighter. But Dylan knows she might settle for him with a bit of persuasion. 'Got some nice powder there,' he says. 'Off the block. Yellow and crumbly.' Instant result. At once, the waglet picks up her £600 furry alpaca bag with chain handle. Dylan notices a patch of the fur is matted with spilt, sticky drink. They go into the disabled bogs for a line.

Back in the club, Dylan asks her again, 'D'you wanna drink?'

'Rosé champagne, lad. Cristal. Bottle of.'

The tray is delivered ostentatiously by a retinue of barmaids. They part the crowd, carrying Roman-style torches topped off with industrial sparklers. One barmaid is dressed in a gold lamé swimsuit and a purple sash saying 'Cristal' on it. Close-up, Dylan notices that the gold costume is faintly dirty, smudgy and sweaty as though she's worn it night after night, got it from a stinky box in the staff changey. But the cups of the swimsuit are metallic-smooth and full. Dylan gets half a tingle on. She places the bottle in a foot-high golden champagne bucket on the bar. Dylan notices that the bucket is slightly dented. All hands in the club are looking over, groups of gangsters and their girls huddled around tiny VIP booths, hate and envy in their eyes. Dylan feels like a cunt, but his WAG is beaming, although she's trying to hide it. She's got one over on everyone in one fell swoop.

She's called Casey. She doesn't talk to Dylan. She just stands next to him and dances, looking into the distance, pouty, concentrating hard to keep the detached look on her face. She stays clear of the Cristal on the bar so maximum hands can see it, to savour the fact that it's hers. Within minutes, sparklers and lamé birds are criss-crossing the club as the jealous desires of the other WAGs are satiated.

Nogger is on the dance floor, shadow boxing on the spot. Does a few high kicks in the direction of a mirrored column, his fists in fighting position, held tight to his cheeks, like a picture of the Krays he's seen. He pulls a bird's hair he fancies, spits at another. Dylan's like that: 'He's only having a dance, girl.' He knows it's time to go soon, to the brass-house, before murder breaks out.

'Come 'ead,' says Nogger. 'Let's get off to the massage parlour.'

'OK, yeah.'

Dylan explains to the waglet, apologetically, 'Just to get him sorted, girl. Otherwise he'll start kicking off.'

'What d'you mean, lad?' asks Casey.

'Just gonna take him down to The Cathouse. Get him a bird, girl. Then we'll get off somewhere nice.'

The waglet puts on a hard-done-by expression, scowling and pouting like an R'n'B diva, eyes wide, arms crossed. 'Where, lad?'

'Got a nice little caravan, there. On the path, girl. It's boss, la. Nice and warm. Get in there, have a weed.'

'What? D'you think I'm some kind of fuckin' dickhead or something? Think I'm waiting around in a brass-house then getting walloped all round a caravan by you? In Nogzy?'

'What d'you mean, girl?' asks Dylan, genuinely hurt.

'I wanna go to a hotel for the night. Like any other normal girl. Think I'm some kind of fucking scrubber, lad?'

Dylan has never been to a hotel. 'What d'you mean? Go on holiday? I've only known you five minutes, girl.'

'No, you prick. I mean take me down the Malmaison or the Radisson like normal fellers do. D'you think Pauline goes back to smoke weed in a caravan? What are you, you little fucking ming?'

Dylan shakes his head in disbelief. They jump in a cab and Nogger gives the driver the address and launches his chippy – shredded crispy duck in hoisin sauce with pancakes (untouched in their plastic wrapper) – onto the floor of the cab, then boots it upwards so that the polystyrene tray sticks to the glass partition just behind the driver's head and slides down, like blood. The driver says fuck all and Nogger falls asleep.

Dylan gets to work on the waglet. She gives him a wank under his Lowies, saying ta for the Cristal under her stinky breath, letting him know the connection between his orgasm and her satiated consumer desire, for future reference.

When they get there, Nogger wakes up from his alcopop slumber feeling aggressive. He throws a 50-quid note at the driver and tells him, 'Wait here, you fucking scruff.' Then he tells Dylan, 'Leave that slag in the back, lad.'

Casey, air-drying the come on her hands, retorts, 'Who you calling a fucking slag? You fucking victim. I'll phone someone now, lad. Turn you into a fucking sieve, you fucking drip.'

Nogger just laughs. Dylan's wiping the fast-drying come off his kecks with her furry alpaca bag, laughing as well. 'Just wait here, girl,' he says. 'Look after her, will you, lad?' he says to the driver. 'I'll sort you out later.'

Dylan and Nogger slip through the steel security gates into the camera'd-up alleyway and ring the buzzer.

'Can I help you?'

'Here to see Gabby, girl,' answers Nogger.

'There's an hour's wait.'

'Yeah, as if. Buzz us in, girl.'

Clank. The big metal shutter opens. It's like a prison. They're up the stairs fast. The receptionist opens the gate at the top. She's 50-odd, short, grey, chemically hair. Sometimes wears a rubber catsuit for a bit of extra dough. Dylan's shagged her before now.

The place is packed, sweaty, smoky. Lads are wandering around half-undressed, waiting to go into a cubicle, stoned and carrying their trainies in their hands. A Liverpool FC youth-team player is stood naked in reception, high, too horny to wait, trying to cop for a wank off the other receptionist, a young mum. There's the smell of green and a couple of lads are snorting.

Nogger clocks Rocky O'Rourke, asks him, 'What are you doing in here, you fucking Crocky rat?'

'Same as you, lad.'

'Fuck off, you twat.'

O'Rourke shoots off, back to a semi-circular booth with a couch covered in thin red velvet, lies down next to several Liverpool and Everton youth-team and reserve-team players.

Nogger can't be arsed queuing, so he bursts into a cubicle: a red heart-shaped bed covered in threadbare, red school-play-quality satin, a wonky oil heater, the enamel burned brown because it's never switched off, a packet of antiseptic baby wipes. Gabby is kneeling on the bed. Forty-ish, bad hair, spots and blackened teeth from the drugs. She's wearing a cowgirl suit and a beige felt cowboy hat, a souvenir from a Blackpool seafront shop. Her top's off: pale skin, smooth, bowl-shaped breasts, tiny, red raspberry nipples. She's bent over a disabled man in callipers, giving him a blowie, his wheelchair at the side.

Nogger pushes the cripple over to the other side of the bed. He curls up into the foetal position and Nogger tells him, 'Look at the wall while I'm shagging her, lad. If you look up, lad, I'll break your legs.' He laughs at his joke. 'She'll finish you off after me, lad.'

Nogger snarl-smiles at Gabby. 'Fucking biff. What's he doing in here?'

'Ah, he's lovely, Nogger. I've got a few disabled clients.'

'What? Shut up, you fucking dickhead,' he says as he pushes her head downwards, her mouth locking onto his knob.

Nogger wallops the cowgirl on the heart-shaped bed. He puts her on top. His legs stiffen as he desperately tries to ejaculate, pushing the disabled man onto the floor at the side of the bed. Nogger kicks out slightly several times to make sure the man is completely off the bed. No interruptions while he's about to jizz up his brass, the heels of his trainies ragging up the red satin.

Afterwards, Nogger pushes the cowgirl off the bed on top of the disabled man. He tears her hat off and wipes the come on the soft felt. She's trying to get the man up from the floor and onto the unmade bed. 'Nogger, give us a hand, will ya?'

'Fuck off with him, will you, girl? Fucking Joey. Who d'you think I am, girl? Bob Geldof?'

'Are eh, Nogger.'

Nogger laughs. He pays the receptionist fifty quid and waits for his fiver change, sparks a Liverpool player on the way out.

CHAPTER 8

ON THE MEET

Big day today. A meet with the Imperator at the hotel. *At the hotel, lad.* Dylan keeps beaming to himself as he jogs on to the bus stop.

The hotel is a tall, deep rhomboid-shaped building clad in white, streakless marble. The ground floor is a wall of glass with heavy curtains behind. Expensive, expansive. Dylan steps into the huge revolving door. Warm air, sterile, blasts from jets above. Through the door's curved partition, he sees a blaze of colour, shape and gloss inside, dazzling even through the tinted glass. His eyes ache at the newness of it. He wants to lunge in, fast as, soak up the freshness of it.

Inside, Dylan stands helpless in the atrium, awestruck at the opulence. One wall as big as two buses is covered in solid, shiny plastic, delicately frosted, gently, hazily morphing into different colours: azure blue, faint pink, pale purple. Dylan breathes out, relaxing, gorping. *What the fuck is this?*

To the left, clean lines, curved white tables, thick swooshes of wood. Immaculate. To the right, the reception desk, a streaky, dark teak, curvily carved into big boxes, divided by narrow sheets of smoked glass.

No caved-in walls. No kids slowly destroying everything, chipping away at brick walls with a centre punch. No shards of shattered windscreen. No piles of shitty washing. No decay. No caravan on the front path. No plastic windows held in with brown tape. No little motorbikes lashed in the garden. No black-tyre fires. Only shiny gleam, dreamy order – and Dylan in his Lowies.

He looks up. Twenty floors, stacked up. *To the stars.* Thick, curved triangles of polished concrete on top of each other, glazed white, seamless and symmetrical, to the height of a tower block. Tiny ice-blue lights twinkle in the roof, thousands of them. *Fucking millions of them.*

'Maaate.' The stretched-out word is half-shouted from behind. *Paul.* Dylan about-faces. 'How you doin', my mate?' asks McQuillum. Big grin, big hug, then one hand round Dylan's shoulder. 'Come over into the office, my mate.' Dylan flushes with pride at being invited into the court, the inner sanctum.

'You OK, lad?' Paul asks.

'Sound. How's life at the top?'

'Wouldn't know, lad.' A knowing half-smile from the Imperator. He stops, gestures at Dylan's head with his hand, fingers together, palm slightly cupped. *Here comes the big-up.* 'Listen, mate, there's only one man around here who moves up there – and that's *you*.'

Dylan flushes at the use of the word 'man'. They laugh and shake hands, not formally, but with Paul's hand swooping downwards in front of him at 45 degrees, like a dogfight Spitfire, and Dylan's coming upwards like a southpaw uppercut. 'Maaate,' as they connect vigorously. Dylan's loving it, buzzing at being on the meet with the Imperator.

'How's business?' asks Dylan, egging Paul on now.

'Listen, lad, if I was doing any better . . . I'd be you.'

Whooah!

Behind the bar – a giant white Corian globe – is a large cordoned-off alcove: the office. They sit off on vast square chrome and leather chairs next to a low teak table. Paul calls over the bar lad, buzzes with him like a mate, shakes his hand, then asks for two seven-pound-a-throw cups of tea to be sent over. *Which he'll get for fuck all, by the way, cos everyone loves the cunt.*

In a mumbly voice, like a long cough, Paul says: 'Might have some work, there. Wages for youse and that.'

Might have. Hmmm. Dylan's disappointed that Paul's not committing straight off, but he remains expressionless, giving nothing away.

Paul's mouth forms a concerned, off-round 'o', then a 'we're not soft' smile, meaning, 'Best not talk in here – too on top.' He tells Dylan, 'We'll go for a walk in a minute. Around the town,' meaning, 'We'll speak outside.'

'Sound. Whatever,' says Dylan, letting the Imperator make the running. At the leige's leisure.

'Everything OK?' asks Dylan, keeping it neutral.

'Can't complain, lad. If I did, no one would listen, would they?'

Paul's biding his time, wondering if Dylan has been followed, if there's anyone moody in the hotel, any foes that Dylan might betray him to, impart his explosive info to.

'Just got a contract there to build a power station in South Africa. Worth 20 quid [£20 million].'

'That's good, innit?'

They shake hands. To toast Paul's good fortune.

It's all true. Paul's never told a lie. That's his power, telling the truth.

What he doesn't say is 'Yeah, I'm building a power station. But as you well know, I've also been bringing in Class As by the tankerful for 20 years. On an industrial scale. I have put myself at the centre of an empire, from Amsterdam to the Andes. But I'm post-industrial now. D'you get me? Richard Branson has got fuck all on me now. Branson, Alan Sugar, the Dragons – they've got fuck all on me now. D'you get me?'

Paul's letting Dylan know that he is super-league, that he cannot be trifled with. 'Abu Dhabi, mate. The other day. To see a man. An oil man. Few million barrels there. Know what I'm saying?'

'Is right,' says Dylan, who has £1.78 on him for the bus and a serrated kitchen knife down his bollocks in case he gets caught slipping on the way home.

'But I can't sell a flippin' drop.'

'What?' Dylan's nearly up off his seat in fighting stance at the unfairness of it.

'Not a drop, mate,' says Paul, a sad smile on his jowly pudding face.

'You're joking, aren't you?'

'Not even a can of oil for your bike, lad, can you sell,' says Paul, his temper rising, 'unless you've got a licence. Boxed off, lad. D'you get me? So the likes of me can't get their hand in the sweet jar. For hundreds of years, lad.'

'By who?' asks Dylan, his voice rising, getting right into it, the *Dallas* drama of it.

'By George Bush. Mark Thatcher. By the flippin' Illuminati . . . I don't flippin' know. Just *them*, innit?'

'No way.'

'Way, lad. But d'you think those pricks are gonna stop Paul McQuillum from taking what's rightfully his?'

'Can't see it, like.'

They shake hands in tribute to Paul's gargantuan one-man struggle against the Establishment, not only for himself but for Dylan as well, and for the likes of. So that Dylan and his boys can have a shot at the super-league one day when the time is right. *If they stay onside.*

'As it happens, like,' Paul continues, 'I knew another man, over there [points towards the bogs] in Uzbekistan – oil type, ten-gallon hat, all that – who's got the paperwork. I put the two of them together in a hotel. And guess what?'

'What?' replies Dylan.

'Got paid. Deals, innit, lad?' They shake hands. 'And I got a new carpet out it. A nice one, know what I'm saying?'

'Mad, innit?'

'There's no one we can't get to, mate. No one.'

Graft meetings can go on for days without anyone really saying anything, just chatting shit and stalling. Dylan knows that. Paul's still weighing it up. He hasn't decided yet if he can trust Dylan enough to work with him. *Work in haste, repent at leisure.* That's the Imperator's watchword. What he's trying to let Dylan know is: *'I can take you into the stratosphere, lad. I won't pull the ladder up. But wo-be-fucking-tide you if there's any behaviour once I've opened the door.'*

Ticker and Jo Jo come in, so there's a break in proceedings, a rest from the head games. They're sharp-witted old-school scallies, purveyors of moody goods to the cash rich, to supplement their pensions. They're selling jarg gear out of a bin-bag. Loads of old-style laughs. Paul buys a jarg Hugo Boss jacket. Dark blue, looks like an Argentinian army coat, Falklands-puffa-style. Seventy buff. *Looks all right, though.* Dylan buys five pairs of Emporio Armani socks, a pair of mad three-quarter-length Lacoste shorts made out of shiny nylon that catches on his nail, with big blocks of different sickly colours. Eighty quid. He doesn't want them, but he'll wear them in bed. Paul insists on paying for the stuff. He sorts it from his arse pocket. Little shake from Dylan, to say, 'Nice one. You shouldn't have.'

But that's the thing about Ticker, Dylan thinks. He's not cheap. But all hands want to keep him onside. Out of the alehouses, on the move in his little Punto. Cos he's flipping nightmare when he's had a drink. Paul notices Dylan's a bit sinkered by the over-the-odds prices and turns to him, one hand round the shoulder, cupped hand to the face, a bit of anger in him. 'He's one of us, mate,' he says. Dylan's taken back by his intensity, but he's back to normal almost immediately.

Paul's pointing at Dylan with his slightly cupped hand. *Here comes the public big-up.* 'You see this man?' Paul asks Ticker and Jo Jo, who get around to all the courtiers, his open hand zooming in on Dylan's face. 'Even if you had a telescope that could look into space, you couldn't look at this man.'

When the other two leave, Paul and Dylan go outside and get into the beige Lexus. 'Have a word in a minute,' Paul says, making a face to indicate that the car could be bugged.

They talk shit about the car for a bit, keeping to safe territory. It's rented, Paul says. 'If you buy one of these new, you lose five grand as soon as it comes off the forecourt. So, for that, the cost of depreciation, I get a free year's worth of use. D'you get me? Plus a service.' All the while, Paul's checking to see if they're being followed and he's thinking, weighing things up. *Are Dylan and his crew safe? Can these upstarts be trusted? Are they too hotheaded?*

They drive past a restaurant clad in shiny steel. The whole three-storey building. Dylan can't get over a whole building coated in weapons-grade steel. Paul's a bit put out at the spectacle of this investment that isn't his, in his city. 'Me mate Louis owns that,' he says. 'Know him, mate?' Dylan says nothing. 'He's all right, Louis. But he's a bit of a mouthpiece, know mean?' Paul's letting Dylan know the guy's the ultimate in scum: a grass.

They stop outside a huge Victorian red-brick warehouse, shut down, for sale. 'See that?' asks Paul. 'I'm developing that, lad: hotel, retail, flats. Planning for 200 units. I'm putting £40 million into that. Do you know what I'm covering it in?'

'No.'

'Gold leaf.'

'No!'

'Like in Dubai.' Paul breathes a sigh of relief, his ego back on track now.

Dylan decides he can't fuck about much longer. He needs to go for it now, get on the offensive. 'Mad about Leon, wasn't it?' he asks. That's all that needs to be said. He's bringing out the big guns. The fable of Leon, the 18-year-old urchin who took on the heavy hitters, in their mansions, in their nightclubs, in their businesses – and won. By spraying up their mansions. By nail-bombing their nightclubs. By burning down their businesses. Leon, who'd won because he was assetless. The heavy hitters lost because they had nowhere to run, trapped by their millions and billions. Leon, a hero to the likes of Dylan, Nogger and the lads.

Paul gets the message, but he just says, 'Mad that, wannit?' He sucks his teeth and a pinched look spreads across his face. What he's thinking is: *I've got no choice, have I?*

Dylan says nothing more. He's thinking: *Deals, innit? Let's get down to business now.*

They jump out and cut off quickly up a side street into a new-build estate. Squat red-brick bungalows, low garden walls, purple wheelie bins looking massive against the shit small houses.

Even outside, Paul refuses to speak openly, paranoid. Suddenly, he starts talking in a mad, twisted voice, throwing it like a ventriloquist. Dylan freaks and instinctively reaches for his knife, genuinely unnerved. Paul's saying, 'Uhiss as e hoary, rythe,' which Dylan works out means, 'This is the story, right.'

'You know me,' Paul goes on. 'I don't usually get involved in all this palaver.'

'Yeah. Go 'ead.'

'But I want you to do us a favour,' he says, still speaking in tongues.

'Yeah? What is it?'

'I want you to rob something for us.'

'Yeah. Anything. What is it?'

'A SIM card.'

CHAPTER 9

SIM CARD

Princess Park gates on a cold, March Saturday night. Old iron gates, black trees swooshing overhead in the wind. Crackheads are moving like zombies across a plain towards the gates, slowly coming together, in the shadows so the bizzies can't see them. They stand just a bit back from the gates, waiting to score.

One of them is a mixed-race kid with black cauterised moles on his skin. He's wearing a big medieval-looking hood with a shiny black jacket with letters on the back over the top – smackhead wear. He bells the dealer, the blue laser glow from his mobile phone lighting up the inside of his hood.

'All right, kidder. I'm by the bench.'

'Be there, in a minute, lad,' replies the dealer.

He's been saying that for more than an hour now. But he won't come until there's at least ten gathered to serve up to, until it's worth his while. Makes them wait, rattling in the freezing rain, for six hours sometimes, pregnant brasses, whatever. But they couldn't give a fuck. They've got the power – it's a seller's market. The mixed-race lad doesn't complain, case he's grassed up to the dealer for slagging him. The politics of scoring: you've got to be careful, grateful.

A skinny, scag-addict prostitute arrives on a bike. A 40-odd-year-old black woman called Chloe mooches out of the street halogens into the dark. Short hair, headband, white-rimmed, grafted sunglasses on, big, colourful bag. The fashiony accessories are to distract the eye from her crack-ridden, blistered face and unsure gait, to make her look normal to the security guards.

'When was the last time somebody phoned him?' she asks.

'Just now,' the mixed-race lad tells her. 'He's on his way.'

'Wish he'd hurry up, kidder. Going grafting after this. Want to get there before it closes.'

'Where d'you go?' asks the lad, chatting shit now.

'Asda.'

A stocky lad with a hard face is waiting too, his black woolly cap pulled right down to his eyes. Someone must be after him. He keeps using the words 'for time', seems nervous. Just got out from a seven-and-a-half stretch for armed robbery, he says. Got moved around the prison system, he says.

'Who's on?' he asks.

'One Arm,' Haden replies.

Haden claims to have been Britain's first crack dealer. He's on the gear himself now. He's done so much he's almost immune to it, though. He's wearing his all-blacks: black hood attached to his 20-quid bargain-basement Lowies with black goggles sown in. Looks like a gas mask. He goes out doing work in it.

Haden and four or five others phone the dealer one after the other. 'Eight or nine of us here now,' Haden tells him, trying to convince him that it's worth his while.

'Just coming now,' he says.

Everyone knows that could mean two minutes or three hours in the freezing cold. One new face appears. People nervously look for reassurance that he's not a bizzy. They make small talk.

One Arm arrives. One Arm is a 19-year-old former heroin addict who had his arm amputated. It had rotted away because it got infected from injecting. With him is a 12-year-old runner, a mixed-race kid called Ray-Ray. One Arm has a face like a *Scream* mask: skin dragged tight over his cheekbones like the membrane across an insect's wings; his mouth is slack, lozenge-shaped, his eyes slanted and drooping. He's terrified, walking very slowly, looking for signs of danger every step of the way. It's a dangerous job. They could be taxed at any moment.

They stop under the black of the trees. One Arm doubles over, like he's going to spew. Instead, he raises his good arm so that his hand is three inches below his nose and begins spitting out some of the tiny wraps of white and dark that are hidden in his mouth so that he can neck them if he gets stopped by the bizzies. Crackhead zombies rush him. They need to be served, fast.

'Get back, you fucking meffs,' says Ray-Ray. He's there to herd the punters into order and make sure One Arm doesn't get taxed while he's serving up.

The mixed-race baghead gives his order: 'Two whisky.'

'Five whisky,' says Chloe.

'Shut the fuck up, you dirty fucking wretch,' replies Ray-Ray.

'What, lad?' One Arm asks Haden.

'One white, lad.'

One Arm spits a dark out by accident. He puts it between his thumb and forefinger for another customer, snatches Haden's tenner with his three remaining fingers and folds it into the palm of his hand.

'Chloe,' he says, 'Karlos says you haven't been calling today. Have you been going to someone else?'

'No, love. Just not been around.'

'Listen, you dirty nigger,' says Ray-Ray, 'if we catch you scoring off those Tocky niggers, we'll fuck you off. And I'll give you a slap, girl.'

The kid has no respect for adults. The only adults he has ever known have been scagheads: the punters, his ma and da. Shit stains on their kecks cos they're too stoned to clean themselves properly. But the kids he knows are all straight, together, all grafting. They've got the power now.

Dylan's sat off in the bushes about ten metres away looking through a night sight he's taken off an SA80. He waits until all the punters except Chloe have been served up, then steps forward out of the bushes with a samurai sword.

'Stand still. Section 60. Stop and search,' he says. Then he tells One Arm, 'Empty your mouth, lad.' One Arm can do fuck all, but Ray-Ray goes for a gun. Dylan chops him a bit on the shoulder, slashes him fully across the arse and boots him into the leaves on the ground. 'That's for the beef you gave the girl, lad.'

One Arm spits the rest of the rocks into Dylan's leather glove. He hands them to Chloe. 'Be off, girl. Keep your fucking mouth shut. Stripe your arse like that little cunt's if you don't.' He's relying on the free gear – 70 quid of One Arm's stash – to shut her up.

Jay and three of the younger lads whizz round the corner in an old Toyota Previa, pick up Ray-Ray and put him in the boot. Dylan walks One Arm over to a bit of gravel by the gate. An old Tranny van pulls up, the side door open. He launches the dealer into the back, gets in and they drive off.

'Where's Karlos, lad? Where's the phone?' Dylan asks One Arm.

'Don't know, lad. Just get the calls from him, lad. "Go the gates." "Go by the doctor's." Whatever.'

Nogger pulls One Arm's trackies down from the back, like messing at school. He bends him over. One Arm has to put his hand on the wheel arch to balance. He's panicky, ready to burst into tears. 'What are you doin', lad? Are eh, lad.' He's suffocating in the helplessness.

Pacer gets One Arm in a head lock. Nogger fishes about with a mop handle, trying to find One Arm's arse.

Slowly he pushes it in until he gets well going, plunging backwards and forwards like he's trying to unblock a drain. 'Woah, lad,' he says, 'got a nice big ring on you there, lad.'

Clegsy, splayed against the back windows (blacked out with bin-bags) to keep his balance, asks, 'Karlos been getting stuck up you, lad?'

Dylan: 'Where's Karlos's ken, lad?'

'Don't know, lad. Don't fucking know.'

The mop handle's about nine inches in now. One Arm's trying to catch his breath. The van's ragging around fast. The graft's on. Big, grating revs, hard, deep gear changes. One Arm's sweating in the cold. Nogger puts on a spurt. Shoves the pole in and out, fast, for about 20 reps, like a jackhammer. Afterwards, he's fucked, his triceps ripped to shreds and burning, like pushing one more out on the weights. Clegsy takes over. Twenty more reps one after the other. One Arm not saying fuck all. Clegsy, breathless, says, 'Must be a fucking rent boy. Used to it, la.'

They leave the pole hanging out of his arse. Nogger steps around in front of him, trying hard to keep his balance as the van flies round a corner. He's holding Dylan's sword. He saws into One Arm's ribs, on the left side, opposite his good arm, so he can't move his hand to the wound.

At the lights, Clegsy nooses a scarf around One Arm's mouth to smother his howls, saying, 'Listen, lad, I'll saw through your cage if we don't find Karlos.'

'He's sat off near Park Road.'

They burst the ken, come through the door. Four young lads who answer the phones for Karlos are sat on the couch. Twelve mobile phones, the key components of Karlos's mini-call centre, are spread out on the coffee table before them. One kid is holding an Xbox gamepad, playing a game. One's got a load of sweets and wash-off tattoos that come free in packets of bubble-gum. Dylan ignores the small fry, runs straight past. He'll let the younger lads following in his trail deal with them.

Nogger steams straight through to the kitchen as well. Karlos is stood over the sink. He's a big cunt – skinhead, roid head, bulletproof vest on. Clegsy jumps on his back, strangling him with a wire coat-hanger, trying to suffocate him. 'You can't knock these big cunts out.' Pacer twats his face with the butt of a pistol. Karlos struggles like a wounded dinosaur. Clegsy's swinging about on his back like a child. Karlos braces his feet against the door frame to stop himself being dragged out. He knows the first rule of being taxed: don't let them get you on the floor or in the boot of a car.

Nogger and Dylan are busy looking for the main phone. Loads of rings and vibrates from the ones on the table. But Dylan's sussed out the MO in seconds, not arsed about the shit ones on the table. He tells Nogger, 'He'll have the main phone on him.' They look at Karlos. 'Those ones [he points his samurai sword at the table] don't take the calls off the punters. They're just the ones the cunt uses to phone the lads.' Dylan spies a Bluetooth earpiece in Karlos's right ear. 'He's holding it.'

Seven lads – Clegsy, Pacer, Iggo, New Loon, Lupus, Bloot and Nogger – are in the tiny kitchen punching, kicking, stabbing Karlos. But Karlos is using the tiny space to his advantage. Little Jay's stood at the kitchen door picking his moments to poke the beast with a sharpened metal bar.

Dylan tugs Jay out the way. Screams, 'Get off him! Out of the way!' Karlos is thinking he could be winning. The lads in the kitchen think it might be time to go, that their opportunity's gone. But lightning quick Dylan says to Nogger, 'Hold his arm up.' Dylan chops the hand, the left one, with an upstroke. Whooosh! It doesn't come off at first. The second chop, the downstroke, does the job. The fist opens. No phone there.

'Must be in the other one. For fuck's sake.' A fast lightsaber downstroke onto the right wrist. Pure Obi Wan in his younger days. 'Fuuuuck Offf!' Jay gasps in admiration. The hand topples off. Nogger's grinning maniacally, loves it when Dylan goes operational. This time the fingers remain clenched but the top of the phone can be seen. It's still going off with punters ringing in.

Karlos is stunned. Both hands severed. Nogger knocks him out with a small steel weights bar to stop him screaming, cuts the Bluetooth out of his ear with a kitchen knife. Dylan goes to pick up the hand with the phone in it from the floor. But it's skidded down the side of the cooker.

'For fuck's sake. Fucking typical.' He pokes it out with a drippy spatula from a chip pan. Nogger tries to nudge it along from above with the sword.

'Fucking be careful, will you?' says Dylan. 'Don't fucking break that phone.'

'Just giving you a hand, lad.'

Lupus and Pacer smirk at the joke. They're all buzzing cos they're seconds away from pure bart.

'Soft cunt,' says Dylan, chiding Nogger.

The hand's now sticking out slightly from the gap. Dylan picks it up with the tips of his fingers and lashes it in the sink.

Nogger peels back the clenched fingers, takes the phone and rags off the sovvies from two of the fingers. Dylan looks at the phone, an old Nokia N73 with a big screen, worth about £15. The number's worth £250,000.

Dylan's worked out the digits. Karlos's round does £50,000 a day, £2,000 an hour. About 80 callers an hour, spending, say, £25 each. Karlos is famous for his aggressive marketing on the street. Buy two get one free – two rocks (whisky) and one wrap (brandy). Bumper wraps for favoured customers. Hence his excellent sales figures.

They pile into the van, get off. Dylan takes the SIM out. 'Wouldn't believe it, lad, would you?' he asks Nogger. 'Quarter bar for that.'

'Back-door it, lad.'

'Can't. Got to get it to him within the hour. Too long and the bagheads'll start going somewhere else. It'll be worth fuck all by tomorrow.'

Dylan unpeels the cling film from five stones confiscated from One Arm before and carefully wraps the tiny see-through squares around the SIM to protect it.

Dylan explains that the client Paul's lined up to buy the card has already set up a call centre to take over the business. 'Two shifts' worth,' says Dylan. 'Two lots of workers. One on from ten till ten, then another overnight.'

'It's just gonna switch over like that?'

'Seamless, lad. Bagheads won't even know Karlos has been neutralised, d'you get me?'

'Mad, innit?'

'Graft, lad, innit?'

Dylan slots the SIM into his side pocket.

GANG WAR

On The Boot, they petrolise the van. The lads head into a derelict house. Lowies burned. Bodies chemical washed. Nasal hairs cut and ears swiped with cotton wool buds to get rid of any residues that might have stuck to them.

Dylan has to attend a prearranged handover at the McDonald's in Page Moss. He gets there early and orders two cups of tea, as planned. Crimson Formica tabletops, stained wooden trim. Good place to graft Mackie D's: big glass windows on three sides so you can see who's coming, one entrance, one car park, one bogs. It's bigger and less intimate than a caff and the punters are less chatty too. Workies in wide-collared rigger boots and hi-vis jackets. A scally dad in Lowies with two kids, mouthing the words to the piped tune. McDonald's is like smoking – an allowed respite from the struggle of daily life.

Dylan necks his tea as fast as, even though it's fucking boiling, then slots the cling-filmed SIM through the slot in the plastic lid. He picks up the full tea and has a couple of swigs.

Bulb Head, Paul's run-around, turns up. 'You Dylan?'

'All right?'

'You all right?'

'Yeah. Cup of tea there for you.'

Bulb Head picks up the empty cup containing the SIM. 'Got to go.' He gets off.

Dylan walks over to the Lidl next door, heads behind the bushes strewn with Big Mac cartons, crisp packets and plastic bottles of Coke. He picks up two brown-paper McDonald's bags. Heavy. £30,000 in cash. Get paid.

CHAPTER 10

FEVER

Next day they go down to Fever to get some new gear for Casey. Nogger pulls up in the black Rangey (a ringer, brand new, two grand, bought with the graft money). Casey jumps out. She's wearing a bright-red bell-bottomed catsuit, right up her arse. Low-cut halterneck round her falling-out, orange, plastic tits, red flamenco frills down the sides. Massive plate-sized sunglasses on. Wagged-up to death.

Nogger to Casey: 'Love to smell your arse, girl.' Romantic talk. They all bounce in the shop. The girl on the till tells Nogger, 'Can't smoke that in here.' Nogger lashes his joint on the laminate floor.

Pauline MacInerney pulls up in her baby Bentley outside, going to get her hair done next door. Nogger's onto her, banging on the window. 'Fuck off, you Crocky witch. Saw your Rocky in The Cathouse the other night, hanging out of some brass.' Pauline fucks them off. Half-snooty media grid on, handbag on arm, she slopes into the hairdressers.

Nogger turns to Dylan. 'Do the car, lad,' he says, looking at the baby Bentley parked outside. Dylan can't be arsed and laughs, but when he looks at Casey her eyes black with jealousy at a real WAG.

'Who the fuck does she think she is?' she says. 'Only shagging a 'baller. Thinks she's fucking Cheryl Cole or someone.'

'Pauline is a proper fucking celebrity now, girl,' says Nogger, winding her up. 'Wages in her own right, her, girl. On telly. In the magazines. All that.'

'All she is is a fucking prostitute, lad. Shags that ugly twat and gets paid in fucking mansions and swimming pools. What's the fucking difference between her and those girls he shags in The Cathouse? Fuck all, lad. Wouldn't shag Rocky O'Rourke if you give me a million pound. Beneath me, lad.'

'Fuck off, you dickhead,' says Nogger. 'You'd suck the fucking shit out of his arse if he fucking spat on you in the Mosquito, you fucking slag.'

'She wears a handbag in a magazine and all you scrubbers buy it,' Dylan tells her. 'Fucking gold dust to businesses, her, girl. Just a fucking walking advert, isn't she?'

'You shouldn't let that gobshite [looks at Nogger] talk to me like that. And are you gonna let that cunt [Pauline] show me up?'

Dylan's under pressure now. Next minute, he's outside. Keys the car goodo, down both sides, sprays it up with a can of robbed turquoise paint. 'RIP Crocky Rats' on the side. All the suck-hole hairdressers in the salon are telling Pauline what's happened, going mad. Dylan walks over to the window and mouths at her, with her curlers in, through the window: 'Call the bizzies and I'll bang you, you fucking Crocky rip. Got bummed by Anthony Mulhearn, girl.' As he's getting off, he mouths, 'Fucking Crocky rat. Tell Rocky I'm gonna smash his auld feller in the Canada Dock.'

Outside Fever are two giant flame burners, like something out of ancient Rome, draped in synthetic pink lace. Inside, the waglet tries on a purple basque and a Roberto Cavalli dress with a big fuck-off split right up to her fanny. 'Yes, girl.' The bill comes to £2,200. The manager takes Dylan into the back to pay and wrap the dress. In the stockroom, Dylan peels off a good few quid, all euros and Scottish notes, graft money.

There's a nice old bint out the back in the stockroom. Looks to be in her 40s. Nice big false tits. Wrinkly, tanned neck, black liver spots on her cleavage. Dylan wonders how you get dirty blemishes on new taigs like that. He gets a lob on. She's wearing just a grey trackie, the zip half down.

'Boss tits, them, girl.' She takes the compliment well. *You don't know with these auld ones.*

'Ta, lad,' she says. 'Might go up one this year.'

Dylan stares down her top. 'No, they're just the right size for you.'

She's got short old woman's hair, fluffy and feathery, over-dyed and chemically. Dylan loves it. Pulls down the front of his kecks. 'Get on that, girl.'

She sucks his young cock. He gets a tit wank off her over the desk, comes all over his Lowies and her black age spots. He has a little play with her falsies.

'Best get back to her in there,' he says. 'Top blowie, that, girl.'

'Ta, lad.'

They go back into town in the Rangey. Dylan drives. Nogger's lying on the back seat. Too on top, too many people are after him.

Casey tells Dylan, 'I wanna go to a hotel tonight.'

'Fuck's sake, girl. Only got ten quid off the graft. Spent two on you there. Fuck all left by the end of the week.' Dylan wants to keep five grand back, buy a quarter ki of white or half a ki of brown. Thirteens on a ki at the present, but he reckons he can get just under half for five grand.

'Well, fucking drop me off at me ma's then,' says Casey, 'cos I'm not fucking wasting me time. You're a fucking minge, lad.'

'It's you, girl. Fucking greedy twat. Want this. Want that. Slaughtered Pauline for being a whore but you're the fucking same. Fucking nightmare, you, girl.'

'You call Rocky fucking O'Rourke a cunt but at least he's got enough dough to take that fucking beast to a hotel. D'you get me? You, a fucking gangster? Know lads who work in Jaguar who make more money than you – *who've done more graft than you.*'

'Fuck off, you prick. Worked in Halewood, I'd be getting £400 a week. I spent more on fucking Cristal the other night, you greedy twat.'

'Be on me for a suck, later, lad, won't you, though? Be a different story, won't it? "Ah, Casey, d'you wanna prawn fried rice from the Chung Ku? Ar, come 'ead, Casey, just give us a li'l blowie." Well, you can fuck off and have a wank. Won't be happening, lad.'

Dylan and Nogger are pissing themselves.

'And don't think I didn't notice that bit of strange in the back of the shop then, you sly cunt,' Casey carries on. 'Fucking state of her. Getting a tug off of a pensioner.' Dylan gets a cherry on. 'Didn't know you liked the bingo-ites.'

Dylan's humiliated. 'Well, if you saw it, why didn't you fucking say nothing?'

'Cos you were buying me a two-grand fucking dress, fucking twat-hooks. Wouldn't have fucking minded if you were hanging out of Pauline or me fucking ma or me ten-year-old sister. Do not give a fuck what you do. As long as you're paying, lad, you can do what the fuck you like. Only problem, don't come sniffing round me after you've had a few lines and want your dick sucked.'

GANG WAR

She hoists her leg onto the dash, digging her heel into the leather, pretending to be in a rage, pretending she doesn't know that her bronzed legs are open a bit. Dylan blimps her snatch under her miniskirt. No knickers. Casey's looking out the window, twirling her chewy round her fingers. For an 18-year-old, she has a top mature fanny on her. Nice and brown, wine-coloured lips, jet-black peabs. As she moved in rhythm with the speeding Rangey, her lips opened ever so slightly. A fine stretch of cunt spittle, like a thread of silk, elongated and disintegrated as the lips kissed and parted. 'OK,' he says, 'Let's go to the hotel then.'

In the room, plasma on, kit off. Casey's wearing white, lacy underwear: thin gusset, high-waisted, *Daily Star/Sunday Sport*-style gear. Her brown skin's mottled from over-tanning. 'Bought these today,' she says. 'D'you like them?' She's pouting in the mirror, lipstick scarring at the crease of her mouth.

'Two hundred buff for a pair of scraigs and a bra? Mind you, fucking hell, girl, a baghead brass off Parly'd look fine in those, girl.'

They put on robes and go down to the health club and into the jacuzzi. The other customers are a few taxi drivers, some gangsters, loads of doormen, just knocked off. Dylan, a scrawny cunt in his long, baggy Everton shorts, follows her in, drags her into the steam room, bends her over, wallops her over the granite, her head pressing up against the smoked-glass door. Outside, the doormen and taxi drivers see her hair and body coming in and out of the steam. One by one, they gather round the door, doggers, having a wank in their Adidas shorts. Casey gets into it, presses her head against the glass. Window-licker.

CHAPTER 11

THE LIBRARY

The next day, Dylan's whacked, exhausted. He's still coming down off the SIM card graft, the adrenalin breaking down now, sinews lifeless. He has combat fatigue off the session in the hotel. He was on the stripes all night, shagging the waglet. His memories are gone already, bleached by the white. He's feeling hollow now.

He needs to get off. Get to *The Place*, quick.

Dylan loves Friday nights. A vague memory from school comes back, of sitting in a science lab as the winter darkness descends outside, relishing the cosiness of the classroom, the comfort of its golden light, but feeling the thrill of the weekend just hours away and the adventure it holds. A feeling of warmth washes over him, cuts through the anaesthetic of the coke for a moment.

He heads for the bus through the drenched estate: charred houses dripping, water pouring through craters in roofs. Silvery yellow light glows from the odd one, still occupied. Pinky, orangey neons flicker on above in Miami colours. He can taste the freedom already, his tummy slightly rolling now at the thought of it: The Place.

He jogs on to the bus stop, moving fast, just in case. There's the odd lad running from building to building, jumping out of the shadows, running for cover. No one standing still, just in case.

Out of the corner of his eye, he spies a lad with a samurai sword stood on the wall at the base of Broadway Bridge. The lad tries to cop for him, gives chase over the roundabout but loses Dylan in the traffic and the dark. Dylan jogs on through the rain. Case of mistaken identity, he thinks. Dylan's hooded up. So is everyone else.

Onto the parade, past the bookie's. Late-night racing. As he passes by, an 18-year-old girl – skinny, on her way to work in the social club, he knows her – gets a slap. Something to do with her brother, a fight at a party 18 months ago. Dylan hears the lad as he gets off: 'Tell him from me, you little sweat, I'll put one in his fucking head.' In an unrelated fight, another lad runs into the chippy and roundhouse kicks a Crocky lad's ma in the queue. Dylan looks the other way. *Got to get to The Place. Jog on to the bus stop.*

On the top deck, the back seat is hot. He zens in on the rough vibration of the engine, enveloped by a cushion of sound, buzzing off it. Not far now to The Place, his only sanctuary. He started going there six years ago to get away from the mayhem. It's the only place he feels safe.

He gets off at the Central Library, a huge, well-kept Georgian building next to the art gallery. Deep within it is an inner sanctum, a 130-year-old rotunda, The Place. The front of the library is well lit, spotlights beaming up the stone, through the swaying trees. The old wooden entrance is bathed in gold from the chandeliers inside.

He takes a look, drinks it in. A dry gulp of excitement. Then he slips off round the back. It's rainy and weedy and dark. Grey slabs of stone. He jumps into a square stone recess, about three foot deep, at the foot of a giant wall. It's a bit sheltered in there. On the wall above him are ventilation shafts, air-con outlets, old, lagged heating pipes. Dylan feels the loneliness of the big building looming, but he's loving it.

First, he takes his hood down, slips off his white plazzie motocross mask. He gulps in the damp air, closing his eyes. The moisture is sharp and sea fresh. He can feel the tingle in his soul already. It's like a metal brace has been removed from his head. He's protected from the downpour, fresh in from the Western Approaches, by the high walls, but a few stray drops of rain cool his scalp.

He unzips his Lowies. The shell falls to the ground. Air Max top off. Freedom. His whole body is rushing now. Impatiently, he takes off his Berghaus bottoms, pushing them down with the soles of his trainies, the treads catching on the matt, rubberised lining of his waterproofs. He's naked now but feeling alive.

He takes a freshly ironed green Lacoste shirt out of the bin-bag he brought with him. It looks new, except for a tiny row of pinhole burns down the front. Over that he puts on a powder-blue Rohan trackie top, space age, with concealed zip and a neat, short funnel neck. His jeans are slightly baggy, with a straight, 16-inch leg. He's brought a pair of royal blue Adidassler.

The kitchen knife with the serrated edge was down his bollocks. Now he plunges it into the moist, grassy earth. He never brought his gun. The thought of it here makes him sick.

Dylan bombs round the front and inside through the main doors. No one says fuck all. No one looks twice. He looks like any other library-goer – maybe a score-knowing stude from Nantwich or somewhere. He's buzzing now at being near The Place, his breathing gone a bit skew-whiff. The lobby is warm and quiet, shabby but safe. Years of decline during the '80s have eroded its original splendour. Students are sat behind '70s glass partitions, bolted on ad hoc to antique rooms. He goes through the Hornby Library, taking it all in, the beech parquet floor, gilt chairs with red-velvet upholstery. Then into The Place, the Picton Reading Room. His body is electrified now. He feels as if he's walking into a floodlit stadium. He looks up at the huge dome roof: smooth, creamy alabaster, 100 ft in diameter, 56 ft high, latticed into panels, turquoise architraving with gold detail.

Only The Place feels totally safe. Only there does he feel totally free. It's too much for him already. He feels drowsy now, weeks of stress falling off him, coming out of him in waves.

He has a quick mooch. No staff around. Spies a gallery high up in the walls, chooses the furthest staircase, a wrought-iron spiral. He carefully places each foot flat on the iron plates, no noise, just like on the graft. Up three flights. Forty foot up now. He steps into a little recess, a small strip of iron floor with a cast-iron radiator pipe belching out heat underneath. Three sides of books on wooden shelves and in glass cabinets. There's dust on the floor. No one's been up here for months. He can't be seen from below. Dylan lies on the floor, switches his mobile off, takes a book about Serbia off the shelf, reads a bit – and crashes.

* * *

Bang! Dylan's head flies up instinctively then slams back onto the ornate, cast-iron floor of the gallery. Panic. He goes for his thing down his kecks. But no Lowies, no shiv, no heater, nothing down there. He remembers putting the knife in the grass outside, feels the denim on his legs. *Where am I?*

Then the vision. Medjugorje-style. That beautiful. Too lovely. Her reflection in the brown, wine-bottle glass of an old book cabinet next to his head, the bottle-green of her dress swimming into the reflection, flowing into the green of his Lacoste, blending as one in the glass. He remembers where he is.

He looks up over his shoulder. The girl has a round face, a dot of a nose, freckles and strawberry-blonde hair in long, twisty curls. She's bending over him, looking down.

'I'm sorry. Did I wake you up?'

Dylan's speechless, shamed.

'Are you all right?' Little smile.

He's confused by her beauty, her openness, her loveliness, and angry that she's found him in this state, like a tramp, crashed in the foetal position, head wrecked by sleep.

She offers a thin, moist hand. Bony arms and alabaster skin. Dylan's eyes dart around for an outro. He wants to get off but there's nowhere to run. Forty foot up. His eyes settle on her. A sail of green dress billows away from her chest as she crouches down. Dylan blimps a pale, solid tit shrouded in a pearly satin vest with a delicate, creamy strap. Her eyes collar him, but she doesn't move. She remains crouched confidently beside him. Dylan, shamed, has a cherry on now.

'It's OK,' she says, seeing that he's blushing. 'Nothing to worry about. I never come up here. But I've got to put those back.' She glances at a small stack of old, dark-red books near the top of the spiral staircase.

Dylan's lost for words, enraged at his own inability to communicate.

'By the way, the library's closing in five minutes.' She gives him a gentle smile, partly because of the mischief of the scenario, partly to calm him down. 'I wouldn't want you to get locked inside.'

Dylan is hypnotised by her teeth: the purity of white emulsion, square, healthy. He's never seen such a lovely grid. Not orange off the tea crawls, not yellow off the green or black off the munchies. Just skirting-board white, every one. He says fuck all.

'I didn't want to wake you. You were in such a . . .' She hesitates to use the word. 'A beautiful sleep.' She blushes a bit, strong, wine-red patches flaring up on her creamy cheeks. Dylan looks into her pot-brown eyes. 'Come on,' she says. 'Most of the doors are shut now . . . and the alarms are on.'

Alarms? What's she on about? Does she think I was trying to hide from them?

The girl senses his unease. 'I'll walk you out, if you want. So you can get out OK. Wouldn't want you to get lost in here. Locked in of a Friday night.' She's firing off smiles.

Dylan springs to his feet. She's wearing woollen, ribbed navy-blue tights, flat, matt red shoes tied with a ribbon. Downstairs, they cross the parquet floor. Dylan wants to say something to her. But what? Confusion grows in him, then rage. She opens the big oak doors, another set of thick, bevelled frosted glass, smiling at him as he creeps through each time.

Why the fuck is she doing this? She going to get me nicked or what? Dylan's trying hard not to be suss. He wants to be nice. But he doesn't know how. He wants to do something for her. Impress her.

Near the main entrance, he sees the security guards waiting to close up and knock off, having a little banter. They stop silent when they see him. Dylan knows their look inside out: sharp eyes, prison-screw smiles, bitter.

Rage wells in Dylan. Should he bang one of them out? Break one of their jaws? Would that impress her? Make up for the lost words? Would she buzz off that? Dylan knows what they're thinking. *How the fuck did he get in here?* But mostly they're jealous and that makes them look down on him even more. Because the bird's with him, their bird, their librarian, the posh bird who they perv off day in day out. The bird who they desperately try to cop for but never can. *Sad twats. They don't like it one fucking bit.*

One of them pipes up, ''Ere y'are, love, we'll take him.'

Don't be pretending you're hard, lad, in front of her. Break your fucking jaw, right now.

The girl senses the tension. 'He's with me.' Dylan feels a tiny bit stung off her need to explain, to defend him. She looks at him. 'I mean . . . I'm showing this guy out. Just a little late from the Picton Library.'

The security guard's a bit suss. 'Oh yeah?'

'He didn't hear the bell.'

The girl gently touches his arm and starts walking, getting out of their way, guiding him through a switched-off security detector, through the hot-draught door and into the tingly cold.

'Well, see ya,' the girl says, watching him go and waving. She wants to say more but Dylan's silence is starting to dent her confidence. All she says is, 'I didn't mind, you know . . . you having a sleep . . . it's OK.'

CHAPTER 12

GRAFT NIGHT

Dylan's home by ten. Friday night, graft night. The older ones all go out, all pissed, desperate for charlie, tablets, weed from the younger ones.

Dylan throws his ma his big bag of powder and says to their Will, playing *Scarface* on the Wii, 'Go and get me scales, lad. They're in next door's back bin.'

Will, ten, fucks him off immediately, zoned out, busy wasting whacked-out Indians at the Sunray Motel.

'Will, you fucking prick, go and get the fucking scales, lad, before I knock you out.'

Dylan's ma, screaming, gets the plastic Wii gun and smashes Will across the head. 'Go and get your brother's thing, soft lad. He's got to get his graft on the go if he's going to make any wages. Ten o' fucking clock already. They'll all be heading into town soon.' Her face lights up in anticipation. She'll be getting a few quid off Dylan. Plus she'll snide a few grams off the block as she's bagging it up for him.

'How you been, lad?' she asks Dylan. 'Haven't seen you for a week.'

'Just grafting.'

'I know. You're the only cunt who works in this family.'

Dylan's ma screams at their Michelle, his sister, 14: 'Make him a fucking cup of tea, will you?'

Dylan follows her into the kitchen. Gives Michelle £200.

'D'you hear what happened in the ePod last Saturday? Fucking twat Connor started chatting shit to some girl, so I went over, ripped the face off the fucking slag. Guess what he does?'

'What?'

'Starts fucking calling me all kinds in the queue for the taxi.'

Just then, they see Connor through the front window. He's coming out the front gate across the other side of the street. Dylan bails out with a golf club and a kitchen knife. Connor's on his toes right away. Dylan shouts up the road: 'Get him!'

A few of the lads by the entry chase after Connor as well, cop for him by the bend. Dylan smashes his head with the golf club. 'Fucking ever start on our Michelle again . . .' He stabs his ankle bone with a kitchen knife and walks back to the house.

Michelle's giggling at the edge of the path: 'Serves him right, dunnit?'

Back inside, settling down, Dylan points at the bag of powder, and says to his ma, 'Bag that up into 20 and 40 bags, will you?'

Dylan's ma's a wizened smackhead, loves to show off her prowess on the scales. Dylan throws her a small lump wrapped in bright-blue cellophane, tells her, 'Got you a few Subutex there. Better than that green you get on the script, I'm told,' he says, referring to her methadone.

'You're a lovely lad, getting those for your ma.' She looks daggers at Will and Michelle for never getting her anything like her favourite son. 'Knock you out for about eight hours, those. Don't make you feel sick, though. That fucking methadone, lad, fucking ruthless.'

'Just stay off the brown will you?' replies Dylan.

He says to Tommy, his younger brother, 'Have you had any tea? 'Ere y'are, go the shop.' He gives him fifteen quid. Ten minutes later, he's back with the tea: bag of Haribo Yogi-Frutti, bag of Haribo Tangfastics, bag of Haribo Milky Mix for the baby, Haribo Lite for his Michelle. She's on a diet, she says. Walkers Gary's Special Lamb Curry Flavour crisps, Quavers, Golden Wonder, Nik Naks. Frazzles, Space Raiders, Wotsits, Dairylea Dunkers Baked Crisps, KP Skips. A massive bar of Galaxy for afters. Michelle gets a few plates out and serves the meal up with a bottle of cream soda. Their younger sister, Stefanie, breaks off from watching the telly. After tea, the kids start going off their heads, banging off the walls. 'That was lovely,' says Michelle. 'First tea we've had at home for ages.'

Dylan reads the *Echo*, a court report about a drug dealer. Making mental notes of the latest police technology so that he can brief the lads. CBeebies is on the telly for the baby. *In the Night Garden.*

'Everything OK?' Dylan asks his ma.

'Great. Will got statemented this week. Hopefully get him taken out of school this week.'

'What's he been up to?'

'Fucking slashed one of his teachers, didn't he? So I went up and the head said that they couldn't control him. They said that he had one the highest IQs in the year but that he was disruptive or something. I told them he'd been on medication since he was eight.'

'Mad, innit?'

'He would have been all right but then some student teacher said that Will had put his hand up her skirt. And had been having a wank in front of her. Felt ashamed when the teacher was telling me.'

'Mad, innit?' says Dylan, head in the paper, not taking much notice.

'Should have seen the state of her, though. The teacher. Went up to the school and, I'm telling you, only one word for it: slag. Am I right, Michelle?'

'Scrubber, Dylan,' Michelle confirms. 'Should have seen her. Felt ashamed.'

'Little short mini on,' Dylan's ma goes on, 'little fucking skimpy top. I said: "She's asking for it. Imagine wearing that in front of a load of young lads. Lads get crushes on their teachers, don't they? Not surprised our Will wanted to fucking shag you."'

Dylan perks up, thinking of the nice student teacher, imagines bending her over the desk. He shouts to Will, who's now chipping away at the plaster and breezeblocks on the landing wall with a tiny hammer robbed from metalwork, 'Dirty little cunt, aren't you? A fucking wank in class? Is she nice?'

Will's embarrassed. 'Yeah, all right, like. Wasn't fucking having a wank, though. Just grabbed her arse while she was on the whiteboard.'

'Is right,' says Dylan, getting up and stomping around the room pretending to hold an invisible cock. 'Have you told her you've got an older brother with a fucking big snake. Lash that on her fucking table.'

Dylan's ma carries on: 'But the fucking head was having none of it. Said that the young girl had been traumatised. Felt as though she was gonna get raped. Off work and all that. I said to the head, "Fuck off. She's only after a pay-out and six months off work."'

Michelle, crashed out on the couch now, adds, 'I know. Lazy twats aren't they?'

'The head said that the teacher had made a statement saying that she'd collared Will wanking over her.' Their ma looks over at Will and says, 'Just like your fucking auld feller, you. He was a dirty twat, as well. Caught him shagging that auld one from the pub on that couch. Anyways, I says to the head, "The fucking slag only wants to put in a claim. Go on the sick."

You know what them teachers are like. They're worse than the fucking bizzies for going on the sick.'

Dylan's still half-reading the *Echo*, but has one eye on *Granada Reports*, watching CCTV footage of a raid on a shop.

Dylan's ma continues her story. 'The teacher said Will was having a wank under his desk and when she asked him to stop he wiped a load of stuff on her hair. She said it was come. I said, "Fuck off. The little prick is only ten, he hasn't even had a wet dream yet. All's the little cunt does is play on the fucking Wii all day. Wouldn't know how to play with himself. I know he's a cheeky little twat, mind you, giving everyone abuse and banging everyone out, but he's not a fucking rapist, is he?"

'But the head said, "No. He's going to have to go on the sex offenders' register."

'I said, "What?" Grabbed the little fucking scrubber, ragged her by the head, threw her on the floor. Bizzies called. Fucking Asbo'd from going to the school again, aren't I?'

Dylan: 'Mad, innit?'

* * *

Later that night, the lads are in an alleyway divvying up the gear. Some lads from the park are putting on a show with a robbed Audi. New Loon's on a robbed Suzuki Kx crosser, winding StreetSafe bugs up, waiting for them to come after him, letting them chase him, then burning them off.

Nogger and Dylan head down to the pub to sell some tablets to the older ones. They go in hoods down, everyone making a fuss of them. They pass the gear under the tables but seconds later the punters are snorting off the tabletops in full view of the bar.

Jay's in his school uniform still, hasn't been arsed going home yet. 'They made me go back to school,' he complains to Dylan.

'Mad, innit? Still getting shit off all those Walton lads?'

'Fucking right, I am. They pulled an auld .455 on me in double CDT today.'

Nogger hears this. 'Let's go and see them now.' He jumps into a private hire, spins up to the shops in Walton. He jumps out, runs into a pub, machetes the auld feller of one of the Walton gang. 'Tell your prick to stay away from Jay.' Chops him on the forearm as he puts his hand up to defend himself.

CHAPTER 13

THE DATE

Dylan's been waiting for this all week. Every day thinking about her, her carefully teased hair, her loose, solid breasts. It's a bright winter's day, sun so strong it makes him smile. It's even warm when the wind stops blowing for a second.

He lashes all his gear into a black Adidas bag, headed for the South End. He loves going to the Golden Gloves gym. No one knows him there. He feels like it's his secret. There's something about the dock areas, about those old sloping streets, that's less oppressive than The Snow. Fresh air from the river, silver light, freedom.

Downstairs the Gloves is packed with lads. It's the same as it must have been 50 years ago. There's loud stomping from the circuit training and army-style shouts off the coaches. Everyone's charging off the loud house music. Afterwards, Dylan has a strong, hot shower, washes away the cold and the sweat.

He gets the 82C into town. Beige Carhartt cords on, new pair of brown Berghaus mountaineering boots, a £70 T-shirt (grafted off Bold Street, bought off a lad in the bookie's), a plain, dark-green Peter Storm kagoul.

As soon as he gets to The Place, he's on her right away. She's helping an auld feller on a computer in the corner. She's dressed sleeker and fitter today: dark-blue skinny jeans, right up her arse, tucked into shiny, brown knee-length boots; a tight, white T-shirt and a thick tomato-red cardi with three-quarter-length sleeves, a few holes in it. She leans over the auld feller to touch the keyboard, her tits pressing out against the T-shirt, like low-hanging fruit. She's laughing with the old guy, patient, not fucking him off. He loves her more for it.

'You OK?' Dylan asks.

'Oh! It's you . . . Sleepyhead.' She smiles. 'Hi. Are you OK?'

'Yeah,' says Dylan, conscious that he's talking too loudly and of his accent.

'Do you need any help?'

'Just looking for a book.'

'Anything in particular?'

'Erm . . . no, just looking really.'

'Well, books on sleeping are over here . . .'

'Bit cheeky, aren't you?' She laughs. 'What about books on on-top birds?'

Half-smiling, she says, 'Birds . . . ornithology is over in that section.'

Her name is Elizabeth.

He meets her outside the library at half seven. It's already dark but the night is electric with hope. They get a taxi. She slides into the back, laughing, her jeans gliding over the leatherette. As she collapses back, her thighs are angled high for a moment, reminding Dylan of those paparazzi pictures of celebrities falling into limousines. Her boots match the shiny black handles on the doors.

'Shall we go to Lark Lane?' she asks. Dylan nods. She tells the driver, 'Kelly's Wine Bar on Lark Lane, please.' The driver looks at Dylan in the rear-view mirror. It's the same one who took him to the brass-house the other night with Nogger and Casey. Dylan throws him a score as he gets out, even though there's only a tenner on the clock.

He's never been before but Dylan loves Kelly's Wine Bar. Wooden benches, candles dripping down the sides of wine bottles. He loves the fact that she's come straight from work, wearing the same clothes she had on in the library. She's ravenously tearing at the bowl of bread on the table, juggling menus and ordering. A young working woman.

'Excellent, isn't it?' he says.

'Haven't you ever been here? Do you mean you've lived in Liverpool all your life and you haven't been to Kelly's or Lark Lane?'

'No. Is that a problem, like?'

'Where about are you from?'

'The North End. Bit of a different scenario by ours, d'you know what I mean? Bit bleak.'

She's 18, a year older than Dylan. She tells him that she's just working in the library part time. She's a student at John Moores. Dylan makes out he knows what John Moores is.

'What are you learning about?'

'Philosophy.'

'What do you do?' Elizabeth asks him.

'Nothing, really. Bit of graft now and again.'

He's choosing his words carefully. He doesn't want to lie to this girl, or play the romantic urchin to the posh wool either.

'Graft – like work?'

'Just buying and selling stuff.' That reminds him that he has a bag of weed and a bag of charlie on him. Usually, he'd have had her in the bogs by now, snorting, getting a little nosh off her to say ta. But he doesn't feel like getting it out. He wants to eat with this girl, tear up the big chunks of warm bread with her, try the stinking cheeses that keep arriving.

She pours several glugs of red wine into an oversized glass. A lad in a black shirt and slim back trousers delivers a heavy block of well-oiled wood to the table. On it are thick wedges of different-coloured cheeses. Big-value portions. Dylan's never been out for a meal before. Food is for on the move, for in your pockets – cola cubes, sausage rolls, all-day breakfast pasties.

Spreading some Camembert on his bread, he says, 'Wow! It stinks.'

'Lovely. Try some of this,' she says, putting a spoon of something in his mouth.

'Where are you from?'

'A small village.'

'In the countryside?'

'Yes.'

Dylan swigs his wine, laughing. 'That's good, innit?'

'What? Haven't you ever been to the country?'

Dylan, playing the wag, the knowing urchin, tells her: 'See cows, throws bricks at them, girl.' Smiling, he says, 'Sorry. Where about?'

'Have you ever heard of Cerne Abbas?'

Dylan laughs as the candle flames dance in the dark, rain-streaked windows, steamy and cosy. 'No.'

'It's in Dorset.' Elizabeth's smiling now. 'Have you ever seen a picture of the giant carved into the hill, in chalk. The one with the big willy.'

Dylan, buzzing, tells her, 'You live in a mad place, you, girl.'

'It's an ancient thing. A fertility symbol. If you're a virgin, you're supposed to sit on it.'

'What? On his big, chalk cock? That's mad. Do you ever sit on it?'

'Not any more. I'm not a virgin.' She smiles flirtatiously.

Dylan laughs, looking at her, his eyes tracking his prey like a lizard's. She's mischievously biting a stick of celery. He's gonna say something about his own giant cock but checks himself. Less of the behaviourals – for now.

'And where exactly does the mysterious Dylan Olsen live?' asks Elizabeth.

Dylan's made up that she used his full name. 'L11,' he says, not being arsed to give much away.

'A number not a place? And where might this L11 be?'

'North end of the city.'

'And what's it like up the North End?'

'All right.'

'All right. That's it? I've told you about the giant cock on our hill. And all you can say is "all right". Haven't you got anything that can compete with my naked giant? It sounds shit where you live.'

'Well it just goes a bit messy now and again. D'you get me?'

'Messy? Do you mean there's a lot of litter?'

'Well, yeah. And a few of the lads are a bit sick. Bit too sick. Too much sometimes.'

'Do you mean they're all ill?'

'Well, a good few of them have to go to A&E now and again. But it's best not to. Case there's comebacks. Just wear a vest, don't you? No need to go anywhere then, is there?'

'And you all wear vests? You and all these sick men wear vests? And there's a lot of rubbish? Well, Dylan Olsen, I'm glad we didn't go for a drink round by your house tonight. It sounds fucking terrible.'

Dylan bursts out laughing. *You have to hand it to her. She's game. She's on it.*

'Well, maybe I just didn't explain it right . . .'

Both of them laugh again.

They go on to the Students' Union. Dylan loves it. The music's loud and cool, bouncy house, psychedelic. There's a massive crackle of noise at the bar. Loud talk. No hard talk, just lots of laughing and screaming. It's different from the places he usually goes. No shadow-boxing on the spot. No German-soldier faces, shaved head, teeth clenched, grimacing Russian-Front-style on the podium. No punters getting dropped outside with handguns.

The girls are gorgeous – less make-up and Gucci than he's used to, but their boho chic is well crafted and they're fit. There are English-rose types in short black skirts over ribbed woollen tights, white shirts, see-through under the lights. Film-star Asian birds, skinny as fuck with long black hair; there's one trendy Indian girl with a fringe that covers one eye, wearing skinny jeans and an electric-blue pashmina. A group of Spanish girls are stood by a red leatherette alcove. They're neat, rich-looking, conservative, in crew-neck jumpers, with long bobs and thick, sleek sunglasses. Dylan clocks a couple of black girls near the fire exit who stand out because they look more clubby, as though they've got somewhere better to go. The tall one is wearing a shiny lime-green dress with a snakeskin pattern on it, and flicks her hair Naomi-style when she laughs. The other one, pure Sugababes material, twirls on her heels as she craftily blows cigarette smoke out of the open door. Tall girls from down south stride past in jeans and boots, wispy scarves tied around their necks. There are loads of girls in dramatic make-up, plenty of Peaches Geldof/Amy Winehouse types.

But Elizabeth is in a different league. She's back from the bar with two pints already, dancing a bit, smiling madly. Big, mad let-ons to her mates. They scream, kiss each other twice and hug. As they step back, they eye up Dylan, mischievously, lustful. They whisper questions to her about her 'new friend'. 'He looks like a townie,' says one. Dylan hears and laughs out loud. 'Yes, I live in a town. That much is true.' He's gracious, polite, has them laughing straight away. *Throws in a few funnies and that. But not too many – just enough.*

'So you study philosophy here?' he asks Elizabeth. 'Mad, innit? What is it exactly?'

'It's just about thinking about how you live.'

'What do you mean?'

'Well, most people don't think about anything, really. Just get by and do what they're told.'

'Right, like, I only think when I'm out grafting. Planning and that.' Dylan checks himself. 'You can't think that much when you're watching the telly or on the Wii or chillin' to Biggie.'

'That's it. All that shit is just distractions to stop you thinking about what's really important.'

'Like what?'

'Like what makes you happy.'

'Dough, innit? Nice phat car, boss kennel, decent swag . . . these are a few of my favourite things.' Wry smile.

'But that's because you've been brainwashed into thinking that, bombarded with commercial propaganda since you've been old enough to watch CITV and Milkshake. Adverts, celebrity culture, women's mags, Peter and fucking Jordan driving a new Range Rover, footie players in their cribs with their WAGs.'

Dylan shudders at the thought of Casey but quickly gets rid of the image. 'Yeah,' he says, thinking about it, 'suppose they have got right into our heads.'

A lot of people would go laddish on her at this point, mock themselves for not talking bollocks for once, for going off-message, away from the usual shit of guns, beefs, birds, footie. Or they'd slaughter her for being too weird. But deep down he knows she's right.

All he says is, 'But look at this nice little Roley here.' He shows her his £5,500 Rolex (which he steam-ironed out of a drug dealer).

'And?'

'That gives me a buzz, makes me feel happy.'

'But, Dylan – it's an illusion.'

'Why?'

'Because you can't link your happiness to your status and money. If you're rich and happy one day, you could be poor and miserable the next. You'll constantly be up and down.'

'You're right. That's mad, innit? I'll get rid of it.'

Outside at closing time there are no taxis about. They start to walk home in the sideways rain. Elizabeth, shivering under Dylan's Peter Storm, says, 'Let's get the night bus.' Dylan can't be arsed with the bus. He's had enough bohemia for one night. *No fucking cabs anywhere. Twats putting their lights off when they go past scuffians, so that they can pick up juicier fares in town.*

Just then, Dylan spots a Red Road private hire. They're not supposed to pick up on the streets, but Dylan collars him at the lights, leaning into his window. He's made up to see Bunter. He's a graft taxi driver, uses his cab to ferry gear around.

'All right, Dylan? What are you doing around here? Got some graft on the go?'

'No, lad. Just been in town with some bird and . . .'

'Go 'ead, lad. Loads of pussy and that?' Bunter shouts.

Dylan can see that Bunter, in his chippy-stained grey sweatshirt and trackies reeking of groin odour, is turned on. Fucking perv is getting a semi-on, a predatory look in his eyes. 'Where is the little darling, then?' he asks, sliding around in his seat, scoping for Elizabeth, half thinking he'll be on Dylan's strange – back seat, little nosh.

Dylan feels rage rising up in him, but he lets it go. They need the lift. 'Do us a favour, Bunter. Take us round the park. For a score, lad.' More than double the usual, because Bunter's taking a risk by picking up on the street instead of taking a booking through the blower.

Bunter eyes Elizabeth over Dylan's shoulder. She's stood in a shop doorway, laughing with her mates. 'Look at the snatch on that. D'you fancy taking her OT ways? Top flange, her, mate. There's a little field behind the power station in Runcorn. Got some roeys, there.'

'What the fuck are you on about?'

'Rohypnol.' He shakes out four rhomboid-shaped blue tablets from his ciggie box. 'Just knocks the pussy clean out. Don't know what the fuck's going on. Wallop them everywhere. Up the arse and all that.' Dylan can't believe what he's hearing, lets it go at first cos it's too much.

Bunter carries on, oblivious: 'Got this little contract taking kids to school and back. Take a little 12-year-old every day. But she's a fucking darling, d'you know worramean? Fucking big arse on her, big tits, all there. As far as I'm concerned, she's fair game, mate. No matter how fucking 12 she is. Stopped at Mackie D's one night. Splosh! Pill into her Coke. Fell asleep. Took her back The Boot. New Loon, Nogger got on me. Three-piper, la. Boss. Afterwards, put her little knickers on, dropped her off to her ma and da and her little brothers.

'So d'you fancy it?'

Dylan has his blade out, the tip under Bunter's chin. He's leaning into the window with his back to Elizabeth. 'Listen, you little fucking fiddler, I'll cut your fucking bollocks off. I know Nogger's into what he's into. But that doesn't mean it's fucking right. Or that I'm rooting for him.'

Bunter's on a whitener now, the tip of the blade nestling in the bristles on his throat. 'OK, D. Just chatting shit. No offence.'

Dylan, looking from side to side, tells him, 'Don't say another fucking word. Keep your eyes off the bird and just take us to where we want to go, OK?'

Dylan slots the knife back down his bollocks, turns and smiles at Elizabeth. 'Come 'ead, girl. Got a ride.'

THE DATE

The taxi pulls up outside her pad and she runs to open the door. Dylan throws Bunter 30 notes. 'Scruffy twat.'

'Thanks, D.'

Her flat's in an old, creaking Victorian villa. *Amityville*. The wind shakes drops of rainwater off the leaves of the looming oaks that brush the roof of the house. No lights on. Park-black skies.

'I'm here on my own,' says Elizabeth, smiling, the rain streaking down her firm cheeks. 'I live on the top floor but the rest is empty.'

'Yeah?' says Dylan, loving her independence, her fearlessness.

He kisses her, a long, sloppy one, his tummy turning over. She breaks off, gently pouting against his ears and his neck, and then pulls him closer. He cups her hair to his nose: a faint smell of coconut, the red standing out even in the dark. The intimacy of their mouths is strangely at odds with their hands fumbling over thick coats.

'That was nice,' she says. 'Beautiful kisser, Dylan Olsen.'

Her flat is cool. Pure *Definitely Maybe*: stripped wooden floors; a fleshy-pink Indian silk bedcover, old and worn, with swirly silver embroidery; an Afghan rug. Dylan's onto the woven AK-47 patterns straight away.

'Where d'you get that?'

'I got it when I was travelling.'

She takes two mugs out of the Belfast sink in the corner. 'Tea?' Dylan smiles a yes, still looking around. As the kettle whistles on the little gas stove, she takes her damp red cardi off. Dylan clocks how her braless tits battle against the white T-shirt, her dark, strong nipples teasing underneath.

'Here's a postcard of the rude man from where I live.' Dylan loves it: the ancient mystery of it, snuggled above a village next to a stream.

'Looks like a boss little place to go on holiday. Have a little sit down on the hill. Go for a quiet pint in . . .'

'Where do you usually go on holiday?'

'Never been abroad. Not even to a Champions League game. Can't be arsed spending that kind of money. It's only a footie match, innit? Can cost you two grand for three days.'

'Well, Dylan Olsen, we can't have that, can we?'

She disappears behind a three-panelled Chinese screen in the corner – black lacquer, fading paintings of red, blue and gold dragons – and pops out wearing a kimono. Playfully, she pushes him back on the bed and climbs on top of him.

'I want you to pretend that we're on a beach somewhere,' she says, sliding the silk off one shoulder. Dylan laughs, buzzing off the mischief. 'And we're all alone. Under the palm trees.' Off the other shoulder. 'Imagine the sea lapping at your feet.' She unties the belt and the kimono drops on the bed. To reveal her in a bikini, nylon, clean, white. 'The sun beating down. And me lying next to you.'

Afterwards, crashed safe and hot under the heavy, dark sheets, his icy breath lit by the moon, Elizabeth lying across his chest, Dylan knows that this is the girl he wants to spend the rest of his life with. He wants to live with her in this flat. Fuck all that nonsense with Nogger. It seems childish and small-time now. What was all that about? He could get a little job. Maybe even go to college. A world of possibilities lying ahead.

CHAPTER 14

MAC-10

The lads are standing in the door of the chemist's on the parade. Nogger's got an abscess. He's moaning: 'Can't go the fucking doctor's till tomorrow.' There's a big golf ball of pus hanging off his jawbone. He's swigging from a big bottle of Corsodyl mouthwash, holding it like a bottle of Stella, then spitting it out as people walk into the chemist, between laughing and arsing about – and going back into the chemist out of the cold and to chat up the counter bird.

Clean white uniform. She's been Tangoed in Tanorama. Miss Midriff with a McFat face. Britney pigtails and bobbles. She loves the young gangsters.

'She asked me how old I was,' Nogger tells the lads. 'And she didn't need to know that, did she? She wants to know, her.' Neck out like a chicken, head moving from side to side, score-knower smile, certain she fancies him. 'I'm telling you, she wants to *know*.'

One of the lads agrees: 'Innit.'

A stranger walks past. Whizzer shouts 'ocifer' in case he's a jack, to let him know that they know. But he can't be. His face is too skeletor. Nogger collars him before he gets to the chippy. 'Brave, innit?' he says.

'Section 60,' says Lupus. 'Stop and search.'

'Empty your pockets, lad.'

The young ones gather round to help him along and shield passers-by from the mugging. He hands over his phone and £11. Little Marky finds an iPod in an inside pocket. 'Nice one. Look, the prick's brought an iPod to the shops. Imagine that.'

'Taxed that, lad, purely,' replies Clegsy.

Clegsy sees what's on it, one headphone in and scrolling, while Nogger proceeds with the search.

Clegsy: 'Talking Heads, lad. Boss.'

Nogger, dread darkening his face, says, 'Punter music, innit?'

Clegsy talks louder as he listens and bobs his head to the tunes. 'Bit of Floyd here as well.'

'Just another customer if you listen to that, aren't you, though?' says Nogger, searching through the deeper crevices of the punter's pockets with renewed interest. Triumphant, he finds what he's looking for. The proof. 'Told you, lad,' he says, holding up the little wrap of heroin. 'Told you that was punter's music, didn't I, lad?'

'Baghead, aren't you, lad? Fucking degenerate fucking wretch, aren't you? Left your kids at home covered in shit in the cot while you've come out to the shops to score.'

'And not even from us,' Clegsy points out.

'Baby P's auld feller, you, mate,' Marky chips in.

Nogger flashbacks to babysitting his younger brothers and sisters. He continues with his sermon, getting foamy and frothy at the mouth. No one knows whether it's the pus or the Corsodyl or if he's just losing it over the Class As, like usual.

'You're out spending their money on gear and chips while you should be putting the kids to bed, you fucking shitbag. Knew you were a customer straight off – Talking Heads, Floyd.' Nogger shakes his head in disgust.

Bloot's on the iPod now, humming along, nodding, sledging 'Comfortably Numb'-style. Then singing along and speaking loudly cos of the headphones, Bloot says, '*Final Cut*, la. Know it's punter music, but they'll always be there, won't they, Floyd?' Nogger recalls the lyrics from his childhood: his ma chasing on the couch, the smell of her vinyl records on the floor, the bittersweet taste of her heroin fumes catching on the back of his throat.

'But no fucking nigger music, though,' says Bloot. 'All pure headz tunes: J.J. Cale, Genesis, Jimi. Country Joe and the Fish? Who the fuck are they?'

'But no fucking Tupac or Biggie?' asks Whizzer. 'Indecent, lad.'

Nogger's still thinking of his own tooth-rotted baghead ma and da. Monster Munch for breakfast for him and his sisters, half-frozen ice pops for tea. Flapping the crack fumes away while watching CBeebies. 'Don't know why you're doing that, lad,' he says, pointing at the brown, telling the smackhead off. 'Destroying our community. Spitting out crack babies, all fucking twisted up like a fucking biff, little claws rattling away.' Nogger mimics a deformed baby. 'You fucking victim.'

The lad's crying by now. 'Please don't throw that gear away. It's not even mine. It's me bird's for Sunday morning, so she won't be rattling.'

Whizzer throws a coin at the baghead's head at close range.

'Misuse of Drugs Act,' Nogger tells him. 'Strip search. Take your clothes off.'

The pack of hyenas wade in, ragging off his top, shredding his jeans. He's left naked in the foetal position, bathed in the golden light from the broad chippy window. Iggo writes 'Dirty Smack Head' on his back in permanent marker. Nogger writes 'Punter' on his thighs, 'Sneak Thief' and 'Mugger' on his arms. Clone draws a sign on the back of a cardboard box lid – 'Auld Ones And Bingoites Beware. Dirty Man Will Have Your Winnings Off' – and hangs it round his neck with a length of cord ripped out of the lad's jacket.

As he's getting off, Nogger cranes his neck around and says, 'Just doing our bit for community, aren't we, lad?'

'Is right. Vigilantes, us, aren't we?'

..*.

Dylan wanders past the alley on his way home from Elizabeth's.

'Where you been?' Nogger shouts to him. 'Look mad, lad,' he says, eyeing Dylan's Lacoste and jeans, bewildered. 'What's going on, lad?'

'In town last night. Just some bird and that.'

Nogger's devo'd, jealous. 'For fuck's sake, lad. Bloot's been shot. All kinds of Nogzy being terrored. And you're out *behaving* with a bird. Wearing all mad clothes.'

'Yeah, I was out with a bird. Is that a crime?' asks Dylan, remembering what Bunter had told him, wanting to slaughter Nogger for his birds – his very young birds.

'You need to get your head together. You *need* to represent lad. We *need* to get down to Crocky and let off some buck.'

'I know, yeah,' says Dylan, taken aback. He takes the insult, the humiliation in front of the lads. Now is not the time for emotion. There's no way he wants to get involved in full-scale contact now. Not even in revenge for Bleeker's death, nor even to avenge the latest attack on Bloot. Beef just interferes with graft. Leads to serious jail. A distraction is needed again, but the excuses are wearing thin now.

'Just send a few of the younger ones round with the long feller,' he says, knowing they can't do much damage with an unwieldy side-by-side. Most of the young lads always aim high. Ride round there at two in the morning, three kids on a robbed bike. Dylan knows no one will get hurt.

Nogger moans about the long shotgun and how bad their weapons are. 'Need to get some decent squirts, lad.'

This is the distraction Dylan's looking for. 'How much have we got in the kitty?'

A grand. It won't buy them much.

* * *

The gun shop is an old yellow Transit van. It trawls the estates renting out and selling guns to the gangs. It's run by a couple of out-of-towners, biker types from Leigh in Lancashire or somewhere. The lads call them 'the gypos'. But, for a couple of sheepshaggers, they get loads of respect from the lads, because they open the gateway to power. The pieces are shit – old rusty blunderbusses – but cheap and rentable. HP, terms, whatever.

The van's parked up on The Boot. Nogger jumps in the back. It's lit by a car mechanic's light wired up to a battery. He buys an old American-made First World War .455 Colt revolver for £200. It's been officially adapted on import to fit the slightly different-sized British bullets.

He tells the gypos, 'I want a Mac-10.'

'Nothing like that, Nogger. It's too high-class kit for us.'

Later, the other gun librarian is doing his rounds. He's a sharper feller. Has a big fuck-off house and stables in the countryside. He's parked in a nice saloon on a play area behind a burned down pavilion. He looks like a lecturer: steel-framed glasses, blue chinos and a golf jacket.

'What about a Mac-10?' asks Nogger. 'Got a Mac-10, have you?'

'You're talking two to ten thousand.'

'Better squirt, though, isn't it, though?'

'The best. It's a very compact, blowback operated, selective fire submachine gun, technically a machine pistol. Weighs less than three bags of sugar, measures less than a foot long but fires 1,000 rounds per minute.'

New Loon butts in: 'I know they're decent hardware, like, but why so much dough?'

'Because they've got prestige. They're an icon. If you type "Mac 10" into Google, you get 372,000,000 results. Type in "Jesus" and you only get 185,000,000. They're twice as big as Jesus. That's why everyone wants one.'

He's spieling out his well-used pitch. The penniless peasants have come to buy a second-hand Ford Fiesta. Now he's upselling them a top of the range Merc.

'They're all over the telly. See that one on *The Bill*? *Pulp Fiction, The A-Team, Predator 2, RoboCop, Die Another Day . . .'*

Nogger loves the gun librarian's Mac-10 porn. He only plays video games where the Mac-10's a selectable option for the gun. If not, he downloads a skin to replace the image of the stock machine gun with that of a customised Mac-10. 'Good Mac-10 games on the PlayStation,' he tells the dealer. '*Counter Strike, The World Is Not Enough, Operation Flashpoint, Enter the Matrix.'*

The librarian fires back: '*Black, Max Payne, Rainbow Six, The Specialist, Metal Gear Solid . . .'*

Nogger and New Loon get the point. 'Fairsensabough, kidder. You don't have to sell it to us. We want one already. But we haven't got ten quid for one weapon. There's 40 of us in our little team. We're saving up so that every one of us has got a thing if need be, so we just haven't got that kind of dough to spend on one piece of rearmament.'

The gun librarian's leading up to his proposition now. 'The bottom line is this: most Mac-10s you buy on the street now aren't the original ones that were made in America. It stands for Military Armament Corporation Model 10. It was developed by Gordon B. Ingram in Georgia, USA, in 1964. The company went bankrupt in 1975.'

'So what?' asks Nogger, although he's secretly loving all this talk.

'The point is – rather, the beauty of it is – that the Mac-10 is a simple, low-cost design with few moving parts. That results in two things. First, the economy of its black, menacing shape, the ultimate in "form follows function". Second, it's easy to manufacture and maintain.' He's moving in for the pay-off. 'This is the most important bit. Most new Mac-10s are made by amateur engineers in little secret factories, like cottage industries, all over the country.'

'What?' Nogger says. 'Are you fucking jesting? There's places that make them over here in England that just have them lying around? Why can't we have the fucking things off?'

'Yes, that's it. But it's not that simple. The underworld armourers who make them cover their tracks well to protect themselves from the police and people like you who want to steal their merchandise. They make all the separate parts at secret locations because they can't be nicked for having individual pieces. Then, on a certain day, they bring them all together for a short production run before quickly shipping them out to punters all over the country.'

'Well, do you know where one of these places is?'

'I know one on the South Coast that sells to all the niggers in London.'

Nogger smiles. 'Do you know when the graft'll be there?'

The gun librarian returns the sneer. 'Imminently.'

❋ ❋ ❋

Later, Nogger relays the story of the Mac-10 factories to Dylan. Low hanging fruit and ripe for the robbing.

'Sick graft that, lad,' says Dylan. He's secretly made up about the Mac-10 adventure because it'll get Nogger out of town for a few days, distract him from getting revenge on Crocky. Meanwhile, he can sit off with Elizabeth, go and see Paul to get some proper graft. Dylan needs some real money. He's planning to get off. Elizabeth has mentioned that part of her course involves studying and working abroad, and he's half thinking of going with her.

Back at the flat, Dylan loves it. She makes him his first-ever home-cooked meal: tandoori mushrooms with yogurt, salad and pitta bread. They eat it on the bed, then she runs a bath. The bathroom's Victorian, cold, slightly dilapidated, with a big roll-top bath. She puts the heater on, lights candles, pours a few glugs of thick lavender oil into the steaming water.

Afterwards, Dylan carries her, soaking and cold, into the bedroom. Makes love to her while she's still shivering on the bed.

Elizabeth asks him, 'Where do you want to come?' Dylan's never been asked that question before. He smiles. She takes the condom off, running with vanguard semen. She sucks wildly, swallows every bit and smiles.

'That's nice,' Dylan tells her.

'What are you doing?'

'Just filming you, girl.'

'Why exactly?' For a moment, she sounds tough, disapproving. 'I'm not a porno star, Dylan. What are you going to do? Show it to your mates? That's weird.'

'Just normal, innit?'

But she isn't having it. She just looks at him, fierce. He blows up crimson, pure cherry on. The moment's wrecked. It takes an hour to warm her back onside again.

Then she tells him, 'When I found you asleep at work, I thought you were a drug addict, crashed out. We get them now and again.'

Dylan freezes with shame and anger. 'What me? On the gear? No fucking way, girl. Must have got another lad.' He's going off on one. 'You can ask anyone in Nogzy and they will tell you straight. Never fucking touched the brown in my life, girl. Bit of weed now and again but not any Class As. Never in a million fucking years. For fucking meffs that, girl.' He turns away, disgusted. This time it's his turn to be indignant.

She's a bit freaked by his prickliness, by his overreaction. She touches him on the arm. 'Sorry, I didn't mean to upset you. It's just that . . . that it happens, doesn't it? Anyway, when I got close to you, I knew you weren't anything like that, because your clothes were too nice. And you smelled clean, lovely.'

Suddenly, Dylan feels strangely proud, almost elated, remembering his green Lacoste shirt.

'I liked the colour of your top,' she says, half to make him feel better.

CHAPTER 15

EASYDRUGS

Dylan gets Bulb Head on the phone. He's at the match, watching Everton in Belgrade.

'Go on.'

'I wanted to speak to the other feller,' says Dylan.

'Militai, lad,' he says, meaning that he's doing drug deals abroad.

'OK. I just wanted to have a word with him.'

'Well, we'll see you by the swings, lad.'

Everyone loves talking in code. That means 'go and see Stan', who's a dogger and a swinger, but one of the lads, sound.

Dylan meets him in a bar and Stan tells him that the Imperator is in Lebanon but that a message has been got to him to call. Then Stan tells a story about banging someone's wife on a velvet chaise longue at a sex club in Cardiff. Just then his phone goes off and he passes it to Dylan.

'Hello, mate,' says Paul. 'Are you all right, my mate?'

'Sorry to trouble you, mate. I know you're on campaign.'

'No, I'm sorry, mate, that I'm not there to see you.'

'Know you mentioned some wages? The Flat Place and that?'

'Course, mate. I'll come and see you, mate.'

Two days later, Dylan meets the Imperator in a supermarket café.

'We'll get you on the EasyJet flights going to Schiphol, Malaga, Portugal,' Paul tells him. 'All's you've got to do is see the lads over there and tell them one thing and another. Just running messages backwards and forwards.' He says that no one talks over the phone any more. Not by satellite phone, not by Skype, nothing. All messages from him into the hubs are delivered in person by an army of foot-soldier messengers going back and forth on cheap flights, delivering instructions to lads in the cafés and on the terraces.

EASYDRUGS

Dylan gets on the plane at John Lennon Airport. 'Above us only sky' on the billboard. He's wearing his green Peter Storm kagoul, brown cords, Rohan suedies. No hand luggage. As he moves along, in aisle after aisle, he sees similar lads, familiar faces. The cream of the city's teenage outlaws moving up a rung. They're all doing all right, grafting for one of the big firms.

Little half let-ons here and there. All of them have been en route – capable, industrious lads. All of the major cartels in the city must have a runner here.

'All right, lad,' Dylan whispers to a lad he knows. Most of them are wearing normal clothes. Near the back, though, he sees two Crocky mongrels, both wearing their Lowies, trapper hats, balaclavas. Way on top. They're looking smug cos they're on the executive ladder, ordering drinks already. They've got bags of Marksies scran like they're going the match. They're showing off to the mangy hostesses, with big mad voices and loud, rooting-tooting gestures.

On the sly, Dylan cocks his fingers at them like a gun. He leans in to the one in the aisle seat, as though he's asking what seat number it is, for a bit of gentle chiding. 'You're roasting, you, lad. Sitting there *behaving*. Pair of fucking scruffs.'

He scopes the cabin. No one else is wearing their normal street clothes. No one wants to fuck the job up. All hands are on their best behaviour.

In Amsterdam, it's a bleak northern European day. Dylan sits outside a café, gets picked up by a Manc lad in a Porsche Cayenne. No one says a word. Boston are on the CD player. They drive for two hours along tree-lined N roads to a nondescript commuter town on the outskirts of the capital. They stop at a pale-yellow, smooth-walled mansion with a long barn next door.

Inside he meets Dean. No other name needed. He's a living legend, a top act. A 35-year-old former ramraider now worth £400 million. He's one of the wealthiest criminals in British history. Dylan's read every line about him in the papers. There are whole estates full of kids named after him.

'All right, lad?' he says to Dylan. 'Cup of tea?'

'Got a little message off the other feller there.'

'Oh yeah. That's nice, isn't it? Come 'ead, let's go fishing.'

They park up near a frozen lake, nothing else but flat scrubland for miles around.

Dylan feels it's safe enough to pass on his message: 'He said it would be there in two days' time. Said it would be lined up on the dock like a row of new cars. D'you get me?'

'That all he said?'

'That's it.'

'OK.'

And that was it. Another international transaction completed. The final words in a complex operation to smuggle 500 kilos of contraband from one continent to another.

Dylan gets the last flight of the day back. He's back in Nogzy by two. There's no one about, so he goes home. He gets a text off Nogger saying that they're out of town, sitting off on a farm outside Brighton, waiting to have off some Mac-10s.

CHAPTER 16

THE RAPE

The next morning, Dylan gets the video. It shows Elizabeth sitting up on the side of her bed, floppy and laughing. She's nodding and keeling over, so that her head ends up between her legs. She's ro'ied-up, sitting there in just a pink vest, no kecks on.

A masked-up lad pushes her down into the foetal position. No resistance. He shafts her one, up the arse. A fatter, older man in a dark-grey camouflage jacket is on the bed, having a wank in her mouth. He's pushing his soft knob into her mush lips. At one point, she pats it away, winces like she's just sucked a lemon, like someone who's drunk and wants to go to sleep.

Dylan drops the phone. Watches the video still playing on the floor. He sees vague images of flesh and shapes of black material moving across the screen. He picks it up again. The lads aren't brutal. They don't have to be and they don't want to leave any marks. All the hard graft has been done. Getting into her pad. Getting the tablet into her. *Get paid.*

Two of them turn her over onto her back. One of them pulls her torso to the edge of the bed by curling his arms around her thighs. Dylan remembers her milky skin. He spreads her legs. She flinches, resists for a second. He fucks her missionary-style.

Dylan doesn't make a sound. He looks outside into the street, his hands on hips. Then he stares at the floor, not knowing what to do. He begins shadow-boxing, fast, long jabs, packed with power and reach. Sweating, he takes his top off, then one by one, he removes every piece of his clothing until he is naked.

Then he jabs at the thin walls, cracking and creasing the cheap plaster methodically from one room to the next, bending and bashing the wire mesh strips with combinations, then ripping them out with his bleeding hands, one wall after another, the bedrooms, the landing, downstairs.

Looks at the vid again. It shows her being shagged from behind, flat on the bed, then being three-pipered. In the mirror next to her bed, there's the reflection of a fourth lad sat off in a chair, having a wank. Even he's got a condom on. They're all forensically aware. No spunk on her face. There's no soundtrack in case their voices are recognised.

At the end, the credits roll up: 'Smashen Dylan Olsen's Sweat. CYG Croxteth Young Guns.' Crude mobile-phone text, video DJ graphics.

Turned on by the three-piper, Dylan has a wank with his swollen, bloodied hands. Then he takes a shower and puts his special all-black kit on, with full hood and goggles, military-issue. He runs up to The Boot, digs up a silver Czech-made 9-mm pistol, a converted replica, from its hiding place. He runs down the centre of the road to the offices of Red Road Taxis. He waits for a driver to come out of the steel-plated doors and bursts the ken. The dispatcher's sitting off in a bulletproof jacket worn over a shiny silk-nylon trackie. Bunter's in a little side room for the drivers, halfway through a Breakfast Brunch Pasty. Dylan goes for the head with the first shot but the bullet nips into Bunter's neck. Dylan picks up the two-bar electric fire and rams it into Bunter's crotch. His trackies melt and there's a foul smell of groin-odour, burning skin and nylon. Behind Dylan, the dispatcher lets some buck off from a small wooden-stock side-by-side. Most of the pellets hit the door frame and Bunter, but Dylan's OK. He fires one shot off to clear his way, then he's off.

Dylan knew the fat one on the bed was Bunter straight away.

As for Crocky, the CYG, this is it. War is now on. No back answers. Dylan heads for The Boot to burn his all-blacks.

CHAPTER 17

THE ACCIDENT

Nogger and Dylan meet in the park, on the tarmac in the middle: sideways rain, pink streetlamps, bare steel railings, melted wheelie bins like purple puddles on the ground.

'Crocky mongrels have got to go, lad,' says Dylan. 'Been thinking about what you said and that . . .' He doesn't mention the rape.

Big smile from Nogger. 'Sound, lad. Knew you'd come round. Anthony Mulhearn has got to go, lad. Made up you're up for it. Got to do it, for Bleeker, if nothing else.'

'But how we gonna do it, lad?'

'Got a boss idea. Get Casey into him, lad. He'll love that, thinking he'll be hanging out of Dylan's bird. Get her to set him up for a little meet.'

'That fucking rip's costing me two G a week in fucking swag and charlie anyways,' Dylan says. 'Made up to offload her onto that scruffy fucking winnet.'

'Get her to send some pictures of herself in all the tackle, lad, sussies and everything. Bit of phone flirting, get her to get him up to the alley behind the Royal Oak, then we can cop for him as he's getting into her, get Jay to blast him. We'll sit off nearby with the Macs in case Jay misses first time.'

Nogger fills Dylan in on the Mac-10 graft, how him and Jay and a few of the younger lads had screwed the farm – smashed the locks on an outhouse and cleaned it out at four in the morning.

* * *

Dylan arranges to meet Jay in the Lidl car park. 'Bit of work there for you, lad.'

'Go 'ead.'

'We want you to smoke Mulhearn for us, lad.'

It's a big thrill for Jay, the older lads asking him to do a bit of graft. 'OK, D. What d'you want me to do?'

'There's a .455 out the way, there,' says Dylan, referring to a First World War revolver. 'But I'll get it brought on for you, d'you get me? So you can use that.'

'Decent.'

'I'll get Clegsy to bring it to you.'

* * *

Casey texts Anthony Mulhearn: 'Want to see me by the entry, back of the Royal Oak pub?' She turns up in the alleyway in tight black Kal Kaur Rai hotpants that cost £300, a silver ankle bracelet, a turquoise Maillili silk jacket, big fuck-off fake-fur trim round the neck and hip, tied at tit height with a big black silk sash, no top or bra underneath. It's four o'clock on a Thursday afternoon. Anthony turns up on a robbed quad bike, a few of the little rats behind him on pushers. He's in a fresh pair of Lowies, fully hooded up with a gas mask and gloves on.

'All right, girl,' he says. 'You look fucking excellent.' He pervs off her, looking her up and down, doing his mating ritual. He rides round her, staring hard, talking hard, cuffing the young rats, not taking his mask off.

Round the corner, a group of little lads from the posh half of the estate wander over from the new chippy, dressed in their school uniforms – grey jumpers, blue shirts hanging out untidily from under them, striped ties, thick knots. They're eating ice pops, playing footie against the wall, dotting in and out of the busy chippy. One of their mas turns up and calls out, 'Michael! Michael, look after Chalina for a minute while I pop into the chippy.' The little sister hops out the car and joins the boys. She's three, wearing a red top, playing with a doll and a buggy on the pavement.

* * *

Meanwhile, as Anthony's being lured into the trap, Jay prepares for his mission, noradrenalin pumping round his body now. His shoulders are knotted with stress. They're sat off in a derelict house at the bottom of the alley, Nogger being the older one, counselling him, geeing him up.

'It'll be all right, lad,' Nogger says.

'I know, yeah,' replies Jay. 'I'm not worried.'

Clegsy arrives, in a location jacket with a mad hooded mask, a dismantled shotgun in two parts down the front of his kecks and a Hungarian M57 9-mm pistol in his pocket. He assembles the shotgun *Day of the Jackal*-style. As he swings the long, heavy barrel onto lock-on, he says, 'It take no shit. If the beef come down here, they get blasted, lad.'

He keeps the shotgun himself. 'I'll watch over you on the way in,' Clegsy assures Jay. 'I'll be right behind you, all the way,' he says, trying to steel the worried kid. He hands Jay the M57. 'This is your back-up, in case the .455 jams.' Finally, he reveals the big old .455, which he is carrying in the belly of his trackie top.

Jay looks more nervous at the sight of the gunmetal. Nogger tells him, 'Best thing is to have a joint, lad.' Clegsy builds up and Jay gets stoned, gorping, the ancient *hashshashin*.

Nogger takes the .455 off Clegsy and loads six bullets into the revolving chamber. As he hands it over to Jay, he warns: 'Remember, this thing's got a range like a fucking rocket. One side of the park to the other. You don't have to get too close. We'll give you a call when we're ready.'

* * *

Small talk over, Anthony bends the waglet over a crumbling concrete bollard, pulls her hotpants down over her arse, rags the front of his Lowies down and smashes her from behind under the pink neon streetlamps. He gets a good feel of her. As he's walloping her, he puts his hand round the front, down the crotch of her hotpants, to cop a feel of her Brazilian. 'Nice bit of stubble there, girl.' Anthony likes it. She's half embarrassed that she isn't waxed smooth. She reminds herself she must get it done before Ladies' Day at Aintree.

Then Anthony gets his mobile out and starts to video himself smashing Dylan Olsen's bird. Got to ring this one in. What a coup! He gets the hotpants, then tracks up to her bobbing face, her Farrah Fawcett/Beyoncé-style layers gently bouncing. He gets a top profile of her fat Botoxed-up lips. She starts biting them with her bleached-up incisors. He splats right up her, then all over the crack of her arse. He pulls in and out and slaps his dick on her cheeks, just like in the blueys, holding the base of his knob and slapping her with the other eight inches. 'Boss, la.' He stretches a bit of the black material of her hotpants and wipes his dick. There's a bit of come on his Lowies, which he wipes on the fake fur of her coat.

* * *

Nogger leaves Jay to familiarise himself with the weapons and shoots off to meet Dylan, who's lying low in a cluster of bushes with a good view of the chippy. The alley where Anthony and Casey are is obscured, but he can hear the engine on Anthony's quad ticking over and imagines Casey's getting walloped all over the show by now. He checks his phone to see if she's sent the signal. They arranged for her to send a blank text meaning that Anthony was set up. But there's nothing yet.

Nogger creeps into the bushes behind him and carefully fishes out a present from his sports bag. 'This is yours,' he says, handing Dylan one of the stolen Mac-10s, a reward for finally OK'ing a big go-around. Respect for coming onside and avenging the death of Bleeker. They're both smiling, on the same buzz: a bit of Mac-10 porn.

'The Mac-10 needs no intro, la,' says Nogger, talking Dylan through the basics. 'See the hard square lines. Wastes no time in telling you just where to pick it up and which way to point it. But it's not until you handle it, lad, grip the dark cold metal, that it all makes sense. Do you get me, lad?'

Dylan feels the heft and the balance. A big grin like he's dropped a tablet comes over him.

'Check the fast muzzle sweep,' says Nogger. 'Comes over you like a wave, lad, doesn't it? What you've been waiting for all your life, isn't it, lad? Now you're the equal of any cunt, aren't you, lad?' Then the pay-off: 'Let's do it to them before they do it to us, lad.'

* * *

Anthony's gas mask is steamed up. Casey's coming down off her orgasm, affectionately kissing the holed metal casing of the carbon filters where his mouth should be. Anthony tells her, 'Clean me up, you little rip.' His voice is muffled and deep, like Darth Vader's, from behind the respirator. First she cleans herself, giving herself a good scratch of the arse through the hotpants, using the material to try to soak up his jizzum, but the fabric's stretchy and hardly absorbent.

Anthony tries his hand at pillow talk: 'You're a fucking disgrace, you.'

Casey's kneeling down in position for a blowie, giving him a wank to start off with. Looking sheepish and pink faced, she replies, 'Ar eh, Anthony, that's lovely. You don't have to say that.'

Half embarrassed about showing his feelings, he says, 'I know, girl. But I mean it.'

Then she sucks his knob clean and licks the milky blobs off the computer-designed black Gore-tex of his Berg jacket. She slowly moves her hand down into her pocket and presses the send button on her phone.

* * *

Dylan's Nokia suddenly lights up. Quickly, he gives Jay the jump-off call on another pay-as-you-go. Jay, still gorping, rides down the alleyway on his pusher. Nogger and Dylan come out of hiding and take up position behind the pub, making sure no CYG reinforcements make it into the kill zone and that Anthony Mulhearn can't escape. Casey gets the call to get out of the way. Jay sees Mulhearn getting on his quad bike. Out comes the auld 4/5. He can barely lift it, it's that fucking heavy. He's gonna do it with two hands but he sees the young ones – the kids by the shops, the little girl, and the young lads with Anthony – and decides to do a bit of showing off. One hand on the pusher, one on the 4/5. Sideways. Bang! Fuck off! A bullet goes right into the quad bike. *The fucking recoil on that.* Bang! One into the chippy wall. Bang! One into the crowd of kids.

Out of sight, Dylan and Nogger hear the shots go off.

'Go 'ead, Jay, lad. True Nogzy soldier,' says Nogger.

They raise their weapons, waiting for Mulhearn to come running round the corner, but instead they see three flashes of black run in between the buildings, like soldiers running for cover. Nogger spurts the Mac-10 in their general direction but the fierce recoil sends his aim skyward. The magazine's emptied. Dylan, charged with adrenalin, fires his, copycat, but it sprays all over the show. Dylan and Nogger look at each other, faces stretched with joy, laughing.

Mulhearn and the three other lads have already made it into the chippy. They jump over the counter and arm themselves with knives, ducking behind a stainless-steel counter in the kitchen, bobbing up to see if anyone has followed them in. Mulhearn has his phone to his ear, belling one of the lads hiding outside. 'Have they gone? Have they gone? Where the fuck are they, lad?'

'Can't see 'em nowhere. Fucking hell . . . there's just fucking bullets everywhere.'

'What the fuck was that?' shouts Anthony, who can hear the shots simultaneously in the background and over the phone. 'Fucking madness.'

Everything's turning chaotic. Phones are going off everywhere after the contact.

'Have they gone?' Anthony yells down the phone.

Jay pedals like fuck, the .455 weighing heavily on him, angular in the belly of his Lowies, stopped from falling out by the tightened toggles. Dylan and Nogger run back to Nogzy over through the backs, phones all over the show lighting up.

PART TWO

THE AFTERMATH

CHAPTER 18

GLORY

The lads meet on The Boot. They're still coming down.

'Better one, wannit?' says Dylan. 'Madness.'

'Did you get him?' Nogger asks Jay. 'Did you get him? Did you drop Mulhearn, lad?'

'Fuck knows. Just let rip. Shots going everywhere. Ting! Ting! Ting! Just saw them run off by the chippy, fall over and that.'

'True solja, you, lad.'

Jay beams with pride, his pasty, additive-riven complexion looking healthy for once, as Nogger pays him the highest accolade, the most meaningful honour. But he shows humility in his response. 'For Nogzy, lad, innit? Protect and serve, innit, lad?'

'Protect and serve. That's us, lad,' replies Nogger, justifying the offensive. 'We're serving the community, lad. Protecting everyone. Not just the lads but all hands: mums, schoolies, kids, shoppers, auld biddies. Stopping them from being had off by Crocky mongrels. People should be thanking you for what you did today.'

'Nice one, Nogger. I know, yeah.'

All their phones are buzzing, ringing, bleeping. A symphony of ringtones. News of the attack is spreading fast. 'Listen to that. Don't worry lad,' Nogger tells Jay. 'That'll be all the congratulations. "Well done for putting Mulhearn in a box."'

'We've got to get off, la,' says Dylan. 'Out of the favela as soon as possible. Place'll be roasting with bizzies soon.'

'I know, yeah,' agrees Nogger. 'Just waiting for the pick-up.'

There are lookouts all over The Boot coordinating the extraction. A black Volvo four-by-four pulls up outside, takes them down to a big coachworks on an industrial estate. All three of them strip naked,

Nogger cupping his bollocks, nothing on but a gold chain around his neck. Jay's wretched adolescent corpse is exposed, underfed but with a pot belly caused by a diet of Haribo and Coke and still partially frozen microwaved scampi.

Dylan shivers as Bloot and Lupus pour petrol over his head from two plastic containers. The organic solvents will dissolve any gun residues and DNA that could link them to the shooting. Then they pour some down his back.

Casey turns up. She stands in the doorway with one hand on her hip, smoking a ciggie even though there's petrol fumes all over the place. 'That was some boss graft, that, lad,' she says to Dylan.

It's time for the post-match analysis, everyone wanting to know the details, share the gossip. 'You were fucking spot-on,' says Dylan, rubbing his cock with petrol.

'Had to fucking tempt him with me charms, like, but the dirty twat was all over me, trying to a get a grip.' Casey's making out that she didn't like Anthony Mulhearn's advances, but Dylan knows that she enjoyed fucking someone who was minutes away from death. In fact, he's sure she's still turned on by the dead man's cold come inside her and in her kecks. That is, if he is dead.

New Loon bursts in. 'Just heard on the radio – the bizzies say there's one fatality.'

Nogger rubs his hands together in jubilation. 'Go 'ead. He's dead, the stupid cunt. I've put him in a box,' he says, greedily claiming the kill.

'Fucking boss,' says Jay, not arguing.

'That must have been my one, lad, with the Mac-10. I saw him go down,' he pretends to remember.

Dylan feels a buzz, like he's coming up on a tablet. A job well done. But the edge is taken off it because he feels jealous that Nogger's already claiming the *coup de grâce*. Dylan knows the power an incident like this had. By the end of the night, grafters in Amsterdam, Spain and Portugal will be talking about it. Dylan can make his bones off this if he plays his cards right. The Imperator might not approve of petty squabbles, but he'll quietly respect the operator who carried this one off. Everyone could use lads like that.

Casey hugs him. 'Well done, lad. You're a fucking hero. Fucking love you.'

'Love you as well, girl. Couldn't have done that without you.'

With just an old brown towel around him and still reeking of petrol, he pulls her into a little room off to the side. He slips her hotpants off, like Mulhearn did a couple of hours before, fucks her. He likes the idea of mixing his live sperm with the Crocky rat's dead ones.

Afterwards, high off the death sex, Dylan is buzzing. *This is what it's about. Letting off some buck with the lads. Having a boss bird with top tits who's game. Come on! What other bird would do what she's done? Get shagged by a Crocky rat to set him up. That's one proper bird. Marriage material.*

Then he looks at Nogger, arsing about as he's getting dressed, their old Lowies being petrolised and torched behind him. *I fucking love that lad. That's what it's all about. Doing some boss little graft with your mates. That's what it's all about. Sticking by your mates. So they stick by you.*

In the hazy high, he's forgiven Nogger for raping Elizabeth. The girl he loved. He knows that Nogger was the lad sat in the chair. It took him a while to figure it out. He watched and rewatched the vid in the days between deciding on the ambush and carrying it out. He spotted the white polystyrene chippy container on the bedside cabinet, studied the delicate transparent film sticking out of the top, streaked with curry sauce. Pure classic Nogger. Exhibit A. Then he analysed the shadowy figure sat down having a wank at the side. *If you've known someone all your life, you just know how they walk, stoop, sit.* He knows that Nogger set her up, sat there while the taxi driver raped her, having a wank in the chair. Probably walloped her later, off-camera, while she was crying. That would be classic Nogger.

Elizabeth wasn't raped by Crocky Young Guns. The credit on the video was just a smokescreen, a nice detail that only Nogger could have schemed up, not only to cover his tracks but for maximum impact on the crime's intended victim – Dylan. The rape wasn't about Elizabeth for Nogger. It was all about Dylan. Once he figured that out, Dylan worked backwards, reasoning everything through. He imagined how Bunter had gone to complain to Nogger about Dylan pulling the knife on him, then Nogger getting Bunter to show him where Dylan's mysterious new girlfriend lived, seeing the perfect opportunity to teach Dylan a lesson.

But Dylan tells himself he's over it now. After all, how long had he known the silly bint? Two weeks at the most. And at the end of the day, he was gonna have to choose between her and Casey at some time. Would Elizabeth have done for him what Casey had today? Dylan laughs and walks over to Nogger.

'I know it was you, you know.'

Nogger gives him daggers. He's onto it immediately. No denial.

'I'm not arsed, by the way. I know you did it for the right reasons.'

They hug.

'I just needed to get your attention, lad,' says Nogger. 'You were being distracted.'

'But why didn't you just come and see me? You didn't have to get her. Not that I'm arsed, by the way. Hardly knew her, d'you know worramean?'

'You were being dragged away from us by a silly bird, lad. I was angry. I didn't even know what the fuck was going on. You just got off.'

'Only for a fucking day, lad.'

'A day alive round here, lad, is a lifetime.' Dylan says nothing. 'Listen, Bleeker's been dead fucking months, his fucking head chopped off . . . and you hadn't done nothing about it. It was as though you wanted Crocky to get away with it, as though you weren't arsed about getting revenge.'

'Fucking hell, lad,' says Dylan, his head down, ashamed, feeling the great dishonour.

'I knew that if you thought Crocky had smashed your bird, you'd go mad. Which you fucking did, mate. So I was fucking right, weren't I?'

'Suppose so.'

'Fucking right, I was. If I hadn't have given you a kick up the arse, you wouldn't have dropped Mulhearn today. And you'll remember this for the rest of your life. Fucking legend, lad.'

Dylan looks into Nogger's eyes. It's clear to him now that Nogger raped his bird because he loves him. Simple as. Didn't want the lad he's grafted with since he was a kid dragged away from the gang by some girl. The rape was a means to an end. Dylan knows the score. If the truth be told, the bond between you and your gang is stronger than between you and your mum, dad, sister, all put together, stronger than your ties to Nogzy itself, never mind a silly bird. End of story.

* * *

Ninety minutes later, they're fully decontaminated, every molecule of compromising forensics gone. Casey's even manicured their nails as a special treat, scraping the dirt from underneath them and pushing back the cuticles just to make sure. Nogger is surging off the military pride as they leave the garage in a convoy of blacked out cars. Untold texts and congratulations are flooding in from allied gangs. 'Is right. Fucken skum had it comen.' 'Congratulations.' 'Anthony Mulhearn in a box. Little cunt.' They're even coming in from Spain and The Dam, from Dylan's new Easygraft mates. 'Fuck's sake,' says Dylan. 'Gone global, lad.'

It's time to stage a ticker-tape parade round the barrio. They dress in plain white T-shirts, like army heroes. They switch cars, into a robbed rag-top Lexus. Nogger and Dylan ride in the back. Jay's sitting up on the back boot, presidential-style. They've got a full complement of outriders: quads, an exoskeleton scooter, a couple of Segways, a few Boardwalk 20-inch-wheel BMX scooters. There's a Rangey up front, with New Loon sticking out of the sunroof. There's a belt-fed M42 heavy machine gun under the seat – force protection, green zone-style. The younger ones are riding in a robbed Omega at the tail. They've got IEDs made of industrial fireworks wrapped in sheet metal with a two-inch fuse, to ward off any insurgents bent on quick revenge, and a white phosphorus smoke bomb, to cover an aggressive getaway if need be.

As they progress through The Boot, clusters of well-wishers line the streets: grateful campesinos, a few young mas in pyjamas clapping, kids letting off balloons from the party shop. There's clapping, loads of shouts: 'Fucking great stuff, Dylan!' Footie chants from some of the teenagers: 'Nogzy, Nogzy, Nogzy.' A couple of banners hang from bedroom windows, dripping in fresh red paint: 'Mulhearn you fucking maggot. Dropped by Nogzy Loyalist Fighters', and the date underneath.

'Look at that,' says Nogger. 'Fucking boss, innit? That's the thing about a ticker-tape – you've got to let the community know who did this, who struck revenge in their honour so that they can sleep safe in their beds, who were prepared to go onto the battlefield for them, d'you know worramean? No one knows the half of what we do to help them.'

'You know what?' asks Lupus. 'We should get a fucking big mural done. Like the ones in Northern Ireland. Painting of us with our hoods on and that, holding a few pieces. Battle honours and that.'

'Fucking boss idea, that,' says Nogger. 'Sort it out and I'll sign it off.'

They put the foot down, doing over 70, when they reach the parts of the estate where no one's out, slowing back down at The Strand then heading up to Broadway. Jay stands up, one hand on Nogger's shoulder, on the mobile to a well-wisher who's giving him big-ups.

There's not many older ones paying their respects here. Everyone's just out shopping, picking the kids up from school, chatting shit with the neighbours. A few of the younger ones are smiling, though. One shop lad, carrying a box of cheap bananas, shouts 'nice one' to Nogger. 'True Nogzy soljas.' A few LA-style gang signs are going up on the sly.

Meanwhile, a team of cleaners is bombing around the estate, disposing of the evidence, hoovering up the trail. Bloot stows Jay's .455 with Warren, a kid he knows on The Boot.

Bloot turns up on the doorstep carrying a faded blue JD Sports plazzie bag with a cord on it.

'Go 'ead,' says Warren. 'What do youse want?'

'Jay wants you to look after this,' says Bloot.

'What d'you mean?'

'Just fucking take it, will you, you prick?'

'What d'you fucking mean?'

Warren's ma's drinking wine on the couch, Jeremy Kyle on the telly. 'Who is it, Warren?'

'Nothing. Fucking shut up, will you, you fucking witch.' To Bloot, he says, 'Go on. See you later.' He scowls and snatches the bag, slams the door.

He wraps the gun in cling film and hides it under the gravel at the bottom of his dirtiest fish tank. A few days later, he reluctantly takes delivery of the Mac-10s and moves all three to an old drain near a sewer.

Pacer rides Jay's bike a few miles across the city to Childwall Woods, next to where *Hollyoaks* is filmed. He throws one wheel down a deep, overgrown gully with high sandstone sides, the other in a patch of tyre-ribbed mud near an abandoned porno mag and a half-burned tree stump where goth schoolies pretend to devil worship. He carries the frame into a field used after the war to dump bomb debris, covers it in shite and fucks off, gets the bus home.

* * *

For tea, Nogger buys in a load of pizzas and they chill out in an abandoned house on the estate. Lupus bowls into the pad. Shocker. 'Fucking hell. Have you seen d'*Echo*?' Dylan rags it off him, half-stoned.

GLORY

GIRL, 3, SHOT
Toddler Fights for Life
Gang Shoot Out

'Fuck's sake,' says Dylan. 'What's going on?' To New Loon, he says accusingly, 'Thought you said there was one dead. Fucking Mulhearn, wannit?'

New Loon gets defensive: 'Well, there is one dead. But we don't know who it is. I thought it was fucking him as well. Obviously.'

'People are saying it's this girl now,' says Lupus, 'that she's fucking dead. Just met some girl in the street and she says to me, "Have you heard about the baby being killed?"'

Dylan's on his feet. 'What fucking baby?'

'Fuck off, lad,' Nogger tells Lupus. 'What d'you think I am? A fucking Crocky-head that fires the gun anywhere, doesn't look where he's shooting?' He mimes firing a gun, with a heavy recoil, accidentally shooting into the air.

Dylan reads the story in the paper:

> A three-year-old girl is in a critical condition after being shot while playing outside a shop with her mother. Merseyside Police confirmed that the child was hit near the Royal Oak public house in Croxteth, Liverpool.
>
> Ambulance chiefs said the girl, who has not been named, was rushed to Alder Hey hospital at 5.30 p.m. last night with a serious gunshot wound.
>
> She was initially said to be in a stable condition but a spokesman for the hospital later said that a bullet had entered her head and that she was fighting for her life in intensive care.
>
> A Merseyside Police spokeswoman said: 'We can confirm that a girl aged three has been shot near the Royal Oak public house. Police were called shortly after 5.20 p.m. An investigation is under way.'

Dylan feels stressed, a white haze of worry bleaching out his thoughts. Nogger's reading more of the story. 'Says that she was wearing a Liverpool top. Serves her fucking right, the rednose twat,' he says, trying to make light of it.

Dylan's fucking seething, straining to stop himself saying, 'Bet you'd fucking shag her if you could, you dirty nonce wretch.'

Everyone's getting wound up. Nogger stops messing about and starts to focus. 'Can't fucking remember a girl in a footie top, can you?'

'No way, lad,' says Dylan. 'Cannot have been fucking us, can it, lad?'

'It must have been those cunts firing back,' says Jay.

Whizzer butts in, reading on from the newspaper story: 'Witnesses told how the girl was shot in front of her older brother whilst her mother was looking on a few yards away. The victim was playing near a chip shop with her brother while their mother was inside being served. Another witness said the family may have been walking back to their car when shots were fired and the girl fell to the ground. A teenage boy rode past on a BMX bicycle with his face covered by a hood and opened fire from a large black handgun, a local resident claimed.'

A secret pang of pleasure sparks through Dylan. *Nice one.* They've not mentioned his and Nogger's guns. Only Jay's. *That's good. Let's hope it stays that way. Jay. The poor cunt.*

Jay instinctively senses that he's being manipulated by the older lads, that they are subtly putting a bit of distance between them and him. For a moment, he looks alone and worried. But then he smiles, secretly buzzing off the notoriety, showing his age.

The next paragraph reads:

> Other shots, described by an onlooker as 'automatic gunfire', were also heard coming from behind the pub. According to a local shopkeeper, there were several guns firing in quick succession, suggesting that there was more than one assailant.

'Fucking hell,' says Nogger. 'Who are these fucking witnesses chatting shit to the paper? Croxteth, la. Full of fucking snitches. That's all you get over there: grasses. If that would have happened in Norris Green, no one would have said fuck all, even straight-goers.'

Jay, trying to help, adds, 'Says this grass is a fucking shopkeeper. We should blow up his shop.'

'Doesn't say what fucking name it is, though,' Dylan points out.

'Just blow the fucking lot up,' suggests Nogger. 'Tonight or tomorrow, when the bizzies fuck off. IEDs into every fucking one, la. Boom. Gone. No more jangling, innit?'

GLORY

Dylan looks at the picture illustrating the story. A night shot of a police van, officers at the scene of the crime wearing yellow hi-vis vests, white fluorescent stripes glowing, others in white Noddy suits. He reads the story's conclusion aloud: 'The Croxteth Park Estate was formerly the biggest private housing estate in western Europe. Merseyside's Assistant Chief Constable is appealing for witnesses.'

Everyone laughs at this ridiculous statement. There'll definitely be no witnesses. Not by tomorrow night there won't be, anyway. As soon as the bizzies have left, shops/residents/passers-by/mates/family/the fucking lot are getting told, getting it if need be.

Dylan's desperate for information, can't stand the uncertainty. He phones Casey, looking for someone to blame.

'You know when you were doing the thingio before, with that other fucking prick, did you see a little girl in a Liverpool top?'

'Erm, what are you fucking on about? Was fucking busy, lad, if you remember, giving the poor cunt a nosh.'

'Shut up, you fucking spunkbucket. Just answer the question. Did you see her or fucking not? Says she's been –'

'I'll split your fucking wig if you speak to me like that again.'

Dylan buttons the call, goes outside, purely fucking gutted.

CHAPTER 19

PUBLIC OUTCRY

Dylan knows the script. He keeps focusing in on the key facts, trying to work his way through it. *She was fucking three. Girl was wearing a fucking Liverpool kit.* His head's blown by this new revelation. He's shaking his head, tutting.

After dark, they reconvene in one of the younger lads' bedrooms. Dylan turns to Pacer. 'D'you realise what that means in this city? This fucking dickhead city. Liverpool kit – three years old – shot dead. They'll hunt us to the ends of the earth.'

New Loon agrees but tries to play it down: 'Only if she fucking dies. If she lives, there's half a chance it'll fade away.'

Dylan stares at him. For a moment, he hates this fucking wretched city. Full of opinionated pricks with their fucking footie. Dylan knows these hypocrites off by heart. He's spent a lifetime around them, sitting on their couches, talking shit, agreeing, arguing. They'll spend £2,000 to go away with Liverpool to Europe but won't give their wives fuck all to feed the kids. Fanatical love for the Reds but they come home bevvied and bash their birds up when they lose. These pricks would be casting the first stones. Just you watch.

Dylan's exasperated. But then he remembers she's still alive – just a-fucking-bout. So he tries to keep cool. Just then Karl, one of the younger lads who's been drafted in as a runabout until the heat dies down, bursts in with a robbed laptop, Voda-netted-up. They look at the news on the BBC. 'She's fucking dead all right, lad,' says Karl.

That's that. Dylan puts his head in his hands. 'Oh no. Oh fucking no.' *For fuck's sake.* He just wants Elizabeth now, wants to put his arms round her and cry. Aches for it. But then he thinks about Nogger raping her, depriving him of the one thing he ever loved as soon as he'd fucking

118

got it. He hasn't seen her since, or even tried to phone her. He blames himself for the rape and he can't face her.

The guilt overwhelms him. He springs up like a ninja. He punches the giant flat-screen. The LED crystals shatter. A combination of jabs and high knee kicks dislodges the TV from its steel wall mount. Dylan throws it at the window but it bounces back off the plastic frame. The younger ones are looking on speechless, still holding their gamepads. He breaks down and sobs on the edge of the bed. No one knows what to do, seeing their leader crumble before their eyes.

A few minutes later, Nogger arrives and Dylan gets his head together. Karl whizzes through to the Sky website for confirmation: 'Three-year-old girl dies after being shot in Liverpool.'

'What are the fucking papers saying?' asks New Loon. Karl brings up the *Daily Mirror*'s site: 'Breaking news: Prime Minister Mourns Shot Girl.' He scrolls down, speed-reading the story: '. . . the girl has not been officially named but locals say her name is Chalina.'

'Chalina?' says Nogger. 'Never fucking heard of her.'

'Anyone know her? Anyone know that name?' asks Dylan, looking round the room at the lads' faces, trying to get a grip. No one says fuck all.

'Chalina? What kind of a fucking name is that? Sounds like a coon.' Nogger's trying to make light with the lads.

Dylan. Panicking. Looking for anything to hold onto. Dylan: 'Maybe that isn't such a bad thing. Cunt of a thing to say like – but if she's black, no one will give a fuck.'

'What d'you fucking mean, lad?' asks New Loon.

Dylan understands the gravity of the situation now, knows that it's fucking murder. If they're collared for this one, it'll be life sentences all round. 'What I'm saying is . . . is that if she's white, it's twice as fucking bad for us. D'you get me? But if the little fucking girl is black, then it doesn't fucking matter as much. That's good for us. Because no matter what anyone says, a white life is still worth more than a black one. As far as the fucking papers and the bizzies are thinking, anyways. That's just the way it goes.'

'Is right, lad. White power!' says Nogger, not getting it. Dylan just looks at him.

Lupus doesn't get it either: 'What are you on about, lad? Coons have got more rights than us now.'

'Fucking point is, let's hope she's black. Cos if she is, the bizzies might fuck it off and the papers'll get back to writing about shit again.'

'Well, I reckon she's fucking white,' says Karl.

'Why?' New Loon asks.

'Cos I've just heard that there's all kinds of people from the telly down at the Royal Oak. From the news. And they wouldn't come in force if she was black.'

Dylan has to see it for himself. He throws on some civilian wear, a pair of jeans and his green kagoul, Everton scarf over his mouth. He just looks like any other pot-head urchin on the way home from work.

At the site, there are outside-broadcast vehicles, a couple of space cruisers, a few underpaid reporters in shabby crombies or too-tight North Faces doing pieces to camera. All the locals are giving them a wide berth, fucking them off when asked if they saw anything or, 'What's the feeling in the community?'

Dylan says to New Loon as they mosey past: 'That's good. No one's grassing. If anyone, fucking anyone, says anything to these cunts, I want to know, OK?'

After a little suss, they find out the vans are from Sky, ITN, Five and the BBC. 'Well,' says Dylan, 'it doesn't look that bad.'

He walks home in the drizzle, under a cloud of stress. When he thinks about it – 30 years in the jug – his mind becomes clouded. He tries to stay calm, thinking it through. *Just a kid killed in an accident. It'll all blow over in a few hours.*

But then he gets home and his ma asks him, 'Have you seen what's happened round the corner? Poor kid's been shot. What kind of a fucking world is it coming to? Hope you had nothing to do with that.'

Dylan fumbles with the remote, trying to put the Sky on. 'Just turn the fucking sound up, will you, you fucking prick, and fucking shut up?'

His ma storms into the kitchen for a ciggie and a chase. A school photo of Chalina pops up on BBC News 24. Blonde hair, snub nose, strong glasses with pink frames. She's dressed in a lime-green Boden coat with a red lining.

No chat with her mother yet, but the reporter says: 'Witnesses have told of the moment little Chalina was struck down by a bullet in this car park behind me. Her mother, named locally as Lynda, was, like millions of other families, buying a take-away meal from a chip shop. Witnesses say she heard the shot and ran out. There on the floor lay her daughter. She held her in her arms until the ambulance arrived . . .'

'For fuck's sake,' mutters Dylan, not feeling sorry for Chalina or her ma but feeling sure that because the victim was posh and white it'll be worse for them.

Within hours, the media frenzy has begun in earnest. The road outside the Royal Oak is chokka with TV vans, more than 20 of them. Before long there are at least 60 as foreign correspondents from Germany, France, Japan and the US roll up. It looks like backstage at a concert: electrical generators, rows of cables, massive umbrellas, camping chairs, bright white lights. The fucking OJ/Wacko Jacko circus.

The regional correspondents, who arrived first, are quickly ousted by heavyweights flown in from London. ITV opts for a mobile news desk; a whole team's brought up to Liverpool. Their anchor is running the show from the Royal Oak car park. The BBC responds by buying up a whole floor of a hotel for its news teams and technicians. The mobile news desk gimmick spreads. Winnebagos are lined up Hollywood-style for the special correspondents. Most of them are petite, skinny, well-groomed and expensively dressed – tight-fitting jackets, blonde-streaked bobs. They're led carefully down the steps of the trailers, tottering under umbrellas. Dylan recognises one of them, the girl the lads twatted after Bleeker's funeral, security all around her. Now she's ramping up the hype on the telly, getting her revenge. The papers have joined the pack too, trying to outdo each other, buying up space in hotel suites, conference rooms and even an indoor stadium.

Dylan just sits with the lads, listening, taking counsel from his boys. But he knows that they're just trying to convince themselves that everything's OK. Finally, he says, 'Bin lid didn't fucking look like a meff to me, lad. On that fucking picture they showed on the telly just then, she looked posh, if you ask me.'

The late edition of the local paper carries an interview with Chalina's dad. In it, he says, 'God must have needed an extra angel. Because he's taken another one today.' Dylan says that it's the final nail in their coffin, that the police'll throw everything at them now.

'Fuck off with all that bollocks. That's just paper talk,' Nogger tells him.

'That's exactly what it is. And don't you forget they fucking rule this country. They say what goes. If this blows up in the papers, we're gonna be hunted down for ever, lad. Worse than fucking nonces, we'll be. Mark my words.'

GANG WAR

The newspaper reporters and photographers are going round knocking on people's doors now. The lad from the *Mirror*'s bald, smartly dressed, in a Ford Mondeo. The *Sun* reporter's tanned, his eyes and attention darting about with animal hunger. He's blagging that he's a freelancer, because of Hillsborough. They're all giving it the patter: 'We're putting together a tribute piece for little Chalina, looking for people who might have known her.' But everyone's onto their graft straight away. They're just desperate to get their hands on more pictures. When they get fucked off by the residents, they trawl the nurseries, child minders, church playgroups and school photographers offering £500 for a picture. Eventually someone sells some shots.

The media frenzy explodes the next day. *The Sun*'s front page reads: 'GIRL, 3, SHOT DEAD. Victim named – Chalina Murphy.' The *Mirror* goes with: 'Mother Cradles Dying Girl'.

The *Mail* talks up the middle-class background of the family. Dylan's sinkered when he sees that. Chalina's ma is self-employed, runs a designer curtains company. Her dad's a manager at a health club. 'Fuck's sake. That means the bizzies'll have to do something about it.' The story goes on about how the family live in a new build in a good area but describes the nearby council estates as 'poverty-stricken and blighted by drug abuse, gang violence and single-parent families'.

Next to it there's a comment piece written by a famous criminologist talking about 'boundary crime' – how the rate of crime goes up on the border between a nice area and a bad area. The article tells of 'poor criminals preying on rich pickings'. 'What a load of shit, lad,' Nogger says. But Dylan, thinking about it, knows it's at least partly true.

Nogger and Dylan walk down to the Royal Oak to scope out the latest. They watch as a shock jock from the local radio station moves down the line of TV news crews giving interviews, prodded on by his agent. 'We're pulling together,' he tells the reporters. 'The city is grieving.'

'Fat cunt,' says Dylan. 'Look at him. He was in fucking panto last year.'

But all hands are running for cover from the press. The wall of silence is going up; witnesses are being threatened.

'Everyone loves this,' says Nogger. 'It's a fucking circus, lad. The telly and the papers are doing good graft out of it. Fucking Iceland and Currys'll be made up cos their adverts'll get read by more people – type of fucking punters who goes there, as well, lad. All the fucking experts queuing up to get on the telly, getting wages out of it, getting famous. Good excuse for the bizzies to clamp down on the shitheads, too. Government'll bring in more laws. Everyone loves this. No one gives a fuck about the girl. No one gives a fuck about us. You watch, la, it'll all blow over.'

But later that afternoon it gets worse. The Prime Minister puts out a statement, saying, 'Chalina's murder was a callous act that has horrified the country.' Dylan knows it's bad now.

'As if the fucking politicians are fucking arsed,' says Nogger. 'What the fuck is the fucking Government saying that for? It was a fucking accident. Jay didn't mean to do it,' he says, cutely putting the blame on Jay.

The next day it gets well worse. The *News of the World* puts up a £1 million reward 'for the scum who gunned down little Chalina Murphy' and launches a 'Save Our Cities' campaign 'to rid Britain's towns and cities of gun-toting yobs'.

* * *

The bizzies have flooded the area. There are roadblocks and increased ARV patrols. Merseyside's Chief Constable phones the Home Office for permission to designate Croxteth and Norris Green anti-terror zones, and gets it. This means that every person and every house can be searched without even the suspicion of a crime. Riot police are brought in to patrol on foot.

But it's not enough. The papers want more. The Metropolitan Police offers Merseyside 100 of its top officers, including some anti-gang Trident teams, to boost the local force. Not since the miners' strike has the Met deployed so many outside the capital. They arrive in a fleet of coaches in a stage-managed flourish. The London bizzies are billeted at an army firing range near Altcourse.

A feller from Altcross Way puts a home-made poster in his window, a cartoon of a bizzy giving a Nazi salute, underneath the words 'Police State'. The next day, he's slaughtered in the *Echo* for being pro-gang. His door goes in. An early morning call off the Vaderis unit and Special Branch.

Even the new measures aren't enough for some. *The Sun* calls for British police to be routinely armed 'on the beat'. The leader says:

> British bobbies are respected around the world for upholding
> the law with decency and common sense. No one doubts their
> bravery in the line of duty. But to send them up against the

armed gangs that seem to roam freely around some of Britain's estates is asking too much.

Would little Chalina Murphy still be alive if the gangs that shot her knew the police were armed?

Chief constables have long been saying that sending unarmed police into our inner cities is like sending lambs to the slaughter. We know they're not lambs. They are lions who face danger every day to keep our streets safe. They are heroes – but they're not superheroes who can fight with their bare hands against enemies armed with lethal weapons.

Merseyside's Chief Con responds by thanking *The Sun* for its support. But he says that he wishes his officers to continue in the tradition of not carrying guns. That's the line for public consumption, anyway. Secretly, he's all for arming every single one of his men and women, but he doesn't want to put his head above the parapet yet.

For now, he makes do with more specialist units. Other forces send ARVs, armed officers and helicopters to help. They even hire in civilian helicopters and pilots to beef up air surveillance.

* * *

The next day, Dylan's woken up early by banging at his door.

'Have you heard?' New Loon shouts up to him at the window.

'What?'

'Your name's being thrown in everywhere. You're roasting, lad. All over the Internet. You, Nogger, Jay.'

New Loon makes him a cup of tea, while Dylan gets onto YouTube and searches 'Crocky Crew – latest video'. He doesn't even bother watching the vid. Skips straight to the comments: 'Dylan Olsen. Fucken baby killa. Shot Chalina Murphy. Split her wigg. Wit a Mak 10. Ur ded. Revenje.' 'Chalina shot by Little Jay (scruffy twat) Dilan and Nogga u fucken peydohfyle.'

'What the fuck is going on, lad?'

'It's all over Facebook,' New Loon tells him. 'MySpace too.'

Soon, Nogger and Jay arrive with the lads. They're worried about their names being thrown in. There are pages and pages of tribute vids to Chalina as well.

One from an Asian gang in Tower Hamlets. 'RIP trak out to the phamilee and m8s of Shaleena Moorfie hu was tuk from dem fru gun cryme.' Dylan plays it, thinks it's quite good. There are pictures of Chalina and her family cut in with messages on a bright blue background. Just like a Nogzy vid. Then pictures of their crew posing up near the waterfront at Canary Wharf. The lyrics are: 'Everyone. Yeah. Complicated. Many. Respect.' That's it. Those are the words.

'Don't usually like that MC-ing chipmunk music,' says Dylan. 'But it's all right, innit?'

'Got to watch those sepoys, though, lad,' Lupus tells him. 'Might look like little skinny cunts, but they'll have a go. Especially if there's a good few of them,' says Clegsy. Nogger doesn't like this.

Dylan scrolls through the comments: 'Propahh in Tears When I herd bout Herrrrr dieing,' posted by Emoshaun. Another one saying, 'Sikenns me wen kidz tayk potshotz at the publickz,' posted by a social networking rapper who calls himself 'I can't keep my nine straight'.

CHAPTER 20

AGENDAS

It goes off all over the estate. Everyone's buzzing on the news, excitement coursing through the cul-de-sacs and bungalows. All the younger ones are supporting the lads but most of the older ones are hoping that the police will finally steam into the gangs, once and for all. They're only saying it behind closed doors, though.

On Dylan's street, most of the neighbours are stood outside on their paths, sat on the gates and wheelie bins with the kids, looking up the street, pointing at Dylan's ma's house. It's the same at Nogger's and Jay's. The pavements are chokka with wheelchairs and electric shopping baskets. Even the people on the sick have come out of their houses to see what's going on.

Everyone's gossiping about how they were dragged up by their mothers, how Dylan's ma was a brass and she's still on heroin. Nogger's ma's oblivious, shuffling down the street in her slippers, zombied up on psychiatric drugs. Jay's ma's only 27. Clegsy reckons he's got stuck up her a few times when she's been pissed and had a tablet after Jay's gone to bed. So he's told Dylan, anyway. But no one's seen Jay's ma for three days now. She went clubbing with her new feller, a cage fighter, left Jay and his brothers with hardly anything to eat.

The Orange Lodge takes advantage of the carnival atmosphere to whip up support for the cause. They're out marching in red tam-o'-shanters, blue shirts and red trousers. The Derry Walls band, playing 'No Pope of Rome' – an estate classic. But a drunk old woman snatches the mace from the leader as they go past, for a bit of impromptu cane-twirling at the front.

Someone's told Nogger that it's an anti-gang march. So Nogger and Clegsy bomb out of the entry, chase after them with a samurai sword.

They twat the old woman with the mace, even though she's an IRA supporter and was just taking the piss. The rest scatter. Roberto Griffin's laughing at his front door, holding up an anti-abortion banner, trying to taunt the flute-players with a poster saying 'Crusaders for the Unborn Child'. Dylan's brother Will and his mates rob the drums and cymbals and start going mad.

Dylan's ma's in bits. She drags him off to a solicitor when Will shows her Dylan's name on the Internet, a tweet saying that he killed Chalina. In the lawyer's office, Dylan, Nogger and Jay are sunk low in armchairs behind the grilles on the windows, saying fuck all, as Kieran Keenan LLB is shining his cufflinks, telling them to say fuck all, especially if they get arrested. Dylan says to him, 'Are you mad? We know the drill. Just get all that shit off the Internet and get the fucking papers away from outside of me ma's.'

Keenan says that because they're 17 and Jay's only 14, they've got to be treated as minors and that naming them is a breach of their human rights. He says that he can deal with the legal side but that the papers are a different matter. He says that it's a nightmare because everyone will use Chalina for their own ends. The police to argue for armed bobbies, the council for some grant money, the Government for tougher laws. The agendas are the dangerous bit, he says.

Nogger explodes: 'It's only some little fucking girl been killed. And it's got fuck all to do with us.' Keenan says that it's got nothing to do with the girl and that it's all about power. But the lads know that he's got his own beef with the police. Keenan's under investigation for washing money for Dean. The police are threatening to get him struck off, but he's buying them off with tickets to the match because he also represents Rocky O'Rourke.

All the estate cranks – the bar-room briefs, the conspiracy loons, the letter writers – are coming out the woodwork, wanting to give the lads advice, to get onside with them, to suck-hole them and get in on the action. Gus Reed is a former burglar and pimp turned criminal reformer, makes out he's a reformed gangster trying to stop the kids from falling into a life of crime, a youth worker and anti-gun campaigner. But it's just his latest graft, to con grants out of the Government and the council. He just likes to get on the telly and the local radio, making out he's an expert. He comes round playing the big time with the lads, telling them that if they cough to the bizzies and make a statement, he can guarantee them immunity. Dylan's like that: 'What? You want us to go guilty even though we haven't been questioned? Are you mad?'

But Clegsy finds out that he's working for the bizzies anyway. That they've promised to sponsor his grant gravy train if he can get a confession out of the lads on the sly. Nogger finds out where Gus's ma lives the next day, lashes a nail bomb through the front window, blows her arm off below the elbow. She's 84.

Even Roberto Griffin's sucking up to them now. He comes and tells Nogger and Dylan that he'll act as their enforcer on the estate, lean on any witnesses, go round the older ones telling them to show the lads some support. When the older ones are pissed at night, some of them saying that they're behind the boys, Roberto stokes up their twisted patriotism towards the area. Nogger and Dylan can't work out why he's being their mate. Clegsy says that he's trying to get in with the younger ones cos he's getting on now, that he's an old gangster who's scared of the new generation coming up.

Then Roberto tells them about 'the Devil', a corrupt solicitor who's half lawyer, half underworld PR man. They call him the Devil cos he's more bent than the grafters he represents. Roberto says that the Devil'll find out all what shenanigans the police are getting up to behind the scenes and deal with the papers as well.

Roberto takes Dylan to see the Devil at his office. He tells Dylan that it doesn't matter what goes on in court these days. He says all that matters is what's said in the papers about you, that it's trial by media, end of story. He says the bizzies aren't arsed about solving big murders, just about making themselves look good and getting more power. If Dylan and the lads want to stay out of jail, they've got to improve their image. Dylan doesn't know what he's on about, but he's impressed so he gives him his last two grand graft money. The Devil says that he'll do the rest for free as long as he can sell stories about them out the back door.

A few days later, the Devil rings Dylan with all the inside info on the investigation. He says that for the time being the bizzies have control of the Murphy family. Press liaison officers have been assigned to babysit the grieving parents. The Devil says that the police are boasting that they're giving the family help and support. The Head of Marketing has said, 'We need to help them deal with the hundreds of media enquiries they have had. They are an ordinary family with no history of dealing with the press. We're going to relieve them of that pressure.' That's the justification for strictly controlling access to the story everyone wants, but the real motive is to keep Lynda and Keith Murphy 'on message', to make sure they don't criticise the police for failing to stop the gang violence that led to the death of their daughter.

At a press conference, one reporter asks the Chief Con, 'Your force has known about these gangs for a long time. The number of gang-related incidents has been increasing exponentially for years. There were 300 shootings in this postcode alone last year. Why didn't you stop it?' The reporter is quickly quashed, bought off with the promise of an exclusive interview and threatened with being banned from press conferences.

Lynda breaks down on camera in her first broadcast interview. It was heartbreaking, the Devil reckons. 'The bit where she completely lost it, collapsed on the floor screaming like a grieving Arab woman on the Gaza Strip, all that was cut out,' he says. A communications intelligence report that the Devil's got hold of states:

> Lynda Murphy is an excellent asset to the Force. As well as defending our position on the Chalina incident (CM34. 86. 7497 MP), Lynda may have a limited role in promoting some of our broader objectives.
>
> Part of her appeal to newspapers and TV appears to be her classlessness. A Sky News producer commented off-camera to a civilian member of our PR team that Lynda went down well because she is seen as a yummy mummy with a lot of 'middle classiness'. Newspaper reporters have commented to us, with the benefit of reader feedback, that her appearance in particular is pleasing.

A second interview is broadcast the following day on *GMTV*. Lynda tells the reporter: 'As a family, we were healthy eaters – oily fish, salads, pasta. But once a week we had our one treat – fish and chips from the local Chinese. Just a family tradition, going back to when I was a kid. Chalina loved it. She looked forward to it. It was meant to be an extra little treat because it was her birthday the next day. So she was excited, asking who was coming to the party. Taking all the kids out to Digger Land. When we got there, like usual, I let her stand outside with her brother. Chalina always wanted to be the big girl. But I always kept an eye on her.

'And then I turned round and she was on the floor. I didn't even know she had been shot – cos there was a telly on in the chippy and I was watching that. All's I could see was the other kids running away. Then I saw a little flash of red on the ground. That was her – that was her Liverpool top. I ran out and put my arms round her but she was already unconscious. Blood over her hair. Couldn't even see where it was coming from, there was that much. As I got up I slipped over on my back – I never knew blood, our Chalina's blood, was that slippy. It was like a tap which you couldn't turn off. Tried to stop it with my coat. She was still breathing but I could feel her going in and out, like kids do when they got a fever or something. And then she seemed to go. And that was the last I saw of our little Chalina.'

CHAPTER 21

SPIN

Lynda's interview blows the nation away. Despite the other stories they have, every paper and news bulletin runs the story, emotionalising, demanding justice. Several comment pieces call for National Service to be brought back. All in all, the Chief Con's plan to lobby for his force to be armed is falling into place. A few big set pieces are organised. The *Times* crime correspondent is invited to go out with an ARV to be shown that armed police are the only solution. The papers are filled with pro-gun stats. A police commissioner from the States is flown in to argue the case for arming the force.

By the second day after the interview airs, however, the debate's become even more inflamed. On Sky News, pundits call for the SAS to be put on standby to attack the HQs of teenage gangs. Suddenly, the issue of arming the police seems neither here nor there, such is the strength of public outrage at Chalina's death. The Chief Con is seen as out of step, asking for too little, too late.

The Devil tells the lads that the Chief Con's agenda is not the only one they need to worry about. A pundit on Sky News has been talking about how the army is equipped to deal with civil disorder. The retired lieutenant colonel, who commanded units in Kosovo and Iraq, told the presenter, 'The armed gangs, that now control vast tracts of Britain's cities, are no different from insurgents in Iraq or the warlords who terrorise decent, law-abiding people in places like Somalia or parts of the Middle East. Our indigenous gangs may not be political, but they're just as dangerous in military terms. Some people say it's unfair to ask the police to deal with these gangs – and they're right. Our bobbies are simply not equipped with the urban warfare tactics necessary.'

The presenter gasped. 'But this sounds like martial law. You might see it in a totalitarian regime, but surely not in Britain today?'

'If the police use these tactics, they're accused of being heavy-handed or the civil-rights brigade say we're living in a police state. If you back up the police's brave effort with support troops, it's a different matter. It's a case of winning hearts and minds, getting back the trust of these forgotten communities, taking away the fear, so that ordinary people can come out, take the streets back and rebuild their communities. It's just like reconstruction in Afghanistan. Look at the way the Brits dealt with hearts and minds in Iraq. We took our helmets off, put our berets on and reached out.'

The Devil phones Dylan and tells him that they've been turned over on ITV. Dylan and the lads flick through the channels to find it: 'ITV News has found disturbing evidence that the teenage gangs in Liverpool linked to the murder of Chalina Murphy have armed themselves with military weapons and terrorist-style bombs. One home-made video shows a cache of heavy machine guns and an SA80 army-issue assault rifle.'

There's loads of laughing and finger-clacking as the latest Nogzy video appears on the screen. It shows New Loon hooded up in the full complement of Lowies, holding up a British Army General Purpose Machine Gun, a golden belt of 200 rounds of ammo slung over his shoulder. There's also a Bren gun, with its distinctive curved box magazine, 30 rounds of 7.62-mm bullets, a conical flash hider and a spare quick-change barrel, all videoed on the pea-green carpet at Clegsy's ma's a few months ago. The ammo belt belongs to an American M60 machine gun – the gun used by Rambo, the reporter says.

An expert on the news identifies the weapons and talks about them. Then the presenter says, 'Police are also investigating claims that the gang have made their own bombs. This video, made by gang members, shows a stolen car being blown up by a roadside IED, similar to those used by insurgents in Iraq and Afghanistan.' They cut to a pair of gloved hands cupping a silver box with a small, wiry detonator sticking out of it – a home-made bomb.

The next day, media pressure is mounting. *The Sun*'s splash reads:

Soldiers on the Street – SOS Message to PM
Today, *The Sun* calls for British army troops to smash teen terror gangs. A petition signed by 30,000 people has been handed to the PM at No. 10. It's an SOS message from Our

Readers to get Our Boys to take back Our Streets.

The PM said: 'It's a tribute to Britain's greatest newspaper that so many people have come out to support the *Sun* campaign. I will certainly be looking into their demands.'

Squaddies joined *The Sun* to support Operation SOS.

Paratrooper Peter Naylor, 24, whose unit has just returned from Afghanistan, said: 'We can sort these lads out. We read the papers and we see what these gangs are doing to old people and women and kids back home. It's disgusting. Everyone's too scared to have a go – not us. That's the problem. They haven't come up against people who are harder than them. Let us at 'em.'

Richard O'Brien, 22, of the King's Regiment added: 'The British Army is mostly made up of lads from poor areas – estates in Newcastle, Manchester, Liverpool and Glasgow. So these lads are just like us, except we've chosen to serve our country instead of smash it up. Let us deal with it.'

On the back of the blanket media coverage, a 'March for Peace' protest comes together the following day. They carry banners saying 'Mothers Against Guns' and 'Stop the Violence'. They were in floods watching Chalina's ma's interview. Sombrely, they march past Lynda and Keith's new build in silence. 'To represent the wall of silence that surrounds gang culture and guns,' the organisers say. They asked Lynda to take part, to make a speech. But, through a spokesman, she fucked them off. She was 'already busy with other media commitments'. She was going to be on the couch on breakfast telly. But she phoned them from the back of the car (a Merc SL) on her way to the studios, her hair in curlers. She wished them luck, half getting down with them, putting on a slightly stronger accent.

The PM makes a speech in Parliament calling for Britain's streets to be taken back from armed gunmen. He reiterates his commitment to fighting the gangs 'force with force'. Commentators say it's significant that he doesn't refer to the police once in his speech, or pledge, as is usual, to increase the number of coppers on the beat. The Chief Con's very worried by this. There's speculation that troops will be deployed, but spin doctors play the idea down, and rumours begin that a new special force will be formed.

GANG WAR

Nogger reads the stories but can't work out what's going on. Dylan reads between the lines straight away. *They want the army to come and sort us on the streets. Mad or what?*

* * *

Over the next few weeks, Lynda Murphy's emotionally charged interview becomes a worldwide Internet hit. March for Peace gathers momentum, with similar events staged in Manchester, Nottingham, Leicester, Birmingham, Newcastle and Glasgow. Then a national million-man march is held in London. There's a massive outpouring of emotion. The Metropolitan Police Commissioner gladly makes a speech. The Merseyside Chief Con is furious. He's been branded a 'provincial meddler' on a major political blog.

The day after the London march, the PM announces in the House of Commons, 'This week, I will be announcing a series of measures aimed at smashing the gangs and their heinous influence for ever. I have asked the Home Secretary to form a new type of anti-gang force made up of the best professionals we have to offer, drawn from a wide range of our security and emergency services, and supported by social services and the judiciary. It will be called YCTF: Youth Crime Task Force. As part of this process, I will designate areas such as Croxteth and Norris Green "Gang Exclusion Zones".'

The PM leaves it vague at first, but it soon becomes clear that there will be 'an armed-forces contingent'. Officials play down the involvement of soldiers, insisting that the army will have 'an educational role', trying to help and support young men, possibly talking to them about signing up, rather like travelling emergency recruiting officers.

The general in charge tells the press: 'We want to solve this problem. We don't want any young man to be lost to a life of crime, and if we can, we will try to show them that a life in the military can be rewarding.'

'Fuck's sake, lad,' Nogger says to Dylan when he hears this. 'I'm not joining the army.'

'They're not trying to join us up. That's a fucking blag. They just want to put fucking squaddies on the street. They can do it, lad – anti-terror laws.'

Before long, Dylan, Nogger and Jay get arrested outside the chippy. They give a no-comment interview six hours long. The forensics come back negative and no witnesses come forward. The Devil's got them out of the police station the next day.

CHAPTER 22

CULT CELEBRITY

Dylan's out of his pit quick. 'What the fucking hell is that?' The noise is different from the usual bizzy helicopter – the 'wop, wop, wop' of the rotor blades is faster, the sound bassier, heavier. He pulls the curtains back to take a look.

It's a sand-coloured tandem-rotor army helicopter. 'A fucking Chinook!'

The press pack are camped outside of Dylan's waiting for him to come out. They've got their long lenses out, trying to get a picture of the army helicopters, which caught them by surprise, coming in from behind. They turn back to the house again when they see the curtains twitch. Dylan gets off in his full Lowies and a balaclava, says fuck all to the reporters, as usual. Just blanks them. Not like Nogger and Clegsy who batter them and get the lads to smash their cars up.

A tasty bird from the *Mail* rushes up to him. 'All right, Dylan? What do you think about the troops on the street? D'you think they're gonna get you?' Unusually, Dylan stops. He didn't know they'd sent troops in. The reporter, encouraged by his hesitation, carries on: 'The King's Regiment have got 100 soldiers in Norris Green and Croxteth, on patrol as of today. What do you think of that?' She's watching his face, trying to gauge his reaction. A reporter from *The Sun* chips in hopefully, 'Yeah, there's a few paras as well,' thinking he's in, desperate for a few quotes from Dylan.

The reporters need him so much now, they've actually begun to like him, even though he's never said fuck all to them. The Devil says that Dylan has the power now because he's a celebrity, that that's why all the journalists are matey and deferential with him.

Dylan marches on, the main body of reporters outside his house thanking him, grateful to him for fucking them off. A few doors down

GANG WAR

are the ghouls, a group of about twenty fans who've set up camp in the
neighbours' gardens: a few truants from around the city, a few wool
wannabe gangbangers from places like Hull, a couple of Asian lads from
Luton, autograph hunters who usually stand outside the hotels in town.
Some freaky arrivals over the past few days: a lad and a girl, backpackers
from Spain, anti-capitalist protester types, smoking pot and thinking it's
cool to be down on the poorest housing estate in Europe, plus three
young Japanese girls who thought Dylan was in a band. They turned up
in short skirts and kilts, brightly coloured leggings and ponytails with
cyber-fashion hairstyles. The oldest one was dressed Harajuku-style, with
lime-green hair, pink space boots and a black top saying 'Motor City
Girl'. She's told Dylan that millions of people in Japan think Nogzy
is a band as opposed to a gang. After snatched pics of Dylan, Nogger
and a few of the lads appeared in mags and on the telly, Japanese kids
started dressing in mountain gear – but with a twist, she says: in red
and fluorescent yellow.

Nogger's round the side of the house, getting a nosh off the youngest
bird, pure mall siren, wearing a grey schoolie skirt, white legwarmers, a
white shirt, a crimson cravat and a cream cardi. She's crouched down,
steadying herself between a couple of wheelie bins. 'Fucking boss, this,'
says Nogger when he sees Dylan coming round the corner. 'Nips birds, la
– they're fucking excellent. Do anything for ya, lad.' After he's finished, he
pushes the crouching girl over, toggles himself up and changes the subject.
'Seen those fucking army at the end of the road waiting for us?'

On the corner there's a checkpoint, a battered yellow Vaderis base
manned by the Metropolitan Police Territorial Support Group. A desert-
camouflaged Land Rover is parked across the road – three squaddies,
SA80s scoping on Dylan.

Dylan moseys through the barbed wire and concrete anti-tank blocks,
off for his breakfast. He notices the red dots from the police Heckler &
Kochs on him straight away. The three paras have their SA80s trained
on him as well, laser-free but sighted on him with one eye.

'Armed police. Stand still. On your knees. Do not approach the barrier.'
It's a force protection search, like they did looking for suicide bombers
in Afghanistan, the para says. Dylan goes through the motions, pulling
up his jacket to show that he doesn't have a bomb strapped to him. He
says fuck all, refuses to give his name, address or ID, won't take down
his trackies to be searched. Nogger's giving them loads, refusing to do

136

anything, saying that he'll phone his brief, that it's against his human rights. A private tells him, 'You have been stopped under the Terrorism Act 2000.'

'As if, you fucking prick.'

'Listen, you fucking scumbag, show some fucking respect when you're talking –'

Before he finishes, Nogger starts up: 'Behave, you fucking winnet. Thinking you're hard cos you've got 30 mates behind you all armed to the teeth.'

'I'll fucking knock you out if you don't shut up.'

'Go on, lad,' says Nogger, laughing.

An officer steps out of the Land Rover. 'Under the Prevention of Terrorism Act, the use of violence for political ends, including the use of violence for the purposes of putting the public or a section of it in fear, is prohibited and punishable by law. We are authorised to search you as a suspected terrorist. As you are known to the authorities for acts of political –'

'Political . . . Listen, lad, I joined the BNP cos you're not killing niggers fast enough overseas.'

The officer ignores Nogger and continues: 'Under the Act, attacks on people or property do not have to be political to be classed as terrorism. It covers any threat or use of violence to influence the public or lawful authorities.'

'Listen, lad, all bullshit, though, innit? I'm only 17, and youse can't touch me. Nick me, lad, and I'm suing you. I'll have your pension.'

'Sir, may I remind you that the UK has suspended Article 5 of the European Convention on Human Rights as a result of the War on Terror and the War on TerrorCrime. So you don't have any rights unless we choose to give them.'

*. *. *.

It's too hot in Nogzy with all the searches, so Nogger heads into town, goes down Sacchanalia with the lads. There's new-found respect for him after 'the accident'. Notoriety – a little bit of celebrity goes a long way in this country, says the Devil. The lads are falling over themselves to give him work, cocaine and heroin on credit – whatever he wants. Loads of lads, even birds, are coming up to him to shake hands and give him a hug.

'Sorry to hear about the accident, lad.'

'Know, yeah. Sorry meself about the kid, like. But it's just one of them, innit?'

'What happened?'

'Fucking accident, wannit? That fucking pizzahead ran across the car park. Let rip with me Mac-10.'

Mac-10 – he's dropping names like Perez Hilton now. All hands are like that: 'Nice one!' Glances of approval, little nods here and there. Then Nogger started doing the actions as well. Everyone's watching, but most can't hear for the music. Loads of WAGs in the VIP booths are looking down, though, picking up the story from his body language. Nogger is pulling up an imaginary Mac-10 to hip height, firing position, his right hand cupped under the trigger. He's gripping the magazine clip, aiming, balancing with the left hand, holding the kick down.

'Pizzahead runs into the chippy.' He mimes a running motion, jogging on, like the Six Million Dollar Man. He keeps running on the spot for fucking ages, upping the suspense. Even the doormen have come in now off the pavement to see and hear it. *Can tell a fucking story, Nogger. That is a fact. Can't hardly read or fucking write, like. But the little cunt can tell a story.* He's reaching the climax. The accident. Little Chalina. He puts his arm right out and down, to show that she's knee high, that there's bin lids on the scene.

The WAGs are turning to each other now, mouthing 'Ahhhh!' to each other in pity. But Nogger jolts them back into excitement by letting rip with the imaginary Mac-10 again. He's Tony Montana now. 'Say hello to my leetle friend.' He makes a machine-gun noise like a kid in the playground, muted in the din of the club. 'Chuch-chuch-chuch-chuch-chuch.' The quick repeat pout conveying the rapid-fire discharge.

He ends on a massive finale, shouts out 'Fuck Off!' at the moment Chalina is hit. Gasps all round. The kid goes down. He motions Chalina hitting the deck, hands up, palms out, falling backwards onto the bar. 'She went down like a bag of spuds, lad. Straight away.'

They're all looking at each other, grids open, eyes on sticks, in disbelief. *Got to hand it to him, like. Could retell* War and Peace *in nightclub mime, that lad.*

All the birds are crying now, in bits. Thinking about their own kids. But they're at home with their nans while the mas are out partying, on the beak, getting bummed in the bogs by gangsters. Fake sympathy for a dead kid.

Nogger is off again, taking his audience through the getaway. He's running on the spot again, his arms doing big wide semi-circles this time, half-windmills, Pete Townshend-style to signify that he's bailing from the scene of the crime, physically and morally.

The payoff. To all and sundry. Nogger asks, 'D'you see worramean, though?' He's beseeching, preaching, palms out, looking up, eyes panning across the club. 'Was a fucking accident, wannit?'

The whole place erupts, like when a boss tune comes on, in agreement. *It was a fucking accident.* Fact. No back answers. Nogger, Dylan, Jay – all fucking innocent. Pure fucking scapegoats. They've been fitted up. Not only by the bizzies, but by the fucking army, the whole country. *By those cunts who are now oppressing us, occupying us, fighting us.* Unanimous verdict: Nogger and the lads are to be honoured, feted – never mind being fucked off.

Spontaneous dancing erupts. Girls in tight black kecks with falling curls are giving it loads on the floor – flailing, shaking, splits, splaying it, giving it up.

Nogger is instantly accepted by the mid-tier drug dealers, who can help him out. The graft's on for him from now on. Loads of birds are on him now. Polly and her twin, glamour models, contracted exclusively to *Loaded* till April, are after him. But he fucks them off. For Pauline MacInerney, recently fucked off herself by Rocky O'Rourke.

The next day, in a derelict house on The Boot, Mayonnaise asks, 'Seen the papers?' Everyone's expecting the worst. But it's fucking mad. Paparazzi pictures of *Nogger* coming out of Sacchanalia with Pauline.

The headline in the *Mirror*'s 3AM column is 'Pauline's Mystery Man'. *The Star*, under the headline 'Pauly Versus Polly Over New Man', reports: 'Super WAG Pauline MacInerney nabbed a new feller last night – after stealing him from a topless model.' The article referred to Nogger as a 'young businessman'.

The papers are suck-holing him already. None of the red tops mention the accident. The other papers, the broadsheets and the *Daily Mail*, aren't so good: 'WAG Pauline Mac Linked to Chalina Suspect'.

The Devil phones Nogger up: 'I did a deal with the tabloids. Said I'd give them more stuff if they didn't mention the . . . erm . . . incident.'

'Don't be talking to those cunts. They're fucking grasses.'

'Listen, you'll have to stop thinking like that. Like a scally.'

'Shut up, you fucking prick. Talking like that. Chatting shit like that.'

'You're not a no-mark now. You're a celeb. So you've got to work with the papers. You could go down for Chalina. But if you've got the papers on your side . . .'

'Not fucking arsed about that. It was a fucking accident. And it wasn't me anyway, you silly cunt. Anyway is there any wages in it, off the papers?'

'Might be able to get you a few quid by selling a few stories.'

'Well, fucking sort it then, you prick.'

Call buttoned.

Within a few days, the backlash against the police and army begins. No one can fucking believe it. The lads are laughing. The residents get together a campaign group against martial law and the overwhelming powers of the anti-terror laws. They arrange a press conference and a march on the edge of the Gang Exclusion Zone.

At the march, a woman walks up to the lads. 'I'm a human-rights lawyer. Here's my card. If you need any help, get in touch.'

Dylan has his hood up, his hands in his pockets, staring at the ground, half thinking it might be an idea to line themselves up with these.

'Martial law doesn't fucking make any difference,' says New Loon. 'Always been fucking martial law round here, girl. Bizzies have been fucking battering us for years. Booted to fuck in the back of vans and that. So it's just the same. Same pricks, different uniforms.'

The woman tells him, 'If you don't stand up, you're going to lose some fundamental rights, freedoms. You're going to be made scapegoats by the police because you're young and poor and voiceless. They're going to stitch you up.'

'Fuck off, will you, you lesbian?' says Nogger. 'We're famous now, girl. Don't need to worry. Fucking celebs, us.'

Dylan's mind is elsewhere. *I wonder where Elizabeth is. Wonder if she's seen us on the telly and that, knows how well we're doing.*

The Devil calls Nogger that night: 'You're a cause célèbre now. All kinds of do-gooders are trying to defend your civil rights.'

'You fucking shitbag. I'll split your fucking wig if you're making dough out of us and not coming across.'

'Let me tell you, there's a few posh mags that want to do fashion shoots with the gang. Urban chic, that kind of thing.'

'Fuck off, you fucking grass.'

'They'll pay good money . . .'

The public are starting to see Lynda Murphy as a hate figure. The Devil's stoking it all up behind the scenes.

'They think she's a gold-digger,' Dylan says, 'trying to make some dough out of it.'

'The fucking slag is,' Nogger tells him. 'She's on all kinds of programmes. She's fucking writing a book. And a fucking film.'

A few days later Lynda appears on *GMTV* to make a fresh appeal for witnesses. But it's a stitch-up. On the couch, she's purely mauled (tactfully) by a hard-faced anchor.

Roberto comes up to the lads on the street, taking the glory for giving them an intro to the Devil. 'Let's face it,' he says, 'you can't be crying for your daughter on one hand and all over the telly the next. Just can't have it both ways, can you? Our stock is rising. Theirs is in freefall like a fucking bank's, lad.'

CHAPTER 23

ASSAULT

Troops build up slowly in the Gang Exclusion Zone. It's Operation Urban Freedom. The mission statement has it as a cross between Northern Ireland and UNPROFOR peace-keeping in the Balkans.

Objective 1 is to secure Lower Lane Police Station. The road in front is blocked off with checkpoints, right down to Altcourse prison, where a 'plywood city' army base is springing up, officially dubbed Camp Photon. Soldiers could have stayed in existing barracks all around the city but the officers say the 'built-from-scratch' camp is good for the papers. Makes it feel like a can-do mission, a spokesman says.

The police station is given the same security status as a British embassy or airport. The perimeter is lined with giant blast-proof concrete caissons. The second, inner cordon is reinforced using a specialist design called 'enhanced building stand-off protection'. A waist-high bi-steel wall system that blends in with the streetscape is installed. An advert on the front says 'Corus Critical Infrastructure – Deterring Attacks from VBIEDs [vehicle-borne improvised explosive devices]'. Glass is replaced with smart windows. They're bulletproof and won't shatter in a blast. They expand in the heat and absorb the energy.

Lower Lane (Operational Command) and Camp Photon form a Green Zone, a secure area not accessible to the public. Civilian workers are bussed in every day.

The Chief Con complains bitterly about encroachment on his powers, on his turf. As a concession, his armed officers are allowed to patrol the Green Zone with Hecklers, like at an airport. It's much trumpeted in the local papers, as if he's running the show, but real power lies with the military commander, the general.

142

ASSAULT

There are regular patrols through bandit country now, soldiers pepper-potting along the street, Northern Ireland-style. One moves forward and takes up position on his knees, scoping the street through his sight (magnified by four), sweeping, covering, while the soldier behind moves up and goes forward.

A patrol's out on The Boot in heavy rain, ponchos out, taking shelter under burned-out roofs and in tinned-in doorways, amongst the rubble and the reeds sprouting through the concrete. In a broken glass porch, two soldiers get out their hexi blocks and brew up. Another squeezes his arse onto a blue-and-red trike he's found in a pile of paper and rocks, the plastic bleached by the sun. He's a Royal Marine sniper, fresh from Helmand, still wearing desert camouflage, sacking and vegetation wrapped around his L115A3 long-range rifle. One round, one kill at ranges of more than a mile. After a while, he takes position in an upstairs bedroom, sweeps the horizon, sighting up on mums walking their prams, grannies out shopping. Fuck all going on.

* * *

Army choppers have been in the zone for a while, but one night they're all flown to Manchester, repainted and rebranded with operational insignia. 'Youth Crime Task Force.' The logo is a silhouette of a soldier shaking hands with a small child. The helicopters are stripped of desert engineering, ready to be unveiled as the new strike force in the PM's War on TerrorCrime. It's all done for the papers, says the Devil, all for show.

The day they're brought back in, all the TV crews are lined up at one end of the prison footie field. For CNN, there's an Indian man in a Sandy Gall-style jungle suit. Some of the foreign crews are sporting flak jackets for show. For extra drama, the BBC correspondent wears a navy-blue combat vest and a Kevlar helmet. He's been driving around in the same white armoured Land Rover they used in Sarajevo, attracting potshots from the lads.

At the other end of the field, Dylan and the lads are hanging off the wire fence, waiting for the spectacle, choking on the dust. It's a sunny day, the first in six months.

At one o'clock, they come in: eight British Army helicopters and two Chinooks in battle formation.

'Wow. For fuck's sake. Fucking excellent,' says Nogger, the life-giving force of the noise and vibration energising him as they fly over. He can feel the heat of the exhausts breathing fumes and dust in his face. At a distance, the rotor sound is bass, deep and slow. Overhead, it's sharper and faster.

Despite being the enemy, Nogger, New Loon and Lupus become patriotic. 'Best army in the world, innit?' says Lupus, brainwashed by a thousand war films watched after a pint on a Sunday afternoon with his auld feller, who did National Service in Germany.

'Fucking right,' says New Loon. 'Those SAS, lad? Can live out on a mountain with just a boiler suit and a live rabbit for weeks – shitting in their kecks and all that.'

'Don't believe the hype, lad,' Dylan tells him. 'These army types are no tougher than you. You'd be mad if you had 30 mates behind you armed to the teeth 24/7. In fact, they're mushes, most of them – because they're told to fight. They let other men tell them what to do.'

Nogger agrees: 'Can you believe that shit? Grown-up fellers doing press-ups cos some posh cunt tells them to.'

The choppers manoeuvre into a straight line and hover ten feet above the ground for a few minutes for the cameras. Noise and power, shock and awe. It blows everyone away. The reporters are charged up, feeling they're covering a good story. It looks like the authorities are actually doing something.

Dylan's less impressed: 'It's just a bunch of helicopters landing in a field.'

The choppers land and cut engines. Behind them, there's a faster, tinnier rotor sound, coming from a small, white commercial helicopter. It looks spindly and toy-like compared with the military might of the army choppers. It's the bizzy helicopter, with its powerful searchlight on to give it more impact. 'It's fucking shit,' says Lupus. It's long been christened 'the Star of Croxteth' because it spends all night hovering above the favelas there. It lands and the Chief Con jumps out, *Top Gun* helmet with a dark, mirrored visor on, flight suit. Everyone laughs, including the press corps.

That night, there's a death in custody. One of the younger lads was choked out while being detained at Camp Photon. When it gets out, two Warrior armoured personnel carriers are fired up with petrol bombs in revenge. One's completely burnt out, but there are no casualties. A soft-skinned Land Rover snatch vehicle is pelted with rocks and two rounds from a 9-mm pistol are fired into the passenger door.

ASSAULT

The day after the attacks, Bloot is shot dead as he tries to run a roadblock. He ploughs a stoley through a manned checkpoint and is stopped 80 yards down the road by a US Army-issue X-Net – a spiked web that wraps around the car's wheels and axles, used in Iraq to catch suicide bombers. A para fires 23 rounds from a light support weapon into Bloot while he's trapped at the wheel. The soldier says he did it because Bloot hadn't slowed down and had a gun. But witnesses say Bloot was smoked well after the car had been brought to a standstill.

After that, the lads plan to get revenge. But Dylan fucks them off: 'Let it go. This isn't about youse. Youse are just flies to them. They'll brush you off. Crush you. Get home. Get off the street. That's what I'm doing.' A few of the younger ones slag Dylan for crumbling on the job.

They go ahead and launch an attack without him. But the petrol bombs and the IEDs bounce off the Warriors, even off the snatch vehicles. A 14-year-old boy is martyred after a riot breaks out. Some say he was killed by a rubber bullet, others that he was run over and crushed by an army vehicle.

The next day at sun-up there's an assault on The Boot. Two Lynx AH.7 helicopters with door-mounted GPMGs. One lands on a disused green next to an old building site. A few paras jump out clumsily. Soldiers secure the LZ. The second hovers above a disused house 150 metres away. Smoke grenades. Several flashbangs. Black-clad SAS troops fast-rope onto the roof and into the garden. Two or three shots inside. Later, Sky News describes this as a successful raid on a well-known gang HQ.

Two hours after the troops go in, four tank transporters arrive, with two Caterpillar D9 and D7 armoured bulldozers kitted up with Israeli Defence Force tractor protection. There's a steel plate over the cab with just a slit for the driver to see through. One's surrounded by an anti-riot cage. A giant dark-green Terex 82-30B bulldozer with tracks as high as a man is also brought in.

They start demolishing the derelict housing, collapsing exterior walls like paper. Inside, the half-exposed rooms are a mosaic of wallpapers and tiles – blues, greens, white, from the '60s, '70s and '80s – a glimpse of the lives once lived there.

The lads squirrel through the gardens and burnt-out houses, digging up their stashes of guns and drugs, hoping to save them before they're covered over with rubble and lost for ever.

GANG WAR

On the fringes of the action, an officer from the Royal Engineers is giving an interview to BBC World. 'This phase is designated Operation Urban Renewal. The Boot estate was a warren of half-demolished houses and decaying streets. In effect, it was a citadel for the gangs to operate in, a ready-made environment that enabled crime and anti-social behaviour to flourish. Liverpool City Council have let it rot for years, despite pledging to demolish it. That delay in decamping this estate has played a role in the rise of gang culture. My soldiers will finish the job in a day so that we can hand this land back to the community in order that it can be put to good use.'

As he speaks, demolition teams are moving systematically from one building to the next. Charges are thrown inside. 'Fire in the hole!' Another house gone. Fires erupt, fuelled by wood, plastic and plaster. Mountains of fly-tipped tyres and rubbish send flames 40 ft into the air. Soldiers move slowly across the landscape, silhouetted against the orange light, bored amid the towers of black smoke, just like after the Gulf War.

On the residential streets bordering the demolition area, communications officers paste propaganda posters onto lamp posts and fences, pictures of smiling British Army soldiers wearing berets, with long radio wires sticking out of their backpacks, chatting with kids and mums: 'The Army – Working With You to Build a Safer Community'. Some Air Assault Brigade paras go round handing out sweets to the gangs of smaller kids.

The Boot is now levelled: piles of broken rubble, smouldering ruins. On telly, the commander-in-chief of Operation Urban Freedom says that his 'number-one priority' is to win the hearts and minds of Broken Britain. No point in building a hospital or a school, he says. There's plenty of them. So they're going to build an adventure playground, he says. The place is going to be completely fucking tarmacked over and sponged-up with dark-green Polymax rubber. A politician chimes in, saying that in the long-term the plan is to build a sports centre so that the teenagers can box and play football instead of joining gangs.

'Fuck's sake, lad,' says Jay, changing the channel. 'Not another fucking sports centre.'

'Know, yeah,' replies Clone. 'Can't believe it, can you?'

'Fucking hated games at school,' Jay carries on. 'Why would you wanna go afterwards and play footie? Don't these pricks understand that?'

'They can't get their nuts round it, can they?' Dylan says. 'Kids round here hate fucking sport. Kids round here are too tired, too shattered from all the mayhem.'

'So you're gonna teach them to box? Even worse,' Jay argues. 'Turn them into world-class athletes. World-class fucking gangsters.'

'Boxing, lad,' scoffs Clone. 'Don't need to box. Why d'you need to have a fight if you've got a gun, lad?'

Dylan starts thinking aloud: 'All's the kids need is a bus shelter with a heater in, innit? Somewhere warm and safe where they can meet their mates. I could draw one now for the pricks, it's not fucking hard.'

'What d'you mean, lad?' asks Jay.

Dylan swallows hard, embarrassed: 'Think about it, lad. Half the reason the kids are off their heads round here is the fucking weather. Pure fucking whalers' weather in off the Atlantic. Six or nine months of the year, you're stood outside in the rain with your fucking hood up in your own little world, sealed off from everything. Can't be arsed talking to anyone never mind making new mates. Everyone stops and talks to each other in hot countries. I've seen it on telly, lad. Give them somewhere warm and dry to chat shit with their mates, and you're laughing.'

Dylan would never have said all that in front of the older ones. But with Jay he couldn't really give a fuck. 'A bus shelter with a fucking radiator in it. Freedom to be safe and meet their mates. That's all kids round here need. But the problem is there's no graft in it. If you build a sports centre, some cunt is making pure punt out it. Someone somewhere's getting a new carpet out it, so they're not gonna settle for making a Perspex hut for four hundred pound, are they?'

* * *

Once the new surface is down, red, white and blue bunting goes up on The Boot playground. At nine in the morning a few fat mums are standing shivering on the rubber matting in pyjamas or old pink sweatpants, a few Liverpool tops. It's a fitness class for the cameras, based on the British Army Fitness Programme, like they do for the homeless in London. *GMTV* are there with their own Green Goddess type. Lorraine Kelly comes out of her Winnebago, says that the army and the locals are working to build an atmosphere of community, rekindling the spirit of the Blitz.

Most of the mums haven't been up before one in the afternoon for years. Dylan looks at the flailing mas out the window, then goes back to bed.

Lupus is sat on a red-brick wall, shaking his head. 'The campesinos – mad, aren't they?'

'Know, yeah,' says Pacer. 'They'll front anything, won't they?'

They see Nogger, a few doors down, run out from his pit in his boxies and a T-shirt. He's spotted his mentally ill ma dancing to 'The Best' by Tina Turner. Nogger runs up to his ma and sister. 'Get in, you fucking pricks. What the fuck do you think you're doing out here in the street dancing with bizzies and those fucking baby killers?' he asks, pointing at the squaddies. 'On the fucking telly, as well. Are you fucking soft or something?' He grabs his ma by her unkempt hair and drags her in. A few of the paras pretend to get aggrieved. Nogger smiles. 'As if, prick. I'll ram that fucking SA80 up your arse.' He laughs at them, fucks them off, knowing they can do fuck all under the rules of engagement.

Nogger's sister tells him, 'I'd watch it if I was you. Those paras take no shit.'

'What? You fucking shagging one of them, are you? I bet you're getting hoofed by half the fucking regiment. Don't you fucking worry about me. I'm a fucking suspect in the Chalina fucking carry-on. If I slipped over on a bar of soap in the bath, they'd be in trouble. D'you get me? I know me rights, girl. They can do fuck all to me.'

Before long, they get an early-morning call off an army disruption team. They swoop on Dylan's at 4 a.m., come through the front door. Bang! SAS-types come through the back gate and the upstairs windows, pure Iranian embassy-style, stun grenades going off in the front room.

They're not like the bizzies – rougher, dirtier, louder. The skirting boards are broken and battered just by them running up the stairs. Wardrobes and cupboards are turned over and tipped up. They're shouting all the time to keep Dylan and his ma and the kids freaked out. Dylan knows the score, though. It's just one of their tactics, so that they can take control of the environment. The SAS live in a world of shouting, so it's just normal to them. Everyone's told to get down or thrown down until they've identified Dylan.

A pointy black sack's put over his head and he's handcuffed to a stretcher and Black Hawked to Camp Photon, where he's put in an orange boiler suit and interrogated. Nogger's there too. They're together in a Portakabin, chained to the floor. There are two officers and a tubby man dressed in civilian clothes sitting behind a trestle table, and about seven ordinary squaddies standing up or sat off behind them.

'You fucking scum,' says one of the squaddies.

Another says to Dylan, 'Sister's fucking tasty, isn't she? Bet she's a good ride.' Dylan and Nogger take the interrogation all day. They've been in and out of bizzy stations since they were 12. Dylan neutralises his body language, giving nothing away. Back straight, hands on knees, palms up. After the hood comes off, he focuses his eyes on a single point on the wall. Nogger slouches and picks his nails, staring the hardest-looking squaddie out.

Neither of them replies to any of the questions. Now and again, Dylan asks, 'Can I ring me solicitor?'

A posh officer tells him, 'You have been detained under anti-terrorism legislation. You are being questioned under British Army regulations. You have no right to legal representation.'

'Is that martial law?'

'Yes. Under the new Emergency Powers and Civil Disorder Act, normal law has been suspended and has no jurisdiction here.'

They start asking about Chalina, and the posh officer says, 'You must feel ashamed when you see her mum. Don't you feel bad that you killed that poor woman's daughter?'

'Don't know who killed her, lad,' replies Nogger, 'but the ma's getting good graft out of it now, isn't she? On *GMTV* and all that. Making a few quid, isn't she? Be on *Big Brother* next.'

'You fucking baby killers,' shouts one of the squaddies. 'You fucking pair of nonces. I'd fucking strangle you right now.'

'Fucking kiddie killers,' chimes in another.

Dylan laughs. 'D'you mean youse in Iraq? Killing all those women and children?'

'Didn't kill no civilians, you cheeky little cunt.'

'Fuck off. All those hundreds of thousands of innocent people youse wasted?' He laughs. 'Fucking rock hard, youse, blowing up all those families in their houses. Those little Paki kids with shrapnel all over their faces cos youse dropped a bomb on a fucking wedding. And now youse've got the fucking cheek to blame us for killing a kid? Full of shit, you, lad.'

The squaddie's seething now. 'You fucking shithead pikey. We're fighting over there so fucking shit like you can be safe here.'

Dylan smiles at him. 'You're fighting over there cos some posh cunt like him' – pointing at the officer – 'has ordered you to. For fucking oil or whatever. They've killed millions of youse over the years in the fucking wars. And you're still falling for it, you silly cunt.'

He goes to punch Dylan now, in the stomach. Dylan's handcuffed, but he roundhouses him in the upper chest as he stoops to hit him, telling him, 'Go way, you fucking prick.'

'Youse think you're fucking hard,' says the squaddie. 'Shit'd be pouring out of your fucking arse if the Taliban copped for you in the field.'

Dylan's buzzing: 'Generations of my family have been sent to war by you pricks. Brought nothing but fucking grief to us. Everyone knows how much arse we've got lad. We're just not grafting it for rich people no more.' Dylan's laughing again, almost relaxed. 'Anyway, what are you doing, fighting for your king and country? Just oppressing ordinary people.'

After two hours, they give up on Chalina. They know they'll get fuck all, despite the constant baiting by the young squaddies. The interrogation turns to gangs in general. Dylan knows this is what they're really interested in. They couldn't give a fuck about Chalina. Finally, they're released.

CHAPTER 24

CIVILIAN PROTECTION AUTHORITY

Everyone's wanting to be Nogger's mate now. A bit of celebrity goes a long way. In the past month, he's been getting some good graft off the older lads. Gets two grand to collect a drug debt from a gangster in Hull. Nogger shoots the feller's bird in the arm and breaks his daughter's nose. He hands over £32,000.

Afterwards he tells the lads about it. 'The cunt owed us 40 grand. But I let him off with the eight. Daughter was fucking fit, though, la. Only 12, but she's a proper little tease. She's got fucking big tits and a big fat arse, and she's sitting there on the couch in skin-tight yellow leggings, legs open. You're not saying that's not legal, lad. That's fair game, innit? As far as I'm concerned. Was half thinking of bending her over in front of the fucking ma and da.

'But fucking scruffs they were, mate, the ma and da. Dirty scags, proper fucking smelly cunts. Fucking spots all over their faces and yellow teeth. Looking too much like the test on the blood, know where I'm going? So I thought, fuck that. Not going near the little bint, am I? Even though she's sitting there giving it loads. So I just banged her out instead. Bang!' Nogger does a little slo-mo jab to illustrate. 'Blood all over her. Running off her leggings. Was fucking funny, though, telling you.'

'And you only got two grand out of that?' asks Dylan. 'They're using you, la. Treating you like a gimp, if you ask me.'

'Fuck off, Dylan. It's business. Do a few little things for the older lads and if that goes OK, you get some more work. Better than taxing little nuggets round here for 700 notes.'

'Sounds like you're being mugged off, mate. Just telling you.'

'D'you know what I did before I got off?' Nogger pauses, looks around the room, hyping the effect. 'Just pulled my hood back, didn't I? Let the feller know who did this.'

Everyone's buzzing off Nogger's outrageous cheek, letting the victims know who taxed them. His new trademark, now he's become immune after the Chalina thing.

On Friday morning, graft day, Nogger's at the wheel of his hired Transit van. Pauline Mac's in the front seat, proud to be sitting next to her feller. Nogger tries to run over a couple of paps as he gets off. They're trying to get pics of Pauline putting on her make-up in the rear-view mirror. She's in *Hollyoaks* now, and she's going for an audition for the lead in some big West End musical next week.

He drives down to Nottingham to a pharmaceutical wholesaler. The place is an old Victorian factory with a loading bay at the back. Nogger shakes hands with the young Asian son of the owner. Nogger, the new businessman. The warehouse lads load up two pallets of benzocaine drums, each one weighing 25 kilos and costing £3,000 – all legal.

They're back up to Liverpool for half two in the afternoon. 'Just be in time for the Friday night rush, there, girl,' says Nogger, rubbing his hands together.

He's renting a new build in Halewood these days, well outside the Gang Exclusion Zone. When they're home, Nogger gets in the back of the van, slices through the industrial polythene wrap around the blue-plastic drums and carries one shadily into the flat, wrapped in a couple of bin-bags.

That Friday, Dylan's up early for a game of footie in the park with the lads. He goes through the washing routine he's adopted. He pours two inches of petrol into the sink from an old bleach bottle he keeps next to the bog, rinses his hands and arms with it, then cleans off the smell with loads of Fairy Liquid, slaps on some Nivea to finish, to make sure his skin doesn't crack. He takes a jacket and trackies off the line. He's washing them every night now, hand-picking the gauze in the pockets to make sure there's no old bits of gear or gun residue in there.

All the lads are getting out of their houses early doors now. The police have bugged all their places up to death. Dylan's even heard the Special Branch are firing microwaves at his windows to measure the vibrations so they can recreate the conversations inside. One of the lads said that was how they beat the IRA and the miners' strike. 'Old technology, like, but it works, d'you know worramean?'

Dylan looked at him as though he was fucking soft. He was like that: 'What the fuck are you on about? The fucking miners' strike . . .' But he told his ma to say fuck all in the house and started staying outside anyway.

He waits in the queue for the checkpoint to get out of Nogzy. Paras and Royal Irish Fusiliers are checking papers, searching bags and doing the rub-downs. Pure Belfast 1981. As well as the pedestrians, cars and buses are backed up all through the rubble of The Boot, paras poking around in the boots of cars.

Dylan and Jay stay in the bookie's all day to keep out the house and off the streets. At the counter, a Royal Irish Fusilier smiles at Jay, who blanks him and puts a fiver on trap two in the 10.50 at Brighton and Hove, just so the girl behind the counter won't boot them out. Dylan's looking up at Sky on the flat-screen TV when the news starts and pictures of the Exclusion Zone come up.

'The British Army handed over power to a newly formed Civilian Protection Authority today. The government body will run the affairs of the occupation zones that were taken over by the army as part of the War on TerrorCrime.

'Troops were ordered onto the streets in the gang-ridden Croxteth and Norris Green areas of the city to restore order following the death of three-year-old Chalina Murphy. Chalina was gunned down during a shoot-out between two of the city's most notorious street gangs. No one has yet been arrested in connection with the murder.

'Officials at the CPA said it will govern the areas until they are safe enough to be handed back to the local council and Merseyside Police. The Prime Minister stressed that the CPA would not be a military organisation. He said it would be staffed by civil servants as opposed to army officers and was an important step towards winning the war on TerrorCrime. Former Joint Intelligence Committee member Robin Farquharson has been appointed to head up the body.

'MOD sources said that the army would remain on the streets indefinitely but that they would be pulled back from forward operating bases to "enduring bases", long-term security facilities outside the gang zones. A spokesman for the CPA confirmed that front-line roles will be taken over by private military contractors.'

Some off-duty Royal Irish Fusiliers come in: skinheads, tight T-shirts, stonewashed jeans. Their aftershave mixes with the smell of the bookie's

– mice and stale cigarette smoke from the years before smoking was banned. Dylan fucks them off and studies the form for the 3.15 at Haydock, a little betting-shop biro between his teeth.

The army lads let on to Pacer and New Loon. 'What the fuck are youse doing in here?' asks New Loon.

'Free country, innit?' says one of the soldiers, laughing. 'Some of us are pulling out today. Or at least pulling back into bases outside the zone.'

New Loon and Pacer high-five. 'Go 'ead. Seen youse off, didn't we?'

Dylan chews his pen and smiles.

'Wouldn't be hanging out the flags just yet,' says the soldier.

'What d'you mean?' asks New Loon.

The soldier winks, collects his winnings and gets off.

That afternoon, Nogger bells Mayonnaise, tells him in crude code to organise a big delivery to his place in Halewood. Mayonnaise organises the transport and the amount – five kilos of real gear, Nogger's own stuff from the Nogzy stash, which was on The Boot but has been moved to a farm on the outskirts of the city. Mayonnaise tells Nogger that it's getting harder and harder to smuggle the gear through the roadblocks now because of the electronic drug sniffers and chemical swab tests they're using.

Mayonnaise heads down to the roadblock on his Segway to scope it out, on a dry run, just to see what's going on. But there's a queue of cars a mile long at Croxteth Hall roundabout. He bangs on some workie's van window.

'What's going on?'

'Need a travel permit now, lad, to get in and out of The Jez,' says the workie, using the new slang word for Crocky and Norris Green, from GEZ for Gang Exclusion Zone.

'Fuck's sake,' mutters Mayonnaise, thinking on how he's gonna get Nogger's gear out on time. He whizzes through the traffic jam to the front of the queue. They've replaced the makeshift army checkpoint with a brand-new complex.

Mayonnaise goes back to the stash. Instead of crashing the checkpoint in one go with a big parcel, he decides to split the gear up instead, gives five of the younger lads a kilo each in a small Eastpak knapsack, so they can bring it to Nogger's new build via the back roads, the cycle paths and the nature trails on the old railway.

They get the stuff there early evening, just in time. Nogger gazes on it proudly, slashes open the brown packing tape. Freshly imported cocaine. Nogger and Mayonnaise are enthralled by its beauty. Their eyes follow the grey veins across its marbled surface. It looks like rough granite. Layer upon layer of compressed flakes arranged in interlocking panels, reflecting light in a spectrum of colours.

'Ah! Smell that. Fucking lovely,' says Mayonnaise.

'Unmissable,' Nogger says, putting the block into a thick, see-through polythene bag. He lays it on his beechwood kitchen worktop and starts smashing it with a hammer, breaking up the brittle slab into muesli-sized flakes.

He weighs out 250 grams on the brushed-steel surface of his electronic scales. He pops the paper seal of the milk-churn-shaped beno drum with his kukri, scoops up two cupfuls, cuts a cupful of coke off and puts the 2:1 beno/coke mixture in his Jamie Oliver blender, which still has a picture of Jamie's head stuck on the side.

'Go 'ead, Jamie lad,' says Mayonnaise as he gives it a spin. 'Happy days.' After it's been bashed up, Nogger puts the diluted coke through a hydraulic compressor so that it looks like pure crystalline gear again. When he runs out of capacity, he takes the back wheel off a car, then lowers the axle down onto the bags to compact them. He's all ready for graft night.

CHAPTER 25

CUSTODY

Dylan, New Loon and Pacer head across The Boot. Nogger's promised them a parcel of cocaine so they can make some money over the weekend. It's dry and hot. Weeds are growing tall over the rubble and shitty standpipes, cracked by the tractors during the demolition and clearance, are drying up now.

'Try and keep away from the T-scans,' Dylan tells the others. 'Keep behind the walls as much as you can.' The T-scan 2003 A and the ThruVision use tetrahertz waves to see through people's clothes even as they're walking down the street, exposing concealed metals, ceramics, plastics, liquids and organic matter such as heroin or skunk. But most of the walls have been knocked down or are paper-thin partition walls and are easily penetrable by their millimetre-wavelength beams. The oversized CCTV cameras are perched on telescopic lamp posts on banks of surveillance equipment, next to the usual sonar sound probes and infrared sensors.

Two Chinooks are flying overhead. Dylan watches their perfect shadows undulate over the bumpy ground, conquering every inch at lightning speed. Dylan has to move his eyes quickly to track the dark blobs, until briefly he is caught in the shadow for a fraction of a second. As the noise of the rotors dies off, Dylan hears the shrieking revving of an armoured personnel carrier behind him, moving down a demolished street. The Chinooks must have radioed the lads' position in on the off chance.

New Loon spots the diesel exhaust. 'It's a Warrior. FV 510.' He catches the little flag on the end of the aeriel. 'Royal Irish Fusiliers – cunts, them.'

The three of them bolt off, trying to find a hole to hide in. But a smaller APC comes round the opposite corner, quickly, to head them off.

It's a nimbler fighting vehicle – a 430 Mk3 Bulldog in desert colours. It does some fancy turns on the length of its own track to come side-on, blocking their way.

An officer comes through the hatch and speaks through a loudhailer from behind the panel of bulletproof glass attached to the mounted machine gun. 'Stop where you are. Put your hands above your heads.' He plays the standard psy-ops 'read you your rights' tape recording. It starts with three bleeps and then comes the message: 'This is a public information film. You have been stopped by the Youth Crime Task Force. You are suspected of TerrorCrime activities, and under the anti-terror laws now in force in the Gang Exclusion Zone if you refuse to cooperate, we have the right to detain you in contravention of those laws.'

Pacer: 'Fuck's sake. We're going to get a stop-and-strip now.'

Under the new laws, the army and police can strip-search suspects in public, drug-test them on the spot and swab them for explosives and gunpowder.

The officer tells them to take their clothes off.

'Not another fucking strip-search,' complains New Loon.

'Shut up, you cheeky cunt, and do as you are told.'

The tank engines roar, the heat and diesel fumes blowing over the lads. Meanwhile, the infantry dismount the Warrior and are taking up positions, scoping with their SA80s.

New Loon and Pacer take off their gear down to their boxies. Dylan refuses and sits back on a smashed-up old sink, lights up a ciggie. The officer sends over two privates to get him to comply. 'Who the fuck do you think you are? You heard the order – take your clothes off, you scruffy cunt.'

Dylan blows smoke rings and squints his eyes. The officer in the Bulldog orders New Loon and Pacer to take their underwear off. New Loon starts protesting now. 'Fuck's sake, you can see we've got fuck all on us.' But the officer gestures to them to take their boxies down.

Dylan's still saying and doing fuck all. Then it clicks with one of the soldiers. He recognises Dylan and whispers to the other, then goes back to the APC to tell his officer that Dylan Olsen is one of the suspects in the Chalina murder and can't be harassed.

'Why the fuck not, corporal?' asks the officer. 'He looks like a fucking scroat to me. Like all the fucking rest of them.'

'Because every time we search him, sir, we get a shitload of grief off the C-in-C. This one's lawyers kick up a shitstorm, sir, complaining that his human rights have been fucked up, sir. Got to be wrapped in cotton wool and all that, sir.'

'But the cunt killed a three-year-old girl, corporal. If you had any fucking balls you'd slot the little fucker yourself, now.'

'I would, sir. But to tell you the truth, sir, we're short. Pulling back tomorrow, sir, to the enduring bases. The quicker we get out of this shithole, the better. I don't want to fuck it up on the last day.'

'I suppose you're right, corporal. But it's political correctness gone mad, if you ask me.'

'I know, it's fucking madness, sir. But so is all this shit, sir.'

'Well, what about the other two?'

'They're just normal gang members, sir.'

'Well, fucking well search them then, corporal. And take a good look up their dirty little arses. Fourth-generation Fenian scum are fucking clever at getting one over on us.'

Dylan carries on smoking his ciggie, looking at a beautiful cloud formation through his robbed £400 sunglasses. One of the soldiers kicks an empty yellow oil barrel over the waste ground. Two of the others get New Loon in an arm lock and drape his naked body over the oil drum. New Loon winces at the sun-heated metal on his skin. Other parts of the drum are muddy and cold. He can feel his cock rubbing against rust and flakes of yellow paint. Two other soldiers splay his legs and a fifth puts a Durex on the barrel of his SA80.

'An internal search for contraband will now proceed under the Prevention of TerrorCrime Act. Do you wish to report to us any illegal substances or firearms that you may have secreted inside your body?'

'No.'

The soldier parts New Loon's arse cheeks with the barrel. 'Who's been a naughty boy then? Not cleaning his arse properly. Look at the fucking state of that.'

The other soldiers laugh. The officer walks over, looks at the small pieces of shit and bog roll stuck to New Loon's arse pubes. New Loon blows up crimson.

'Is that a piece of carrot or red pepper there, corporal?'

'Where, sir?'

'Right on the star of his arse, corporal.'

'Neither, sir. It's a discoloured piece of onion, sir.'

'Well, whatever it is, I'd flick it off with a stick before engaging your weapon. I don't want the undigested supper of a fucking peasant coming into contact with your kit. Is that understood, corporal?'

'Perfectly, sir.'

Smiling, the soldier pushes the tip of his rifle up New Loon's arse. He pulls it in and out at least 30 times until the Durex is covered in streaks of blood and mucus.

New Loon says fuck all. He's been sexually abused on and off since he was four. So he knows the script.

The officer turns to Pacer. 'You're getting this next.'

Pacer laughs. 'Not arsed, lad. Do what the fuck you want as long as it's not your cock.'

Dylan speaks to the prodding soldier: 'If your ma could see you now! She'd be proud of you, lad. The British Army – finest fighting force in the whole world.'

'Only following procedure. If it was up to me, big shot, I'd pull the trigger. But I'm bound by regulations.'

Dylan stares up at the sky and smiles. 'Remember One Arm?' he says to New Loon. He's wincing with pain but forces a chuckle, acknowledging the memory. 'What goes around comes around, eh?' says Dylan. All three of them burst out laughing.

'You'll be laughing on the other side of your faces,' the corporal chips in as he's splaying Pacer across a barrel. He stares at Dylan, having the last laugh. 'The private military contractors take over tomorrow, and they can do what they like.'

The first soldier bursts Pacer's arse until it bleeds.

* * *

The Devil phones up to tell them that two private security companies have won the contract to police the Gang Exclusion Zone. He warns Dylan to be careful, so the lads call a meeting to decide how to play it. The first company is Global Social Solutions, a London-based consultancy run by former British Army officers. Clegsy fills Dylan in on the details: 'They're the ones that drive round in the Mambas.'

Dylan's tired and impatient. He's been running the show recently because Nogger's been spending a lot of time away, grafting. 'What are Mambas, mate?' he asks Clegsy wearily.

'Like armoured-up jeeps, riot-control trucks made in South Africa. The firm's made up of older fellers, old paras and marines. A few of them are a bit tubby, but they'll have a go. They're the ones in charge of putting up the knife arches all over the place.'

'Knife arches?'

'They're like the walk-in metal detectors you get at the airport. Except they're mobile and they move them up and down the street, in the shopping centres and that, searching people at random. Anyone caught with a blade gets carted off.'

The second company is Greyrock, an American military contractor that got famous when it was brought in in the aftermath of a hurricane and runs law and order in several US cities.

'Wraparound sunglasses, big tats, mainly Yanks,' says Clegsy. 'They bomb around in brand-new right hand drive Chevrolet Suburbans. SUVs, lad. Trigger happy, serious. They're the ones who video everything as they're driving along.'

'Why?'

'They videotape the routes to and from John Lennon Airport, to and from Lower Lane HQ, everything. Then they play them back later to see if they've missed any security threats.'

'What d'you mean?' asks Dylan, finding it all too much to take in, feeling as though they've won already.

'IEDs, car bombs, ambushes. Standard operating procedure for them, lad. Their last contracts were in Baghdad and Afghanistan.'

'Mad, innit?'

'We'll have to watch them. Cowboys, them, lad. Shoot first and all that.'

Dylan heads out of Nogzy into town but he can't move out of the Exclusion Zone because of a new roadblock on the border with the city. Gone are the ramshackle huts and barbed wire of the army. In their place are state-of-the-art permanent roadblocks in navy-blue Global Social Solutions livery. For pedestrians, there's a massive walk-in border control centre built by an Israeli contractor. Dylan meets Lupus coming out.

'Watch it, lad. Everyone going through's drug tested and swabbed up for bombs. If you test positive, you'll get nicked on the spot. Fucking out of order.'

'When was that brought in?'

'Just started today. Gauleiter's orders, lad.'

The Gauleiter: Robin Farquharson, the head of the CPA. Lupus gives Dylan the *Echo*. There's a picture of the Gauleiter getting out of his white

Suburban. His guards, with buzz cuts and wraparound sunglasses, are armed with Colt Commandos. Farquharson's quoted as saying:

> We are introducing blanket drug and gun residue testing to protect the community. Anyone who fails a test will go before the special tribunal we have set up, the Community Combatant Status Review Tribunal, which is made up of experts including senior anti-terrorist officers, military advocates and psychiatrists. Anyone who is judged to be a threat to the community, for instance a gang member, can be rendered to one of our facilities outside of the city and detained until that threat is neutralised.'

Inside, there are pictures of Farquharson next to a Little Bird OH-6 helicopter owned by Greyrock, and he's quoted praising them for introducing the right kit to get the job done:

> Greyrock are deploying three Little Bird helicopters to patrol the Gang Exclusion Zone. These helicopters are small, speedy, well-armed scout helicopters, ideal for the challenges we face in the War on TerrorCrime in our cities. It's long been recognised that the army's helicopters were designed for a different conflict and that the Merseyside Police helicopter is vulnerable to small-arms fire.

Fuck's sake. Dylan looks around. Granmas with wheelie shopping bags. Young mas with kids. Workies.

Lupus tells him, 'Don't fuck off from the queue. They've got BSCs behind them mirrors over there.'

Dylan's confused again: 'What the fuck are BSCs?'

'Behavioural science consultants, lad. Special spotters who're trained to look for suicide bombers and oddballs and suspicious types. They look for people leaving the queue, talking to themselves, swearing and muttering under their breath, mad clothes, sweating, all that. They call it TerrorCrime profiling. Fuck the test off now, lad, and you'll end up at a tribunal.'

'Fuck it. I'll take the test.' Dylan knows his clothes are negative cos he's been washing them every night, but there might be old residues in his hair and skin.

'Make eye contact. That's a key one, lad. Don't make it look like you've got something to hide. Don't carry your mobile or your iPod, cos these pricks think it's a remote control for an IED. Remember, lad, these are not long off the streets of Eye-raq.'

When Dylan gets to the front of the queue, a guard takes a small stick and swabs his cuffs, collar and inside his pockets. He then puts the swab in an explosives trace detection scanner. Dylan watches it search for forty different explosives, including RDX and PETN, in eight seconds.

Another guard takes Dylan's ID and puts his name into the Police National Computer and the TerrorCrime database. As the screen flashes red alert, the man doesn't move a muscle. He's good. But Dylan clocks the armed guards behind the Perspex barrier get the message in their earpieces.

The guard puts Dylan's ID into a Smiths Ionscan 400B document scanner that looks for traces of discharge powder, TNT, Semtex, NG, nitrates, HMX and TATP. The colour-coded display blows up green for all clear.

But they badly want Dylan. He can see a snatch photographer in the back of a white Suburban whacking off some shots of him. Another guard moves a Smiths Sabre 4000 up and down his body looking for molecules of cocaine, heroin, cannabis and 37 other banned substances. But again it proves negative.

A massive black American guard wearing a jungle hat pinned up at the sides comes over and tells him, 'We know who you are, fucko.'

Dylan smiles. 'I'm saying fuck all, lad. Fuck all.'

CHAPTER 26

RENDITION

Jay and Iggo have been missing for three days now.

'They've been nicked, lad,' says Pacer. 'Telling you.'

Nogger tells him, 'Jay, the little cunt, best not be snitching about Chalina. Don't care where the fuck he is, I'll smash his head in.'

'Don't worry about Jay,' Dylan says. 'Staunch, he is. No back answers. And I don't think they've been nicked, either. More likely been had off by someone. For all we know they could be in an abode somewhere or in Crocky being tortured, whatever.'

'D'you mean those rats might have shot them?' asks Pacer.

'Don't know. But if they'd have been nicked, the bizzies or the redcaps would have to tell us, or tell their mas or whatever. They can't just hold you for no reason, can they? They've got to tell your next of kin, d'you get me? And the Devil's phoned every fucking bizzy station and no trace.'

'Telling you, lad,' says Pacer, 'they've been purely rendered. Those private security can do what the fuck they like, take you off to some mad place somewhere. Don't have to tell anyone except the TerrorCrime tribunals. End of story, lad.'

'Fuck off,' Dylan tells him. 'If they nick you, you can't just vanish without trace, even under the TerrorCrime laws.'

'There's all kinds of jangle flying around,' rebuts Pacer. 'That the CPA have got secret detention centres on American bases down south, in little shady places off the coast and that. They can do what the fuck they want cos they're on American soil. D'you get me?'

'Fuck off. It's bollocks. Those PMCs, lad, they're just like security guards. No different from the beauts who stand on the door in Asda and can't do fuck all except stop smackheads robbing shower gels. Handy lads, mind you, but they ain't got no special powers.'

'Mate, the CPA are more powerful than the army, the bizzies, the Government, the lot. And they've got their own camps, like those mickey-mouse prisons owned by Group 4. It's covered by anti-terror laws and no one can say fuck all.'

Dylan phones the Devil, puts him on loudspeaker on a robbed iPhone, *Apprentice*-style.

The Devil tells him, 'There's rumours that the CPA have set up a detention centre on the Isle of Man for people arrested in Gang Exclusion Zones all over the country, cos it's not covered by the same laws as the mainland.'

'Well, have you asked them if they're holding Jay?' asks Dylan.

'Yes. And they deny it. They're giving everyone a standard reply. "Rumours that community combatants have been secretly detained at CPA facilities and tortured are false. These rumours are just part of the asymmetric warfare that anti-social elements are waging against the CPA."'

'Asymmetric warfare?'

'Like guerrilla warfare. What they're saying is this: that you're fighting an unconventional war against them and this is your propaganda to try and smear them – saying that they've detained two of your mates.'

'Mad, aren't they?'

Nogger chips in, 'Listen, you fucking bell-end, I'm not interested in your fucking warfare. You're being paid enough, you slimy little cunt, to represent us. So find Jay and get him out of whichever jug he's in.' The Devil LLB swallows hard in his office. Nogger presses his message home: 'If you can't find Jay, we will. And if those CPA pricks want a fucking war, lad, we'll show what some proper soljas can do, not some fucking part-time army pricks.'

Phone down. Nogger's on the warpath, gets a cheer of approval off the lads for taking a hard line on protecting their own. But Dylan tells him, 'Those PMCs are not weekend warriors, mate. They're fucking ex-US Navy SEALs. Fucking Rambo types. They're not soft.'

'Fuck the SAS, Dylan. That's all telly talk and filmies, just to put the shits up us. The SAS? Fuck 'em. Mugs, mate, telling you. Action Men, wearing those snorkels and that, taking orders off posh lads. What kind of a fucking prick would do what someone tells them?'

'If you're saying we should have some beef with them, then I'm telling you, they'll fucking annihilate us. They've got fucking tanks and choppers.'

'Let's go and see those American niggers on that checkpoint. They'll know where Jay is. Odds are they'll have nicked him. Fucking coons coming into Nogzy and intimidating us, getting a fucking 1,000 dollars a day wages while we can't graft cos there's fucking Little Birds up our arses every day.'

Clegsy's with Dylan: 'Nogger, lad, it's suicide. Every one of them's carrying an M4A1 carbine with an RIS-mounted M203 grenade launcher with a fucking telescopic sight perched on top of it. D'you know what that means, Nogger? That everything that gets within an effective range of 360 metres is purely shredded.'

Nogger knows the score. He's even done a sketch of the M4A1 carbine in his bedroom, straight onto the wall, as well as an AK, a Mac-10 and a few other bits. All the lads did gun sketching to relax. Still, he's a bit taken aback by Clegsy's backchat. 'Doesn't matter what kit they've got. What matters is, have they got the arse to use it?'

'All's I'm saying, Nogger, is that one of them has got more firepower in his hands than all of us put together – between 700 and 950 rounds a minute. Face it, Nogger. We're fucked. We've got blunderbusses. All of our decent kit has been taken away by the bizzies, or it's buried fuck knows where. Fucking shameful, lad. Call ourselves a crew?'

Nogger's facing a revolt. Dylan says, 'Nogger, listen to him lad. If we attack the CPA now, we'll get walloped all over the place. Use your head. Gorilla warfare, or whatever, is all about not fighting your enemy head-on. It's about being a bit spicy. It's about ambushing them, using the element of surprise. Bide your time. Use your head.'

'Fucking shitehouse talk,' says Nogger. 'What are we, soljas or scaredy cats? Let's do what we used to do when we'd go down to Crocky, let some buck off. These fucking contractors are worse shithouses than Crocky. They'll run, lad. Telling you.'

The lads vote for an immediate attack.

They all meet in Nogzy Park, around 40 of them. Loads are pissed and stoned already cos it's Friday night. They meet in an old walled garden in the middle because the stonework gives some protection from surveillance. Everyone's given one petrol bomb. Nogger's got access to the two Mac-10s. They're still stashed in a hole near a sewer just outside the Exclusion Zone. But it's too risky to bring them back on just yet. 'Redcaps get hold of them, lad,' says Dylan, 'and it's 40 years each in jail. Leave them where they are.'

GANG WAR

Nogger makes the battle plan. Clegsy and a few of the lads have gone round the estate digging up their bits and bobs, getting the schoolies to retrieve guns that they've stashed in their lofts and gardens. Clegsy comes back with a green canvas army-surplus holdall and a heavy-duty plastic masonry sack full of their guns. There are only nine weapons between them. Everything else has been seized or lost for ever under the rubble of The Boot. Dylan picks up a silver-handled Czech converted replica pistol, three shitty bullets in the clip. Dylan widens his eyes in protest, almost laughing at the thought of using this in an exchange. Clegsy laughs. 'It looks like a toy.'

'Get you a little cowboy holster, Dylan,' says Lupus. 'One of those little brown plastic ones. You'll look sound then.'

Dylan bursts out laughing at the madness of it. Nogger throws them a moody stare. Doesn't like back-of-the class banter while he's generalissimo-ing. He's wearing his Rommel desert-storm goggles, drawing plans in the soil with an NHS walking stick. Nogger tells Lupus that he'll be smashing a robbed car into the checkpoint at the top of Stalisbrook Avenue. Lupus looks unsure, half sinkered.

Nogger stiffens up. 'Don't worry, lad. Be just like a ramraid. Chose you cos you're a better jockey.' Lupus is half beaming with pride now, at being praised in front of the lads. He's like a kamikaze before a mission. New Loon gets his phone out to make the martyrdom vid.

Dylan steps in. 'But, Nogger, the CPA guards'll fire back. Close air support and all sorts. Lupus'll get walloped at the wheel before he even has a chance.' Clegsy and Pacer nod in agreement.

'But we've got surprise on our side. We can steal it on them.' Nogger tries to steel the lads with an eve of battle soliloquy: 'Shock and awe, innit? Won't know what's hit them, will they? And while their heads are turned that way, looking at Lupus driving through their office, we'll come at them at the flanks.'

Dylan narrows his eyes, gives him a stare and half a smile, as if to say, 'The flanks? Who the fuck do you think you are, lad?'

Nogger, not waiting for Dylan to spell out what he's thinking, throws him a green paperback: *British Army Field Manual: FIBUA – Fighting in a Built-up Area*. Dylan flicks through the pages: 'Updated to include tactics used by coalition forces in Iraq and Afghanistan'. There's a section called 'Main Principles'. Dylan reads the first chapter: 'Keep Equipment Light'.

Nogger, pointing at the manual, says, 'See? You don't need loads of mad guns. Keep it loose and light, that's what they're saying. And these are the cunts who make the rules.'

Dylan reads more: 'Attack rapidly, in depth, to dominate killing areas. Use masking smoke.'

'See? What that means is just lash a few petrol bombs before we bail in. Laughing, we are. Laughing. Over the back gardens, from the sides. Bang! Bang! Bang! Innit?'

Dylan shakes his head, waving the book: 'These are just words, Nogger. It won't work out like that for us. Telling you.'

Nogger rips the book out of Dylan's hand and reads from it: 'Employ shock-producing weapons to reduce enemy strongpoints.' He's made up with himself. 'That,' he's saying, pointing at the page, 'is exactly what we're doing. The strongpoint is their little hut. Lupus in the car is the shocker. It'll freak them out. Niggers'll be all over the place.'

All the lads are buzzing now, up for this. Dylan knows it. 'Where d'you get this book from?' he asks. Nogger tells him he robbed it from the Central Library in town. Dylan stares at him and thinks of Elizabeth.

All the lads are bang into the attack now.

Pacer seems cagier, asks, 'But having the checkpoint off won't tell us where Jay is though, will it?'

'We'll have the computers off, grab the paperwork,' Nogger tells him. 'We'll find out everything they've got on us, where they're up to with Chalina. Everything, lad, innit? Mission Accomplished.'

Everyone gets in position, crouched down in the privet hedges and gardens near the checkpoint. Most of the tenants are gone now from the houses, decamped, but the few pensioners who're left are told to fuck off back inside. Dylan, Nogger and Clegsy with ten other lads are on one side of the road. Fifteen others are back-up on the other side, including the younger ones like Clone and Onion. They form the reserve second wave, led by Pacer. A few of the younger lads, with their pitbulls in harnesses, are pretending to be ordinary pedestrians, walking along the street towards the queue for the checkpoint with the usual ragtag of mas and kids passing through the border control.

Lupus, in a robbed old summer-yellow Cavalier from the 1980s – no tax, nothing, with a green sunstrip across the top of the windscreen – joins the traffic jam of back-logged cars waiting to be searched and let through at the checkpoint. When nothing's coming the other way, he suddenly wheelspins out of the queue, floors it and bombs towards the checkpoint.

All the lads in the bushes are going, 'Yeah, Lupus, lad. Putting on a show,' whispering. Dylan's watching it through his field glasses, through a hole in the fence, adrenalin pumping for Lupus the Hero, Lupus the Top Jockey. He just sees flashes of pale yellow and plastic see-through green, sometimes makes out Lupus's black hood in the driver's seat. He's accelerating too fast for Dylan to watch him through the binoculars now. Dylan keeps track of Lupus's progress by the unnatural screech of the robbed car's revs and the smell of burning rubber that's floating over to where the lads are hiding, like a gas attack.

Dylan puts the binoculars up to his eyes again. For a microsecond, he catches the heavy, rusting, yellow bonnet buckling slightly and two wisps of white smoke coming up out of the engine block, almost imperceptible. Lupus's revs go into super-high-pitched overdrive for a second, then there's a rattle of spinning-off parts, an exploding fan belt, before suddenly the engine cuts out and the car rolls to a halt.

Dylan knows what the CPA guards have done without having to look. They've put two rounds into the engine block. He knows it from the two little impacts he saw on the front of the car. Defensive vehicle immobilisation. Standard operating procedure. Force protection.

But Lupus is still alive. Dylan watches him panic, trying to unbuckle the old seatbelt and untangle himself. The driver-side door opens. Bang! The third CPA round blows a chunk out of Lupus's neck, like a butcher slicing out a cut of raw meat. He drops to the ground, holding his neck with his right hand and gurgling.

Nogger stands up, going-over-the-top-style, rallies his troops, making a big 'c'mon' gesture with his arm, like an officer. Clegsy, a few feet away, stands up, carrying the long shotgun awkwardly with both hands. Suddenly, he whooshes up in a big ball of flames. Gone. Blinding orange. Everyone has to look away.

And that's it. Everyone scatters. Guards are pouring rounds into the garden fences and hedges, disintegrating the wood and privet, shattering the front doors of the houses.

Dylan goes to help Clegsy, but his whole body is cooked, smoke and steam coming off it. Like Anakin Skywalker before he becomes Darth Vader. *Star Wars on Earth*. His skin and fingers are crusty and black, his teeth even blacker than usual and pointy. The skin on his cheeks is smooth and bloated. Dylan touches it. Broiled jaw muscle slides off. It's like a chicken fillet. 'Fuck's sake.' Dylan recoils in fright, wincing, his face tight. He spews a bit on the clean grass behind him.

Then he remembers Lupus. Civilians are scattering out of their cars now, kids screaming, bags of shopping spilling dark liquids over the pavement. Dylan pepper-pots over the road, crouching behind the yellow car for cover. He can hear Lupus trying to call for his mum. There he is. Convulsing violently on the floor, crawling sideways on the ground to try to get away from the pain, rotating in a circle like a breakdancer.

He stops when he sees Dylan, but he's still gurgling blood. He stretches his hand out, fingers beckoning, pointing upwards. Dylan looks to the sky. The downdraught blows his hood down and bloats his jacket up. There's an OH6 whirlybird right on top of him, a Greyrock sniper hanging out the side Hollywood-style, a low-slung psy-ops loudhailer underneath. 'Drop your weapon. Move away from the casualty. Armed authorised personnel. Stand still. Do not attempt to move. You will be immobilised.'

Fuck. He's been nicked. Right out in the open. Nowhere to go. He lashes the gun and puts his hands on his head.

He's blinded by pepper spray, the hooks of a Taser ragging at his nipple then blasting him all up with electrification. He's slammed onto the ground by a guard squashing him with a riot shield. Behind him, a five-man squad wearing full padded riot gear, with the words 'Extreme Reaction Force' stencilled in fresh white paint on the chestplates of their bulletproof vests, their boots stomping on the ground as they get closer. 'Comply. Comply. Do not resist. Do not resist. Comply. Comply.'

Dylan is hooded, gloved and shackled, sweat pouring into his eyes. He comes round in the back of a moving refrigerator truck, kneeling, hands behind his back, wrists pinioned and cuffed to a belt, head on the floor – a stress position. For what seems like ages, it gets intolerably hot. He can't breathe, sweating in the hood, lips blistering, eyes stinging. Then it gets freezing cold. His lips are blue, he's shivering, pissing. The cycles of extreme temperatures go on for hours.

Blasts of super-loud techno come through speakers. Then it changes to country music: 'Okie from Muskogee' then 'Mystery Train' by Elvis, dead loud. Then it's the sound of dogs barking non-stop.

There's no daylight. The outside world seems very distant now. Dylan's mind starts to eat itself. After many hours, the van stops. Dylan's dragged out the back, over some crunchy gravel. There are real dogs barking and growling, snapping at his bare feet. They bite through the hood, but the thick hessian stops the fangs causing too much damage. American guards are kidney-punching him, calling him a white nigger and a child abuser.

He's lashed to a sloping board, tilted downwards slightly, so his head is lower than his body. Three layers of towels are put over his face, on top of the hood. He's in total darkness. Dylan feels the coolness of the water first, is glad of it. Then he holds his breath, determined to resist. Eventually, he has to inhale through the damp cloth, close against his nose. A cascade of water floods into his nostrils. Sheer panic. Dylan is drowning.

The interrogator barks questions. 'What is your role in TerrorCrime?'

'Comply. Do not resist. Comply,' other guards are shouting in the background.

Dylan can hear the artificial shutter noises of their camera phones, then one of them saying, 'Video it from this side. You can see the motherfucker's head going wild here.'

Another says, 'Keep it tight. Don't fucking ID nothing, not even my patches, motherfucker.'

The waterboarding goes on. Dylan's gag reflex keeps triggering every few seconds until it's overwhelmed.

'What is your status as a community combatant?'

'Which gang are you a member of?'

'What are the names of the principal members of your organisation?'

The water's stopped and the towels are lifted away from his face so that he can answer. When he says nothing, it starts again.

Water and adrenalin are coursing round his body now, life fighting to the last. But he's crushed now, giving way to a wave of nausea and terror. Just at the onset of unconsciousness, the torturers stop.

'What was your involvement in the execution of Chalina Murphy?' Dylan feels a finger hard on his solar plexus. The interrogator prodding him, putting pressure on him, trying to wind him, get the air out before they pour water into him again. Then the sickly sensation up his nose once more, like his adenoids freezing and contracting. Then he passes out.

Dylan wakes up in a box, in cramped confinement. His hood has been taken off but he's wearing large, blacked-out goggles now. Learned helplessness is setting in now. He's left in isolation for hours. Then the torture starts again, this time psychological. The guards threaten to put stinging insects and snakes into the box. He hears the box open and something's dropped in. He feels large insects falling on his hair, crawling around his nose. At first, Dylan jumps violently in the two inches of wriggle room, smashes his coccyx on the top of the box, presses and strains his arms and legs against the sides trying to get away from them. He spits, clearing one from the edge of his bottom lip. Then he tries to calm down. He's dealt with the claustrophobia. Now tries to reason away the insects, tells himself that they would have stung him by now if they were dangerous. They're just trying to fuck with his head, he tells himself. It's no worse than what those pricks on *I'm a Celebrity* put up with. Then he laughs out loud.

Dylan becomes delirious. At some point, they move him and put him in a cell. When he wakes up, pushing the scratchy blanket off his face, his head and his kidneys are aching. There's a little window, high up, but all Dylan can see is the perimeter wall, a stainless-steel Active Topping System running along the edge of it to prevent prisoners from climbing over it. Just like any other nick. He could be anywhere. The inner fence is a fibre-optic weave bolstered with three tiers of coiled razor wire.

Jay shouts on him from the cell opposite. When he gets to speak to Jay later, he says that he wasn't waterboarded. Maybe cos he's too young. But he was tortured, he says. He doesn't want to say what happened.

'Did you tell them anything?' asks Dylan.

'No,' says Jay. But Dylan knows that he's told them everything.

Later, in the exercise yard, which is no more than a huge metal drum constructed of wire mesh, Dylan asks Iggo what they did to Jay.

'Stuck something in his arse, put him in a nappy, tied him up.'

'Mad, innit?'

'The Yanks say that he shit hisself.'

'Not good is it? Not good at all.' He smiles.

'No one knows we're here, so we've had no visitors. All of them are Yanks. But we had one English feller. The Greyrock guards said he was MI5. I kept asking him when we were getting out. He said, "I don't know. All I know is what's been on TV. Your case hasn't been on TV."'

Dylan laughs. 'Mad, innit?'

CHAPTER 27

MEMORIAL

The Greatest Show on Earth. That's what they're calling it, Chalina's memorial tribute concert at Anfield Football Stadium. There are 70,000 mourners, including the Prime Minister. A Beatles reunion is rumoured, Phil Collins, Robbie joining back up with Take That. It's beamed to an estimated two billion viewers worldwide.

The lads are watching the wall-to-wall coverage on the big screen in the Canada Dock. Sound turned down, jukebox up. New Loon spikes one of the old alkies, big thick glasses on, pure bottle tops, with a tablet for a laugh. Half an hour later, the alky's dancing next to the bar and under the dartboard, to 'Macarena' and then AC/DC, humiliating himself.

New Loon's laughing, shouting, 'Go 'ead, special.' Giving the lads a bit of merriment to pull them out of their sinker.

But Nogger has got a cob on. 'How come she's got a fucking big send-off and Lupus and Clegsy got fuck all?' He's trying to cover up for guilt, deflect the blame for sending Lupus and Clegsy on his doomed raid on the CPA checkpoint. After their bodies were released, the lads were banned from having a proper funeral. The CPA had issued a statement saying that all 'sectarian' events, including funerals, were prohibited under TerrorCrime legislation until further notice. 'Couldn't even get a nice car, for them. Can you believe that? Wake banned from every pub in Nogzy. That's no way to see off proper soljas. But little Chalina's got the fucking Beatles playing hers. D'you get me?'

Nogger's secretly half made up because he didn't have to splash out on a big funeral for Lupus and Clegsy, didn't have to fork out for the cortège and the moonshine at the wake. But then playing the big time, he tells the lads, 'Course, I gave the families some compo, course I did.' Nogger gave Lupus's mum £200 compensation for the loss of his life.

172

He gave Clegsy's grandad £300. He got more because all that was left of his body was his head. The rest of it had been burned to a crisp and fell apart when the ambulancemen took him away. His granddad told them that the body broke into bits like a pile of crispy bacon. The doctors said he'd been hit by a depleted uranium round, a new kind of anti-personnel weapon they were using. Clegsy's ma blew the compo on cocaine and tablets. His granddad bought a half-size kiddie coffin to save money. Said that the charred remains fitted in 'no sweat'.

Outside, the sky starts to fill up with helicopters, TV ones. The pre-concert procession is expected. Crowds are gathering behind the safety barriers. At the front is a Liverpool FC open-top bus, blaring out Robbie Williams' 'Angels' through the PA. A huge framed photo of Chalina is on the top deck, with the family and VIPs: a few Liverpool players, a few *Hollyoaks* cast members, Chalina's favourite CBeebies presenter dressed as a pirate. Most of the players are on the bottom deck with their WAGs, talking about villas in Dubai and whether they're a good investment or not, having a glass of champagne, because Lynda says Chalina 'would have wanted a celebration'. There are police and redcap escorts, the roads along the route closed down.

Then come the press buses, eight of them. They're all pissed and charlied up as well. When the procession's gone past, all the lads pile back into the Canada Dock to watch the concert. A few lines, a few Stellas, settling in for a good day of free entertainment on the box.

Lynda has asked the crowd to wear either red for Liverpool or pink, Chalina's favourite colour. Mariah Carey, Lynda's favourite singer, sends a video message over the giant monitor from her home in Malibu saying sorry that she can't be there. She sings an a cappella version of the Jackson 5's 'I'll Be There'. New Loon shouts 'slag' when she comes on. Mayonnaise, horny off the bugle, slopes off into the bogs for a wank after seeing Mariah's tits struggling to escape her low-cut dress. Whizzer throws a load of ale at the big screen then goes, 'Fucking love to shag her.'

The satellite link crashes just as Mariah is halfway through her farewell speech, crying. The opening bars of 'You'll Never Walk Alone' strike up and Gerry Marsden swans onto the stage: lived-in face, orange tan, black polo neck. The crowd go wild, scarves go up, everyone in floods.

Outside the pub, the crowd turns nasty, lashing the barriers at the police and the redcaps. The police jump into their ARV Volvos and speed off. The redcaps mount their desert-camoed Jackal weapons platform. The driver cuts off-road and races across the rubble of The Boot, laughing cos he's got all-terrain air-bag suspension. One of them throws a Thunderflash to clear a route through the crowd. The auld ones give a whoop, thinking it's a firework.

Several para-reg officers get into a Panther Command and Liaison Vehicle. One of the NCOs comes up through the turret, puts down his head-mounted night-vision goggles to see through the smoke from the Thunderflash, then lets rip with two canisters of Purple Haze from an SA80 A2 Underslung Grenade Launcher. The Panther drives off up the rear of the procession. The army's under orders now not to get involved in policing Gang Exclusion Zones. They come under the strict jurisdiction of the CPA and their private security forces.

The crowd's setting bins on fire now. Thick, quick curls of smoke from the burning rubber, township-style, are cutting through the slower-moving Purple Haze from the obscuration grenade. One bus shelter's already keeled over, too many people standing on the roof, fuelled by the emotion of 'You'll Never Walk Alone'. Then the crowd turns on the lads. A few of the alkies attack Onion while he's serving up some powder to the ghouls in the crowd. He'd been doing some good graft out there today. Always does at a funeral or a coming-home cup parade for Liverpool. 'Best of both worlds, this,' Onion's saying before he gets knocked over by a haymaker to the head from an auld feller wearing an azure-blue jacket from Asda, then spat on.

One of the older ones is saying, 'It was youse who killed little Chalina,' blaming them for all kinds, calling them yobs and Asbos. 'Youse little twats have ruined this neighbourhood.'

Loads of fired-up ghouls march on the pub, determined but mindless, like zombies, to get revenge on the lads. A few windows go in. A feller in his 30s throws a bottle at Whizzer, who's standing outside, gets him heavy in the head. Blood gushes from his temple and he feels dizzy. The crowd's baying for the blood of anyone under 18, anyone dressed in black.

New Loon runs back into the pub, panicking, shouting for Nogger. 'Mad out there, lad. All the auld ones saying that we killed Chalina, that we've been terroring the estate for years, they're gonna get revenge.' A few of the younger lads are panicking because they've never been spoken back to, never taken any shit off the auld ones. Even some of the older alkies in the pub are getting a bit mouthy, calling them 'little shitbags' and 'rats'.

MEMORIAL

There's no messing around from Nogger. He stands up, runs over to the auld alky at the bar who's now sledging off the E New Loon had given him before, muttering under his breath about the lads. Nogger roundhouse kicks him right in his already obliterated kidneys. Then when he goes down, he rags his bottle-top NHS specs off, breaks them and gouges one of his eyes out with the glass.

'Think youse auld cunts are gonna have us off?' he shouts. Then he grabs a set of golf clubs from behind the bar, takes the driver and launches outside for the cull. He jumps into a crowd of angry bingoites, taking long semi-circular swings at head height, toing and froing, cutting the auld ones down like ears of corn. Blood and blue rinses all over the show. He's taking on a rhythmical, methodical groove now, wielding his death pendulum with accuracy, laughing like he's tripping, a big, fat cone hanging out his grid.

The auld ones at the back, try to turn and run. But can only hobble or wobble away. Nogger, grinning, starts twatting their backs and legs with the driver, which is starting to bend and buckle. New Loon's mopping up with a putter, tapping their temples softly to knock them out, stopping now and again to dip their pension books and wriggle their sovvies and earrings off their broken fingers and bloody ears, rag their Our Lady pendants and gold crosses from round their necks. Onion's blasting a CO_2 fire extinguisher over their bodies to scare off the able-bodied stragglers. He robs two bottles of Bell's and a bottle of jarg vodka out of a pensioner's wheelie shopping basket while she's lying on the floor mouthing for help. 'Cheers, girl,' Onion says, before putting the nozzle up tight to her grid and giving her a good blast of gas, laughing like a hyena now. Mayonnaise finds a bottle of cheap bleach in a bag of shopping, starts pouring it over the pensioners' nylon clothes and brown tights, lashes some in the eyes of a young mum with her two kids.

They're near the end of the contact now, Nogger sweating and smiling, soaking up the victory of the cull. 'That should fucking shut them up, the cheeky cunts. After all we've done for this area, and then they turn on us like that. Talk about us being snides. These people . . . fucking savages.'

'Thing about it is,' New Loon adds, getting his breath back, 'with treachery like that, you've just got to stamp all over it straight away.'

'Just got no bottle, have they?'

175

'Always telling us how they fought the war and that. Couldn't of been a fucking bad one, could it? Cos all these shithouses ran away.'

US style-sirens can be heard drifting across the estate, getting closer. Onion, head bandaged up with a pair of 12-denier tights, spots the first Suburban coming out of the smoke. 'Sampon off the port bow,' he shouts, pointing at the four white Greyrock Suburbans heading their way. Slaloming in and out of the debris in the road carefully, then blocking off the junction at the crossroads. They fire off tear gas into the crowd. Nogger and the lads bomb back into the Canada Dock to drink up, watching the end of the concert.

The commentator says, 'Not since the death of Michael Jackson, or perhaps even that of Princess Di, have we seen such an outpouring of emotion.' They're doing vox pops in the crowd. One woman who looks like a VIP says, 'It's sombre and joyful. Everybody's hurt. Everybody's crushed.' Lynda's watching from the manager's box, with Prince Harry representing the royal family. The women in the pub are saying how nice the flowers are. Centre stage is a massive bouquet of tasteful yellows, purples, whites, reds and greens. The finale begins with Ringo Starr singing 'Octopus's Garden' from his house in the South of France, beamed by satellite feed to the giant screen in the stadium. Everyone wanted Paul McCartney singing 'Let It Be' or 'The Long and Winding Road', but they couldn't get him.

On stage, all the other artists shuffle on in a Live Aid-style grand finale to back up Ringo's struggling vocals. Loads of them are pissed and laughing. Only the little kid off *Britain's Got Talent* is taking it seriously. He's an old hand now, after performing at Wacko Jacko's funeral.

The outro is carefully choreographed. Special guest star Robbie Williams sings 'Angels' live. The two big screens on either side of the stage show a home video of Chalina at her third birthday party, wearing a pink fairy costume with angel wings and a wand. She's playing in the back garden, freshly creosoted ranch fencing in the background, a bouncy castle on the lawn.

Robbie launches into the chorus and suddenly a 3D holographic image of the little angel Chalina leaves the screen, floats out of the home vid and up into the sky. Big gasps from the stands. All the crowd's in tears, lighters flickering in one hand, phones out filming the spectacle in the other. It's the resurrection brought to them by Musion Eyeliner HD Projection technology, the corporate logo in the corner of the screen.

Tears are streaming down their faces as the spatial image is beamed up to heaven.

Chalina's hologram rises into the clouds, ascending out of the stadium lights. Circling helicopters film the ascension to heaven, beaming the virtual reality back down onto the big screen. As it gets further away, the interference causes static distortion. The faint blue line around the hologram gets thicker and it breaks up gradually.

'Boss, innit?' says New Loon.

Nogger's mesmerised. 'Like *Stars Wars*, innit?'

CHAPTER 28

RELEASE

A week later, Dylan, Iggo and Jay are released from the detention centre, in secret, at 0500 hours. They're driven to the gates in the back of a blacked-out Suburban. Jay doesn't want to go at first, says he's sick, wants to sit off in the hospital wing until he's better. Dylan knows what's going on. Jay wants to stay in the safety of the nick on his own. But he tells him to get his head together. He can't have Jay going on the numbers cos he's a grass. He picks up the thick see-through plastic bag containing Jay's gear, printed with the words 'Property of Greyrock Correctional Facilities', and lashes it in the Suburban along with his own.

They sit there in silence waiting for the massive electrical gates, little steel-mounted lights flashing at the top, to slide to one side. Dylan's hoping that there isn't a last-minute fuck-up, that they won't get rearrested, dragged back in and tortured again. He looks at the raindrops sliding down the windscreen, clocks the Guttermaster anti-climb downpipes, the concealed tamper-proof fixtures running down the side of the modular outbuildings. No escape from this place, for sure, he's thinking.

When the gate opens at last he can hardly believe it. 'Fuck's sake. Look where we are.'

'Fuck's sake,' says Iggo. 'We're at Altcourse.'

Jay's head is down. 'Oh no!' It makes his grassing even worse, folding in the local dispersal prison.

HMP Altcourse. Twenty minutes' walk from The Boot. A mile or less from CPA HQ at the old Lower Lane police station. 'I thought we were miles away,' says Iggo. 'On a fucking island somewhere.'

'That's cos they drove us around for hours in the refrigerator truck,' says Dylan.

'Just to disorientate us.'

RELEASE

Dylan clocks a big sign as they turn the corner. The old Altcourse sign's been replaced with a high-finish plastic sign saying: 'Welcome to Camp Echo Greyrock. Fighting TerrorCrime. For Freedom. For Justice.' Underneath, there's a row of logos, the project's partners.

Youth Crime Task Force
Operation Urban Freedom
Gang Exclusion Zone Delivery Unit
TerrorCrime Tribunal Partnership
The Urban Conflict Redevelopment and Reconstruction Agency
Civilian Protection Authority

Then a list of banks, property developers and corporations bidding for contracts.

They're driven to CPA headquarters in the Green Zone. News of their release must have got out. Outside the gate, there's a huge press pack. The Suburban edges through, camera flashes bursting through the tinted windows, rolling thuds of reporters and cameramen banging on the sides. 'Which one of you confessed to killing Chalina?' shouts one reporter. Dylan ignores it, carries on smoking a ciggie. Jay has his head down. Iggo has his hood up, making gun signs and telling them to fuck off.

Dylan says quietly, 'Jay, is that true? Did you tell them anything?' He already knows he did, that that was why Jay hadn't wanted to leave the detention centre: partly out of shame for being a snitch, partly out of fear, because he knows that Nogger'll kill him.

Jay's ashamed, but now that the reporter has asked about it, it seems a good time to confront it head-on. He doesn't need to spell it out. 'Dylan, they were fucking me up. Seriously.'

'I know, yeah. Don't worry. I would have done the same,' he says, but he knows that he didn't, that he stayed staunch.

Iggo says to Jay, scowling, 'Know it was bad in there. Me and Dylan got fucked up too. But we didn't fucking snitch.'

Dylan flicks his ciggie, staring at it while he thinks. He needs to be diplomatic here, not belittle Iggo's bottle in taking the pain, in not folding under questioning – the highest honour. But at the same time, he can't slaughter Jay for being a grass. Who wouldn't have caved in? Dylan looks at them both and says, 'Don't worry. I'll sort it. Just say fuck all to the lads. Nothing to Nogger, right? Just give us a couple of days on it.' They both nod.

Dylan, Jay and Iggo meet the lads on The Strand. Nogger's in the middle of happy-slapping a toothless crack whore outside the Post Office. She's jammed her arm in the post box because Nogger told her an old lady posted a birthday card with a tenner in it. The crackhead's baby's screaming in its pram, nicely dressed but starving. Her five-year-old boy's panicking and asking what's wrong with his mum.

The crackhead shouts for a girl called Paula to hurry up, then breaks down into desperate sobs, begging for an ambulance. Her cries disintegrate into demonic moans, her face gurning. The baby keeps crying and the boy's running between it and his mum trapped in the post box. Nogger's filming the crackhead, keeping out of her reach to avoid contamination, saying, 'Don't touch me.'

Pacer keeps saying, 'You look like Sandra Bullock,' to the woman with her gummy, wrecked face. New Loon pulls her grey sweatpants down, with all the lads laughing. She can't do nothing cos of her arm stuck in the slit.

Nogger breaks off when he sees Dylan and the lads. 'Youse all right?'

'Purely rendered, weren't we?' Dylan tells him.

'Any bad happen? Heard all kinds of jangle that youse were getting tortured,' says Nogger, looking at Jay.

'No. Just normal jail, wannit?' Dylan says quickly, hoping to change the subject.

The crackhead's moaning still, the baby crying, the little kid trying to protect his mum. New Loon's slapping her arse.

'Little lie down, wannit?' says Iggo. 'A few decent kips, half all right scran. Laughing.'

Nogger stares at Jay: 'And what about you, Little Jay, lad. Did those cunts ask you about Chalina?' The baby's crying hard, the crackhead trying to pull her swollen arm free.

'No, Nogger.'

'Hope not, lad. Cos you know what snitches get, don't you, lad?' The crackhead's writhing in pain now. The baby's cried itself sick and the five-year-old's pissed himself.

'Fuck off, Nogger. Said fuck all.'

'Snitches get stitches, Jay. Snitches get stitches.'

Jay's arse is going now. He looks at Dylan. Dylan searches for a way to take the heat off Jay, then suddenly jumps up, takes a run-up at the crack whore, kicks the arm that's stuck in the post box. It breaks and falls out of the slot like jelly. All the lads are in hysterics. 'Come 'ead,' he says. 'Enough talking shite. Let's party on. Let's get a weed. Come on, the lads are back.' Dylan signals to Jay with his eyes that he needs to get his head together.

Nogger jumps up, laughing at the broken crack whore. 'One sick puppy, you, lad,' he says to Dylan, off Jay's case now.

New Loon clacks his fingers. 'See that fucking spaz go.' Pacer throws the kid half a tub of Haribo Friendship Rings robbed off the counter from the Armenian shop. New Loon gives the baby some fried-egg sweets. As they're getting off, Onion gives the crack ma a £20 wrap of powder, then snatches it back. 'Serves you right for being a punter.'

The next day, Nogger throws the *Echo* at Dylan. 'Have you seen this?'

CHALINA SHOCK CONFESSION
'We Shot Chalina' Admits Gang Member
Arrests imminent after new breakthrough, says CPA
CPA officials announced a 'significant step forward' in the Chalina investigation.

Dylan's stomach lurches. He scans the copy until he comes to what he's looking for:

Sources close to the probe told the *Echo* that a 'human intelligence source' directly related to the shooting has provided new data. A CPA spokesman refused to confirm that a gang member had confessed but said that fresh leads were being examined.

Dylan takes a moment to control his breathing before looking up at Nogger. Then he laughs. 'Paper talk, lad. Load of fucking jargarooney. It's a fucking wind-up.'

'But they're saying that one of youse is a midnight mass.'

'Fuck off, Nogger. It's just speculation. Look, it says here that they "refused to confirm". That means they haven't said nothing. Just rumours and the papers making it up.' Nogger rereads it slowly, sounding out the syllables and running his fingers under the words. 'They're just trying to put pressure on. They release us from the jug and then say that we've grassed so we'll turn on each other. Classic cut-throat defence. Mind games.'

Nogger isn't getting it. 'But that article basically says Jay has been chatting shit to guards inside.'

'Do you remember when we used to get nicked by Vaderis? They'd give you a slap and then drop you off in Crocky so you had to walk home through enemy territory? Well, that's what the CPA are trying to do us in this article. Make Jay out as a grass, an informant, then drop him off back in the endz. And you're falling for it, playing right up to it.'

'See where you're going now.'

Dylan reads the last few lines. 'Look, it says that the CPA have now officially taken over the Chalina case from the police. Do you know what that means?'

'No.'

'Means the police don't like it. Another humiliation. Not only have they been kicked out the Jez, they've been kicked off the Chalina case. The CPA are just making out they're doing the business where the police couldn't. Politics, lad.'

'Clever cunt, you.'

Dylan gets rid of Nogger. He knows that he's only got 24 hours to save Jay, before tomorrow's papers reveal more. Dylan slips through The Boot, over the border fence and out of the Gang Exclusion Zone, back into the city.

Everything seems normal. Cars going by, ice-cream van serving hot dogs up to the kids, council workies digging up the roads. He walks around the streets on the perimeter of the Zone to the checkpoint. Outside, the usual protests are going on: anti-globalisation people, anti-martial law campaigners, climate-change folk and flower punks, the United Campaign Against Security Force Violence.

The human-rights lawyer who tried to reach out to him before is making a speech condemning the killings of Lupus and Clegsy. Dylan hoods up to avoid the CPA official photographers and cops for her when she's finished. 'Remember me? I'm one of the lads who's been accused of killing Chalina. You said I could come to you if I wanted to fight back.'

'Yes, I remember.'

'Well, I've got something for you.' Dylan tells her about the rendition, the Greyrock prison and the torture, about how Jay had made a confession while he was being tortured. She immediately says that Jay's statement will be worthless in court because it was given under duress. Dylan tells her about the waterboarding and gives her a signed statement about what happened. The next day, it's all over the papers.

CHALINA SUSPECT TORTURE SCANDAL
Gang Members Accuse CPA of Prison Abuse
'I was waterboarded' says teenager

Three teenagers linked to the murder of Chalina Murphy claim they have been tortured by private military contractors.

One 14-year-old boy says he was forced to sign a false confession after being beaten up and humiliated by American guards employed by the CPA. Two others say they were waterboarded, a controversial interrogation technique first used on al-Qaeda terrorist suspects.

The boys, none of whom can be named for legal reasons, say they were abducted from the street in Norris Green's Gang Exclusion Zone and taken away to a secret detention facility.

A spokesperson for the Youth Crime Task Force said that passive rendition of TerrorCrime suspects is permissible under new security legislation, adding: 'Youths characterised as Incongruous Social Enablers as defined by the S41 Emergency Powers Act can be detained indefinitely without charge. However, their rights are protected by the TerrorCrime tribunals.'

But officials at the Zone's governing body, the CPA, denied that any torture had taken place. CPA High Representative Robin Farquharson said: 'Torture of community combatants does not take place. I have complete confidence in our security partners Greyrock. They are professional operatives who have served in the most challenging disharmony zones around the world. They have fulfilled their contractual obligations in accordance with UK law, subject to the Emergency Powers Act and the TerrorCrime legislation.

'Since the CPA took over operational duties from the army and Merseyside Police, under the Youth Crime Task Force mandate, incidences of TerrorCrime have fallen by 37 per cent. TerrorCrime arrests are up by 75 per cent. Stop-and-strip searches have doubled. The population is secure and happier by a factor of two-thirds.'

GANG WAR

Dylan's buzzing. *Thrown a pure spanner in the works.* The scandal explodes the following day. All the papers and TV stations are running the story. The *Mirror*'s headline is 'Torture of the Scallyban'. The press pack is back with a vengeance. Loads of TV crews and journalists flood into the Gang Exclusion Zone, despite TerrorCrime reporting restrictions.

Dylan blows them out as usual. As he comes out of his front gate, off to the greasy spoon for his brekkie, the bird from the *Mail* is suck-holing him again. 'How does it feel to be a hero?'

Dylan, hood up, just says, 'No comment.'

The reporter from *The Sun* asks, 'Will you back *The Sun*'s campaign to stop child torture?'

In the café, Dylan flicks on Sky News, tells the auld ones who were watching *Treasure Hunt* to fuck off. Farquharson is being grilled by a reporter again, unruffled but clearly on the ropes.

'Are you categorically denying that your security forces tortured British teenagers?' asks the reporter.

'All community combatants held under TerrorCrime are treated in accordance with emergency powers legislation.'

'But does that amount to torture, High Representative?'

'No. Under anti-TerrorCrime laws we are allowed to use enhanced techniques when questioning suspects, and that is perfectly appropriate.'

An expert is drafted in to explain 'enhanced techniques' in the next on-the-hour bulletin. 'For years,' the pundit says, 'our communities have suffered from a wall of silence. Gang members will not inform on their mates. Using an alternative set of procedures during debriefings, we are able to extract vital intelligence. These procedures are saving lives. Since alternative interrogation procedures have been introduced, there has not been another significant Terror Crime murder. There has not been another Chalina.'

All the older ones, the same ones who attacked the lads at the pub during Chalina's memorial concert, have been praising them, calling them heroes. A select committee launches an inquiry into Greyrock's 'legally problematic techniques'.

The next day, *The Guardian*'s headline is 'Six Guards Arrested in Torture Probe': 'Six employees of CPA security forces have been suspended as part of the mounting investigation.' On Sunday, the *News of the*

RELEASE

World reports on pictures and videos discovered on the suspended guards' phones, showing Dylan being waterboarded, a naked Iggo being walked like a dog around a cell and Jay wearing a Ku Klux Klan hood and being wired up to a battery. For the time being, the case against the lads has completely collapsed.

PART THREE

ON CAMPAIGN

CHAPTER 29

MILITAI

'You're going to have to get off,' says Paul McQuillum, shovelling his breakfast into his mouth.

'Why?' asks Dylan bluntly, not as deferential nowadays.

'Because you're roasting.'

'But they can't do fuck all.'

'Doesn't matter, my mate.'

'We haven't even been nicked properly yet.'

'I know, but I can't help you. You're going to have to skedaddle.'

'No forensics. No witnesses. No statements. Nothing.'

'On your toes. You know it's best.'

'Fuck all, the bizzies have got. Specially after all that torture carry-on. Can't touch us.' But Dylan knows he's onto a loser. The Imperator has decreed it. That's that.

Two teas are brought over in cuboid Philippe Starck teapots. The Imperator shakes hands with the waiter, slots him a fiver.

'It doesn't flippin' matter, lad,' he tells Dylan again. 'The army are back on the streets. The city's locked down, lad. Looks like flippin' Goose Green out there.'

He starts throwing his voice and slurring his words now, tells Dylan about the SIM card that he robbed for him. It was worth £250,000. Now it's worth flippin' nothing, says the Imperator, cos there's a drought on. The Government have got GCHQ monitoring calls, they've even had the navy searching ships in the estuary. 'Never mind all the swabs and the sensors rattling the punters,' says McQuillum, shaking his head, embarrassed at having to talk openly about graft.

'Not our fault the arse has fell out of it,' says Dylan.

'Know it's not *you*, mate. Know it's not you personally. Know the other thing with the poor kid was just an accident, at the end of the day. But it doesn't matter what *I know*. It's what *you're doing* that's important. And at the moment, you being here is interfering with business. Our business, mate. The flippin' olive oil business. You know what I'm talking about.' The Imperator's trying to be diplomatic, not stand on the young ones' toes. But Dylan can see his patience running out. He says nothing.

'Listen,' the Imperator continues, 'nothing can move, lad. Kids are starving, lad. Not one ounce of graft. Hundreds of families rely on the smooth running of things. D'you get me? It's not just me. I'm happy. Doesn't matter whether I've got this carpet or that carpet. But others aren't as . . . capable as me.'

Dylan's not that arsed about other grafters' problems. But the Imperator keeps pressing home his point, trying to get into Dylan's head, although he doesn't want to go for any last resorts just yet. He starts talking in code: 'Lad, there in Rotterdam, we've got 500 new shirts [500 kilos] on a rail [in a container]. School ones, pale shades [cocaine]. Lined up on the docks like a row of new cars. Can't get it away. No one will go near it.'

'Paul, why?' asks Dylan. 'I'll go and get it. Give us the keys and I'll pull it out and get it back if I have to drive it meself.'

'The problem is there's fleets of flippin' helicopters flying up and down the Mersey. All hands are complaining to me. Asking me to do this, asking me to do that, asking me the other.'

Dylan's onto the mid-powwow pay-off straight away. He means they've been asking him to *do* Dylan, asking him to *do* Nogger, asking him to *do* Jay. The big firms have been asking the Imperator to exterminate the rats so that they can get back to business. Dylan looks at Paul but he's getting nothing.

'You've brought heat onto the whole city. The whole country. I warned you, mate, didn't I? At the funeral parlour, mate. To stop all this cowboys and Indians behaviour with the gangs. But you wouldn't listen. No, youse have brought it on top for everyone. First with the accident, then being in the papers, now upsetting the CPA. People are asking me to sort it out.'

'But it'll calm down.' Dylan's living on borrowed time, seeing the writing on the wall. *Got to sort this one. Can't have him on my case.*

The Imperator's getting a bit aerated now. 'You don't understand. It goes deeper than the graft. You and your flippin' gang are upsetting our friends. D'you get me?' Dylan's stung by the Imperator's disrespect of the gang. 'The CPA, Farquharson, they're our mates now, Dylan. My partners. My company's bidding for the contracts to rebuild The Boot, for miles around. It's gonna be the new Canary Wharf, mate. We're trying to put something back. And you're trying to take it away. D'you get me? You're fucking it up cos you've just embarrassed our mates. Letting Farquharson down like that.' He's so angry he's almost spitting his tea out. Dylan's shocked now at Paul half losing it, shocked to hear Paul swearing.

'Listen, Dylan,' he says, 'you've got to get on your toes. I'll set you up over in the Flat Place. All three of youse. Get you some good graft there. Put you to some proper people. I mean proper.'

Dylan has to weigh it up. Is it straightforward graft? Or is he trying to get them out the way so that he could have them dropped quietly, where no one will know. *End up washed up on a beach in Spain. Or bits of me floating in a canal.*

He looks straight at Paul. Hands on his knees, palms up. Interrogation position. Neutral. Giving fuck all away.

* * *

Before he leaves, Dylan has got one thing to do. He goes to Elizabeth's flat and knocks on the door. There's no answer, just like he'd suspected. He tracks down her landlord and he tells him that she left months ago. But he gives him an old address he has for her. Dylan goes to Cerne Abbas on his way to the ferry to Europe.

He knocks on the door.

Her dad answers. 'Hello.' Dylan just stands there. 'Can I help you?'

'Is Elizabeth in?'

'I'm afraid she's not here.'

Her mother appears behind him. 'Hello,' she says tentatively. 'Are you a friend of Elizabeth's?'

'Yeah. I met her at The Place . . . erm, the library.'

Her mother smiles. Dylan can see Elizabeth's beauty in her. She seems pleased that someone has come all the way down from Liverpool to see Elizabeth. The couple seem lonely and startled, old before their time. House empty, too big, kids all gone.

There's a few awkward silences and false starts, as though they're trying to tell him something but holding back. Dylan feels sure he knows what's coming next. Elizabeth is dead. He's sure of it. He closes his eyes, welling up.

'Are you feeling all right?' her dad asks.

'I'm really, really sorry.'

'About what?'

'About Elizabeth.'

'It's not your fault,' says her mum. 'You weren't to know she wasn't here.'

'What?'

'She's gone to live abroad.'

Dylan opens his eyes. 'Abroad. What? Where the fuck's she gone?'

'I'm sorry, what did you say?' asks her dad.

She tells him, 'She's gone to teach in France, something to do with an American college over there, but that's all she told us. We haven't heard from her since she left. We're terribly worried about her. Something happened to her at university. She came back here in a terrible state, but she wouldn't talk about it.'

He's off into the night, over a fence and back up the hill with the giant's cock on it.

CHAPTER 30

THE FLAT PLACE

Dylan's sitting off in a backstreet square in The Dam. It's a sunny day, but the stone's still moist from a summer shower. The plane trees are damp and shady. Dylan's enjoying a morning coffee. Easy living, Holland-style. Watching the yummy mummies pushing space-age prams, blimping the students going in and out of the little shops. They make him think of Elizabeth.

He's not arsed with the brass-houses and the coffee shops. Jay and Nogger have been on a bender every day for weeks now, the pair of them doing nothing but drinking, smoking, sleeping and whoring. Nogger and Jay ran amok at first, kicking fuck out the Algerian pimps, shivving mouthy punters from Germany. There were running battles in the streets with Albanian traffickers, fighting and shooting with Hells Angels and mad traveller families at their weddings. Now, though, they've settled into a routine. 'Doesn't it ever get boring?' Dylan asks them, half smiling. *In the darkened parlours, shagging and stinking in there all day and night.* 'Youse are like pigs in shit,' he tells them.

Nogger and Jay bowl up to the café with Wade. He's 23, on his toes for a murder back home, but grafting in Holland with Dean's crew now. Scrunched up Rizlas and bags of White Widow and Northern Lights are falling out of Nogger and Jay's pockets. They're laughing like kids, still can't believe it's legal. They chat shit with Dylan for a bit but then they're straight over to the brasses.

They're shagging pale, skinny Moldovans two at a time. Nogger goes mad for their tight, baldy fannies and their wide moon faces, which he likes coming across, aiming onto the planes of their cheeks with his jizzum, then slapping their bony arses with his red-raw cock. Nogger doesn't even wear a bag. 'You worry too much about the test on the blood,' he says to the young girls, laughing, not even paying them extra for a natural spurt up them. He bends their rickety legs over their heads and pokes them from up top. 'By sitting on them, facing the other way,' Nogger explains. 'Like in a bluey.'

Jay joins in, literally. Says he does a bit of sword-fighting with Nogger. 'One up the fanny, one up the arse,' he says.

'Shut up, you dirty little cunt,' says Dylan, 'you're only 15.' Nogger calls Jay a 'smelly-fingered little twat'. Jay rags him back by saying that he could feel Nogger's cock inside one of the brasses and it was tiny. Nogger tries to dig him on the top of the arm, laughing so he nearly spits his joint out. 'Cheeky little twat,' he says, crumbs of glowing pot falling from the joint onto the freshly sluiced pavement. Wade chips in, 'Fuck off, Jay, you're barely old enough to get your grabs off a little sprouter, never mind acting the goat.' Jay says that he's 'cosmopolitan' now that he's moved to The Dam. Where the fuck he picked that up from, no one knows.

Graft's going well. Dylan's working hard during the day, grafting for Dean as a runner. In the first few months, he was just vacuum-packing gear all day, nine to five, in a food-processing unit on an industrial estate somewhere just north of the city. When he first turned up, one of the other lads threw him a white paper Noddy suit, a hairnet and a pair of wellies. They burned the overalls at the end of each day. 'Just like working in a chicken factory, innit?' the lad said. Dylan wrapped a tonne of skunk a week, a tonne of pollum hash, 50 kilos of coke and 60 of heroin. Day in day out, for months.

But Paul sorted out some better wages for him. He was promoted to transport: driving furniture vans all over Holland and Belgium, loading them up with groupage – parcels of Es, coke, brown and cannabis – then handing them over to sweating, arse-gone lorry drivers in Rotterdam, Utrecht and Antwerp, telling them to fucking drive, twatting them with tyre levers if they threatened to cry off. 'That's the problem with using freelancers,' Dean told him. Dylan said that one of the cry-offs would go to the bizzies one day if they were pushed too hard. Dean laughed, confided in him that he's got no choice because he's been forced to get his own transport. 'Got to,' he said, 'because the Dutch and Irish control the lorries and the ports. But the Dutch are dubious about us now cos so much of the gear was being had off by robbing twats like you.' Dylan laughed. 'They won't graft with us any more,' Dean said.

On the other hand, he told Dylan, the Turks, Colombians and Moroccans love his crew because of their work ethic. He says that the Turks and South Americans aren't bothered by scallies from back home robbing too much of their gear because they factor in losing 'so many million' every year anyway. They know that little cunts like Nogger and Jay are going to have them off, but as long as the big parcels get through, it's happy days, he says. And, of course, it goes without saying that they must get paid on time.

Now Dylan spends his days cutting up lead ingots full of gear from Venezuela and Mexico on industrial estates in the Benelux, dripping sweat over the jackhammers, oxy-burners and metal saws. Or he's running bags of money to be wired and washed, sitting in the basements of travel agents and currency shops counting up stacks of Kellogg's boxes with £200,000 carefully layered inside each one. Dylan keeps the burned or ripped notes himself because the money-washers won't accept them.

Sometimes he has to meet up with Khalid and Azzam, the Bradford lads with their flash trackies, their £3,000-a-day rented Ferraris and their hawala transactions reaching from corner shops in Keighley to Dubai and Hyderabad. Scary how much money leaves England on a Monday, says Wade, to pay for gear received before the weekend from Holland.

At first, Dylan lived in a graft flat but he's just moved in with Wade, into a tall townhouse overlooking some wooden barges with little gardens and fences on them. The price of property in The Dam is ruthless, says Wade. Of a night, they go to the City Bar with all the lads. Danny, the Bengali Mancunian who used to graft with the Turks, was shot in here, says Wade. 'Only 25, he was.' Then it's all off to Chopsticks for a Chinese. There's so many of them that it's just table after table of grafters letting on to each other. They're on the run or they've been chased out of the Gang Exclusion Zones. They've got their own five-a-side league, a team for each of the neighbourhoods back home. Dylan plays for Ajax Nogzy, fully kitted out in a brand-new Real Betis strip that one of the lads brought home from a bit of graft in Andalusia. The league's sponsored by a sandwich shop Wade's just bought as a front.

Wade says that you need a little business over here to show that you've got a legit income. Dylan's stashed £90,000 in three different banks so far – a Spanish one, an Irish one and one based in Liechtenstein. Wade says that once you've got over 100 quid you've got to get a front to wash it so the Dutch revenue won't be on your case. They all used to be sunbed shops, he says, but the lads are bang into franchises now. You can get a fast-food business for £30,000, he lets on. He knows the score, does Wade.

Sitting in Chopsticks one night he tells Dylan and Nogger, 'I'm gonna buy a pawn shop franchise next time, because you get four businesses in one – the pawn shop, a money-wiring bureau, a retail outlet and a cheque-cashing counter. That's four ways to make money. But the franchise on that is 750,000 euros.' Wade's talking big now but Nogger thinks he's talking about French fries not franchise. He says he's gonna buy a Mackie D's when he's brewstered. Wade tells him that the franchise on that is a million. But Nogger's lost interest. Suddenly he's running outside, down the street. He comes back with his knuckles bleeding, says he clocked a lad from Crocky walking past so he ran out and twatted him. 'Bet the rat thought he wouldn't get caught slipping in Amsterdam, didn't he?'

The next day is shopping day. Dylan comes back to the flat with three bags from Lidl, gets buzzed off heavily. 'Got to go to Marksies to buy your scran, you meff,' says Richard, Dean's deputy. He's turned up at the flat saying he needs some workers. Richard is worth £100 million plus. He drives round in an old Zafira back home, but he's a proper flash cunt once he's over in The Dam.

Dylan laughs but he's got half a cherry on over the shame of going to the Lidl. Nogger and Jay swap daggers. Nogger would drop Richard now, if he could. Cut his head off with a kitchen knife. Does not give a fuck how much he's worth. No one calls one of the lads a meff. But Dylan sees his face and warns him not to slaughter the golden goose. Not just yet, anyways. Dylan's whispering to him in front of the widescreen telly: 'Take the graft off him. He's looking for workers.' Nogger holds his tongue.

The next day, Dylan pops into Marks. Sure enough, all the lads are bombing round the aisles with their birds, showing off, trolleys piled high with Chinese chicken wings, ready meals, Viennese whirls, salads for the birds. 'The lads won't shop anywhere else but Marksies,' Wade had explained to him. 'Got to have Marksies scran cos they've got to have the best, haven't they?'

The birds are talking dead loudly, letting everyone know they're there, tottering across the tiles in their high heels, wearing slashed tops flown in from Cricket. They're on their cocaine hangovers, massive sunglasses on to soothe away the glare from the strip lights.

THE FLAT PLACE

Dylan flashes back to Casey, almost shudders at the memory of her, but doesn't know whether he's just shivering because it's cold walking by the chiller cabinets or if it's because she was such a fucking horror. But then he gets a semi on in the frozen-foods aisle, the heavy, misted-up doors of the double freezers reminding him of her window-licking in the steam room when he was getting stuck up her at the hotel. Dylan pulls open one of the freezer doors and takes out a box of fish fingers. *The dirty slag.*

CHAPTER 31

THE WORLD IS YOURS

Over the next few months, Dylan moves up the hierarchy bit by bit. Nogger complains that there was never any hierarchy back home. Everyone just grafted with each other, he says. Which is true, as far as it goes. But on campaign, there's a strict pyramid. Dean is number one, in the field, anyway, Richard his number two. Of course, the whole thing falls under Paul's umbrella. Run from back home, it is. No one would dispute the Imperator's strategic significance. Then below the lot of them are the lieutenants, one of which Dylan is rapidly becoming. Some have specific departments, like transport, security, money. Others are general runabouts like Dylan. Then below the middlemen are the workers, your bog-standard grafters like Nogger and Jay.

Dylan fills up scaff pipes with long strips of cocaine, then sorts out the bills of lading for port officials by fax and email from moody hotels or Internet cafés owned by mad Russians. Dean lets him do bits of paperwork now and again.

In the evenings, after Chopsticks it's on to Escape, all the little firms letting on to each other. Dylan says that the lads might as well be back home cos they do the exact same things. Escape is just a Dam version of the Cream.

He cops for an American tourist backpacking round Europe. She's nice but he can't shag her cos he can't stop thinking about Elizabeth. Even though he's peeled her jeans off within five minutes of getting back to the kennel and she's walking round the cream carpet with a pair of pink cotton knickers with a little blue ribbon at the front on, smoking a weed and playing on the Wii. He boots her out at seven in the morning, then goes down to one of the Irish bars in the drizzle. They're the only places you can get a decent English brekkie, says Wade, and a decent roast on a

Sunday. Dylan, Nogger and Jay have never had a roast before, but they're settling in to the good life with the lads in The Dam now. Easy living.

Dylan tries searching for Elizabeth on the Internet but all of her MySpace, Facebook and YouTube pages are frozen in time, on the day of the rape. Dylan pores over the old photos on her Facebook. There are no videos of her but he plays a few of the links he finds on her YouTube channel, things that she must have liked, buzzed off. One shows two Belgian girls dancing about madly to a Coldplay song; another, from Germany, is a montage of romantic photos set to a jangly '90s indie hit. They remind Dylan of her.

Then there's sales and marketing. Dylan goes out on the piss with the diesel Mercs from Green Lanes, North London Turks who look foreign but speak with thick Cockney accents. Dean tells him to take care of them. Dylan lays on 300-euro-a-pop brasses for them. Then, while they're getting their cocks sucked, Dylan loads up a bottle of Cristal with eight grams of charlie, so it goes down their throats nice and numb. Later, they sort out the details for a 110-kilo load of brown, to go through Paris in a coach full of folk dancers from Anatolia.

Then there's the Tony Montanas, the South Americans. The most important ones, the VIPs. Mario and Ortez, salesmen for the Mexicans in Europe. Hector from Cali. He takes them to the match with all the lads in a rented Gulfstream, cos they're footie mad. Six-star hotels, panoramic views, two grand a night spent on Chinese meals. All the top touts flying in to serve them up the best tickets in person, everyone trying to outdo each other, forcing Rolexes onto each other as gifts of lifelong friendship.

Loads of the Turks, South Americans and Moroccans live in a little town in the Randstad region. Dylan gets to know a few of the black lads from Tocky who've set up there. Nogger won't have anything to do with them. Jay's not that arsed cos he's so cosmopolitan nowadays. Dylan likes grafting with them. The Tocky lads tend to do their own thing more. The light-skinned, mixed-race ones are good 'blenders' there, they tell him. They say they don't stand out in this little town cos they look like part of the local Turkish community.

Nogger and Jay aren't allowed front of house. Dean won't let them near the gear end of the job or anyone connected to it in case they rob one and tax the other. Nogger's not jealous of Dylan – not yet, anyway – but he wouldn't think twice about dropping Dean and Richard for lording it over him and Jay while bigging up Dylan with the same graft. 'Not on, is it,' says Nogger.

Dean keeps them at arm's length, farms them out to Richard cos he doesn't know what to do with two kiddies who are well known hotheads. Richard hates the pair of them but he can't do fuck all. Can't fuck them off or even wallop them on the sly, because they're on safe passage from the Imperator. Dean has warned him against any funny business. So he gives Nogger and Jay the moodiest jobs he can find in the hope they won't come back alive.

He sends Jay to iron out a 64-year-old Turkish *baba* outside a smoked-glass casino on the Antwerp seafront. Jay pushes him down an iron stairwell, the foam from the crashing waves lashing over them, and blasts him with a three-foot-long single-barrelled shotgun. The sound of the wind and the waves hid the blast, he tells Dylan later. Then he just walked off down the street and sat off in a park until he was picked up by his driver.

Richard can't believe it when Jay comes back from Antwerp alive. He's only 15. 'He's like the fucking Terminator,' Richard keeps telling everyone, scragging him by the head like he's a kid in a Sunday league team or a pet or something. Jay's waiting for Nogger or Dylan to give him the nod so he can put an end to the humiliation. Then he sends Jay to burn out an old mate of his in a terraced house in Amsterdam. Jay takes the slates off the roof, pours the petrol in and torches it. 'Like a fucking pro,' Richard says, bragging to his mates in Chopsticks.

Nogger's more of an enforcer. Richard drags him into all the firm's internecine wars in The Dam: shivving out-of-order Yardies, going on campaign with ex-'Ra gunmen to wallop Serbs who've stolen gear. Nogger loves it.

Richard tries to put the shits up Nogger before one job in Rotterdam: 'Some of those Jamaicans have killed 20 or 30 fellers back where they're from, you know? I mean, we know loads of lads who've ironed maybe three or four. But 20 to 30 is very unusual, you know.' Nogger laughs. He's not arsed about the stats. He comes back from the job with their thick gold chains spattered with blood as spoils. Richard starts to get Nogger involved in personal stuff, petty stuff between the lads.

After that, Dean moves his crew into the countryside, says it's too on top in The Dam now, with Richard using Nogger and Jay to drop his own workers.

'His own workers!' Dean rants at Dylan. 'Lads he grew up with. Lads who've arrived in The Dam on their toes with holes in their trainies, just looking for a bit of work. And he's getting Nogger to iron them out just for doing a bit of their own graft on the side. Not even robbing his gear – ours even, *our* gear – just making a few quid. I've told him to ease up, but he's got a fucking nasty streak in him, has Richard. Stay clear of him. And your mate. And stay out Marksies as well,' he says, spying Dylan loading up the fan oven with a sun-dried tomato quiche.

'Why?' Dylan asks.

'Because the bizzies are all over it,' Dean says. 'Are you backward or what?' He keeps saying 'Why?' over and over again, feigning astonishment at Dylan's naivety. Dylan laughs and Dean shakes his head in mock disgust.

He tells Dylan, 'Merseyside Police have got Level 3 capability now. There's fucking squadloads over here. And they don't have to work too hard to find youse – just sit outside of Marksies and follow you pricks back to your kens.'

Dylan's still laughing.

'Are you backward?' Dean asks again.

* * *

Easy living. In the countryside, Dylan gets up at half ten. First off, he spends 20 minutes scanning the fields surrounding their commuter mansion through the tripod-mounted binoculars on the top floor of the pale-yellow villa. He checks every bush and hedge for Customs and Excise, searches by the dyke and the canal for Dutch police surveillance, poring over the bland, featureless farmland that stretches for miles around. There are acres of tulip beds. Dean says that's why he bought this house – because he can see who's outside for miles. It's midway between The Dam and The Hague, in a neat little market town.

He gets himself a bowl of Kellogg's, lashes the empty box in the counting room, tramps back to his sleeping bag in the corner of one of the bare, unfurnished rooms. Like all the others, the nine or ten grafters who are here working for Dean, he's kipping on the floor. There are a few flat-screens and laptops dotted about, but mostly their possessions are limited to little piles of shit next to their sleeping bags: ciggies, hardcore Dutch porn mags, key fobs for the anonymous Euro saloons they drive round in – company cars for the Continent's number-one cocaine firm.

GANG WAR

Dylan doesn't like the other lads on Dean's new firm. They're a ragtag of fat-faced jailbirds on the run from all over Britain, cold and twice his age. They've got faces you could strike matches on and they're stinking. They'll wear the same old trackies four days running. They've been in prison that much that they can't wear anything tight around their balls.

Haden's there. Britain's first crack dealer, trying to get back on his feet with Dean's wages. Dylan recognises him from the night in the park when he chopped up One Arm. Haden doesn't get onto Dylan because he had a hood on that night. He spends his free time doing weights in the gym, wearing a dirty leotard and an acid-house bandana, chatting shit about back home, like how B&Q's a bit pricey if you're doing up your house.

There's not much to do in the day. They just laze around watching the satellite. All the grafters in Holland have got Sky boxes so they can watch all the same shit they watch back in England. 'Need little things like that, don't you?' Wade says. 'To make life comfortable when you're on campaign.'

One afternoon, Ste Ellis suddenly jumps up. 'Shall we all go fishing?' So they all troop out to go fishing in the canal, swigging cans of lager. But Ste keeps getting paranoid about a Dutch angler who repeatedly uses the wrong bait. 'Definitely customs, him,' Ste says. In the end, he phones Dean to tell him that he thinks they're under surveillance by a plain-clothes officer disguised as a fisherman. Dean laughs and tells him that he's off for a massage.

The next day, they all go ratting around the dykes. Dean comes along to take a look at the suspect fisherman. He brings the Neapolitan mastiffs that he's just bought as guard dogs. He's on the phone all the time, first to a South American scrap dealer who's selling them X-ray-proof lead ingots so that they can drill them out in Venezuela and stuff them up with a tonne of cocaine each. Meanwhile, Yorkshire Phil is setting the dogs on the wildlife in the scrub. They're chasing otters up the muddy banks and crunching their heads. Then Dean rings up a Bulgarian feller to tell him off about a winery he's bought outside of Sofia.

Suddenly, they see the moody angler by the canal again. Stephen sets the dogs on him straight away. 'Now we'll see if he's kosher,' he says. The dogs maul his face. Yorkshire Phil pushes him in the canal and throws his flask and keep net in after him. Dean is still doing business on the phone, has to cover the handset and say, 'Don't be doing that, you pricks. You'll bring it on top for everyone.' He climbs out the other side with his cheek hanging off from the dog bite, in shock. It turns out the feller's not customs after all, but a sheet-metal worker from Ostend enjoying a few days off. Yorkshire Phil tries to say he's sorry from the other bank. Ste robs his rod. Then they all head back, still swigging lager.

That evening, Dylan fills up the plastic roof of an old Land Rover with vacuum-packed skunk and drives it to the Hook of Holland to hand it over to some lads from Bolton.

Next day, Dean's sat in the jacuzzi in the tasteless pine-panelled gym under the mansion. The water's foamy and greasy because none of the lads ever clean it, jizzum and hair-dye stains from the cheap brasses Stephen uses all up the sides. The steam room and sauna is dark and dusty because no one has sussed how to work it. Damien's in there putting a new bulb in one of the '70s-style heat lamps. He's a divvy doorman with a stripy top on and a fierce false smile, suck-holing Dean for more graft.

Svetlana, Dean's favourite brass, swans in, a purple silk dressing gown clinging to her small tits. She's got a little pot belly but she's as fit as a fiddle. She starts arranging her things on the pine rack – johnnies, massage oil, KY jelly, hand cream, a nice Dutch dildo that Dean likes to get stuck up her if he can't shag her cos he's on the phone.

'Gonna get blew off in a minute, mate,' he tells Damien.

Damien puts his stepladder down and says, 'Best way, isn't it, mate?'

Dean has arranged to have his new Merc delivered straight from the factory. He says that he never buys a car from a showroom now cos it gives the bizzies a chance to put a listening probe in. He's sending a private detective he knows to pick the car up from Germany. Dylan says he'll go as well. Him and the private detective drive it back to Holland. Turns out the PI is an ex-para. Dylan tells him about when they used to fight the paras in the Gang Exclusion Zone. The feller says that it's calmed down a bit now back home. Says that the Government have got what they want now. The army's in seven cities now and the police forces are all armed, with special powers of arrest. There's a new division of militarised police that's half army, half bizzies, 'like the Carabinieri,' he says.

After they bring it back to the villa, the PI strips the car down and scans it to make double sure. Then Dean asks him to debug the mansion. It turns out he's able to track people down as well. Dylan asks him to find Elizabeth, but two weeks later he says that there's no trace of her. Dylan gives him a good drink for trying and says that if he ever does get an address, he'll pay 30,000 euros for it.

CHAPTER 32

FRANCE

One of Dean's partners turns up from back home, a drugs financier who puts up millions to underwrite shipments. His hair's in a greying wedge he must have had since the 1980s, but he's well groomed, sporting casual golf wear from Florida. Dylan's onto him straight away: shrewd ex-docker type, started off by grafting out of the port, been en route from day one.

Dylan's met a lot of higher-ups but the banker's in a different league. Most heavy hitters are on a conveyor belt: graft, make brewster's, go to jail; come out, graft, make brewster's, go to jail; come out, graft, make brewster's, and so on. But this one's done less jug than Dylan and Nogger put together and he's three times older. Even the taxman back home can't get on him.

The banker asks Dean to send a worker down to Paris to make a bank transfer. Dylan's spider sense goes into overdrive. France means Elizabeth. Dean asks the lads for a volunteer. They're in the kitchen, eggs and bacon on the go, keeping their heads down. None of them wants to do the business. France is too on top for their moody passports and false IDs these days. 'Especially for messing around in banks,' moans Yorkshire Phil. They're scooting about and making themselves look busy now that there's proper graft to be done.

Dean goes off on one, calls them shithouses, says he doesn't fucking know why he pays them so much to sit around, to go fishing, when there's graft on the go. Then to save face, he ribbons Yorkshire Phil in front of the banker and the lads, tells the banker how Yorkshire Phil took his bird with him *to help him buy a new car*. 'Can you believe that? Taking your bird with you to buy a car. He's backward.' Guffawing from the lads. Yorkshire Phil blows up crimson, sheepishly not looking up from his frying pan full of eggs.

The banker shakes his head. 'You take your mates with you to buy a car, not your bird.' He taps his foot against the side of the kitchen table, mug of tea on the go, hands in his slacks, pretending he's doing a bit of tyre-kicking.

'And that's not the worst of it,' says Dean. 'Holding hands with her, he was, yesterday. On the couch. *In the daytime*. Can you believe that?'

'I'd sack the lot of them, Dean. I can't believe what I'm hearing.'

Dylan sees his opening, butts in: 'I'll go to Paris for youse. Give us the paperwork and I'll front it.' The lads are sniding looks at Dylan, jealous of him because he doesn't even look like he's trying to suck-hole.

The banker turns to him suspiciously. 'You're the lad who Paul sent over, aren't you? The one that was involved in *the accident*.'

Dylan says fuck all about that, just asks him, 'D'you want your graft doing or what?'

Dean smiles. The banker takes out a bank statement, scribbles some instructions down on the back. 'Once you've read that and got your head round the numbers, give the piece of paper back to Dean.' He looks Dylan in the eye. 'And I mean memorise the accounts before you go. Ring it in when you've done it.'

'Nice one, Dylan,' says Dean, laughing. 'I knew I could rely on you.'

Dylan gets off early doors the next day. It's still dark when he leaves. He jumps a sea-green bendy bus. The day-glo sign on the front says Schiphol. It winds through the thin, spindly streets, passes the canals and the rows of bikes. Black skies over the flat roofs.

Schiphol's busy with backpackers and school trips, kids crashed all over the departure lounge. A few business types are propping up the breakfast bars, drinking beers and eating cheese rolls. Dylan feels tired and trippy, his mouth dry, off the early start, but the space-age fountains and modern art wake him up a bit. He pays cash for a mid-morning flight to Charles de Gaulle, breezes through security with a mad Jersey passport stamped up with a jarg Schengen visa.

In Paris, he checks into the Hotel Costes first off, but quickly decides the other guests are sneering pricks – a few footballer-player types in there. It's too high profile, anyway. So he gets off to the Normandy Hotel to get lost amongst the tourists. He sits off in his room, curtains blowing in the warm air, then lazes around in the brasseries near the Opera and Bastille.

Dylan takes a walk past the bank and goes through the drill. The graft looks straightforward. A transfer from the Dutch Antibes to Paris,

22 million euros. Dean and the Banker wouldn't tell him what it was about, but he collared Wade on the sly before he left to see if he thought it was too mad, to ask him if he was being set up. Wade told him that it was 'pretty safe', as long as Dylan looked and spoke the part.

'What d'you mean?' Dylan asked.

'Listen, you're not going over the counter, lad. It's white-collar stuff. You'll be all right. It's money-washing, that's all. Pinging money between one computer and another. But the older ones won't go near it in case someone's following the money. Plus Dean is half-caste and this is a white man's game. Stick a white boy in front of the bank manager – that's what he's used to. You've just got to fill in a few forms and wait around until the dough lands. Fill in a few more, then send it on to wherever they want it stashed.'

Dylan was still a bit suss. 'What if it goes wrong and I'm stuck inside the bank?' Thinking about it in the cold light of day, after he'd said he'd do it, his arse had gone a bit. It was a big risk to take just to hang around in France on the off chance he might bump into Elizabeth.

'It'll be all right if you do it right,' Wade reassures him. 'Don't go in like a scruff. Pretend you're an accounts clerk for a big company or something like a cashier, who does this day in, day out. The bods in the bank won't give a fuck as long as the paperwork looks shipshape and they're getting their wire fees and all that bollocks.'

Wade filled him in on the back story. Dean had got stuck with 40 million pounds' worth of out-of-date Dutch guilders that he couldn't change over when the euro had come in 2002.

'Wow, fuck's sake,' said Dylan.

'Telling you, they'd kept their money in guilders and not pounds for storage reasons. Back then, guilders came in 1,000 fl. notes worth around £300 each – high-denomination notes so the cash piles were smaller and could be moved round or buried easier. They thought they were being clever but they got caught with their pants down big-style when the Euro came in and they had all this buried dough that couldn't be changed up.'

'So what's that got to do with me?'

'They've paid a little crew of ex-Dutch marines to take the old guilders bit-by-bit over to the Dutch Antibes, where some dodgy banks'll still change them up – but at a huge loss. The hard graft is getting it wired back into the Eurozone and cleaned up. So that's you. That's your graft. When it lands in Paris, you've got to sign the paperwork to get it sent off again, on to fuck knows where, so that the trail is clean. D'you get me?'

'I get you.'

Before Dylan left, Dean offered to get him make-upped up with a prosthetic mask specially made by some pop-video people they knew in Belgium. But Dylan thought it would look even madder, sitting in a smoked-glass bank in Paris with a mad mask on. So he laughed and said no. 'Just in case you felt a bit exposed,' Dean said, 'sitting in there on your tod. Just looking out for you, kidder.'

Dylan wanders round the Left Bank near the Sorbonne, hoping he might see Elizabeth, pining to see her badly now. But nothing. He phones up a few places, a few universities, runs her name by the offices. But no joy because he doesn't speak French. He gets fucked off by snooty French women cos he's a bit nervous on the phone.

Then he gets back to the graft, goes and buys a nice 800-euro suit from a decent shop on the rue Saint-Honoré. Gets it fitted properly, double-cuff shirt, silk tie, decent pair of slippery-soled brogues. He goes for a shave, sauna and steam at a posh health club he's found in the 2nd arrondissement, near the Stock Exchange. He still looks young, but he's half smart now.

The first visit to the bank goes off OK. He's shown into an old office. Everyone speaks English. Dylan reactivates the account the banker told him about. It's in the name of a wine-shipping company that has offices in France, Bulgaria and Chile. Dylan scans the recent transactions while he waits. Four million euros came in from Chile two weeks ago. And before that 7.2 million from a big leisure chain in the Bahamas. Dylan guesses they're jarg transfers, legit money pumped through the account so it looks live and on the up and up. Dylan goes through the instructions, telling the woman that he's expecting a deposit of 22 million to land overnight, that he wants to move it on to the Bank of Sofia in Bulgaria. They fill in the computer forms together. The private banking manager tells him to come back in 24 hours.

He buys a second set of business clothes in case they think he's a scruff. But when he scopes the bank out the next day, he notices that it's a different woman at the desk he went to before. He spied the guards on the doors, whom he hadn't noticed yesterday.

He gets Dean on a safe sat phone number he's been given, bells him from a bar opposite the bank. 'I'm telling you, it's on top.'

'What are you on about?'

'It's not the same bird that was here yesterday, for a start. It's what's going on in the background, as well – security, all sorts. Just doesn't feel right, d'you know what I mean?'

Dean is calm, placatory: 'Listen, just go back in, will you, finish the fucking thing and come home? It's safe. You're imagining all this shit. We've been monitoring it from this end and there's no red flags. It's just nerves cos you're not used to this kind of graft.'

'Fuck off, Dean. Something's gone skew-whiff, telling you.'

'It's just the peasant in you. If I was asking to go over the pavement on it, you'd feel comfortable. That's what you're used to. But because it's business, proper fucking graft, you're fucking flummoxed by it.'

Maybe he's right. Or maybe Dean isn't arsed whether he gets nicked or not. Maybe Dylan's expendable. Either way, Dylan can't lose face in front of the lads. And if he backs out now, there'll be untold, not only for him but for Nogger and Jay as well. They'll either have to get on their toes or go back home, back into the Gang Exclusion Zone again, and deal with the Chalina thing. The spectre of the accident is a distant memory for him now. Strange how he hasn't thought about Chalina for months, as though it never happened.

He marches into the bank, right over to the foreign bureau, to the different woman. She's polite but firm, almost off-hand, speaks English. He signs the forms, she gets off. Dylan clocks the two security guards at the sliding doors. Foreign Legion types. They're wearing earpieces but they're unarmed. Dylan has to try hard to resist staring them out. He picks up copies of *Paris Match* and *Newsweek* to distract him while he waits.

The woman returns with two men and introduces one of them. 'There's an issue with your account,' she says. 'Would you care to step into the office?' Dylan thinks about making a run for the sliding doors. He might make it through the exit. At a push, he could ask to go for a piss and slip out. Tell them he has to move his car, whatever. But he thinks about the 22 million dangling there. He thinks about Chalina. His stomach churns. What would happen if he lost Paul, Dean and the banker 22 million euros? He could run. But Nogger and Jay would get dropped for sure. Tortured, dropped and burned. And Richard would love to do it.

Dylan fronts it out. Into the office. 'Would you like something to drink?' the woman asks him.

Dylan fucks her off. 'What's the problem?'

'It's not a problem as such. For now, anyway. It's purely administrative. We've noticed the recipient account has been dormant for a while, except for a couple of recent deposits.'

'Yes. So what?' He doesn't know what the fuck she's on about. The two men stand behind the woman, one looking over her shoulder at the computer, the other grim-faced.

'The account history is mostly concerned with transactions of a global nature – international transfers, some of which pass through unusual territories.' Dylan says nothing. 'We've noticed that the status of the account hasn't been reviewed for some time.'

'Yeah? What's your point?'

'Well, our personal banking arm can offer you a free review that might help save you and your company money.'

The cunts want to sell him insurance to guard against wire fraud or money getting frozen in dodgy banks. Dylan fronts it out. After fifteen minutes of spiel from the two men he buys eleven grand's worth of insurance and opens a premium online account that costs thirty-five hundred a year in fees. 'Just charge it to the account,' he says as he shakes hands with the salesman. The woman comes back with confirmation that the 22 million has been sent on to Sofia.

Everyone's happy. Dylan's buzzing.

Near the hotel, Dylan does three go-rounds of the neighbourhood to make sure he's not being followed, then he phones Dean on a pay-as-you-go number he's been given.

'Sorted.'

'Told you, didn't I? You little arse bottler,' says Dean, chiding him for nearly crumbling on the job.

Dylan tells him the story about buying the insurance.

'Eleven grand,' says Dean. 'Just like buying a toaster from Comet and them trying to sell you a five-year warranty on it. You were ripped there, lad.'

'Fuck off,' Dylan tells him, both of them laughing.

Dylan heads for a travel agent, one he'd seen earlier on a buzzing street near the hotel, to book his train ticket back to The Dam. He thinks about getting a sleeper to Germany first, then bouncing back to Holland through Belgium, either on a bus or in a hire car.

The travel agent woman is lovely. She's in an air-hostess-style uniform and a white shirt. Dylan blimps her bra through the see-through cotton. A silk scarf is tied around her neck and she's wearing a fruity perfume. She clocks Dylan perving off her, so he looks away at a poster on the wall, a picture of an old church on a hill with the word 'Lacoste' underneath. 'Is that where they make Lacoste shirts?' he asks, covering up his cherry-on at being caught blimping her.

'No,' she smiles, holding his gaze. 'That's a little village in the southern part of France. Are you familiar?' Dylan shakes his head. 'It's in a very beautiful, touristic place. But still very quiet. Most of the town is owned by an American university.'

Dylan's tummy rolls over. Her dad had mentioned an American college. 'A what?'

'They have an art school there. The town is very beautiful.'

Dylan knows that's where she is. 'How far is it?' he asks, his impatience showing in his voice already.

'A few hours on the train. I'll check. There's a high-speed link to Avignon. Then it's a branch line.'

Dylan throws 200 euros on the counter. 'Get me on the next one down there.'

CHAPTER 33

LACOSTE

Dylan's on the branch-line train in rural France. Wheels shuddering, night blackening, sky sparkling up. Deep blue-black space studded with crystal-clear diamonds. *Star Wars on Earth.*

The train clanks along the tracks, the polished wood and brass lampshades glinting. Dylan's crashed on a worn, bare bench. The only other person in the carriage is an old woman in a cardi, knitting. Dylan gets up and takes his tea out of his rucksack. He hasn't eaten since early this morning in Paris. Fresh baguette, big fuck-off block of cheese, two big brown bottles of foamy French beer. He cuts up the cheese with his kukri on a square of wax paper on the bench. He smiles at the loveliness of it, letting on to the auld biddy with his chunky sarnie, the first fuzzy glow of the ale kicking in beautifully.

He has a little kip until the train pulls up at a village called Rustrel. Dylan jumps off. He's decided to find somewhere to get his head down. In the warm night air, crickets are buzzing and pylons crackling.

Dylan follows a sign for a campsite, walking down the hill, out of town, through a trail of sandy bushes. The campsite's next to an old ochre quarry. Huge red and yellow cowboy-film rocks shoot up, glowing against the night sky. The girl in the reception shack says there are no small tents. Dylan pulls 200 euros off a wad and asks for a massive family tent that's already been set up. She smiles and walks him down the grass paths with a torch. Threw his bag on the metal-framed bed, then heads for the open-air restaurant. Even after the sarnie, he's still famished, the anticipation hollowing out his insides.

The night's full of promise and freedom. Ropes of fairy lights are hung like bunting around the restaurant. Dylan blimps the drop-dead French girls chatting with their families, playing cards, sipping Oranginas, scratching their arms. One comes over while Dylan's eating his pizza. Honey skin, sun-bleached hair, pale-blue shorts. 'How come you're alone?' she asks in perfect English, fearless, bursting with confidence.

Dylan's blown away. *How can you just walk up to someone like that?* Wondering where a girl like that might have come from, to have no fear. 'Better, isn't it?' he answers. 'Being on your tod.'

She laughs. 'Your tod? What's "tod"?'

Dylan laughs, tells her that he's just passing through, 'backpacking round the place'.

Her name's Agathe and she's 18. Dylan likes the fact that she still goes on holiday with her ma and da and younger brothers and sisters. Dylan just looks at her. The cooling night air's catching her nips, gently poking through her thin, white cardi. She doesn't look away.

'Bye-bye, funny English boy,' she says, turning round, giving him an extra-good blimp: sandy dust on her boyish shorts, dirt on her bare heels. She smiles and gets off.

The next morning, Dylan's up early for the final leg. He jumps in the open-air swimming pool, taking three run-ups to pluck it up for the freezing water, laughing at himself. Then he's cutting silently through the calmness, only dead mosquitoes bobbing on the surface for company.

The wooden gate clicks behind someone and he looks up. It's Agathe, a small white towel over her shoulder, wearing a brown, well-played-in nylon bikini. Dylan clocks the yellow waistband, almost loose across her waifish stomach. But her bikini top is a different story. The piping trim is stretched to the max, barely holding the weight of her plump tits. She's giving him a full-on view of her profile, throwing her hair over to one side, showing off a full hand's length of neck. Then she pulls her hair back and dives in like an athlete. Dylan knows it's all on, but he gets out, a semi-on clearly visible under the dripping, long black Valencia shorts.

He's off to the little bakery, a washed-out blue clapboard shed with a sign saying 'boulanje', to get some croissants and a loaf. He's decided to walk the rest of the way. He fills his flask with coffee, buys a map and gets off with his backpack on, his old green Peter Storm wrapped around his waist. He waves at the French family packing up their car. Agathe comes out of the shower block, hair wet, fruity conditioner, skinny jeans showing off her tummy, faded top showing off her tan. She kisses Dylan on both cheeks and says goodbye. Later, their black Audi estate passes him on the dirt track. Agathe turns around and smiles at him, waves and mouths 'take care', her eyes lingering out of the back window. A possible future gone.

He makes his way up and down the wooded hills. It's so beautiful it makes him slightly nervy, almost angry. Reaching a small town, washed out in ochres and purples, he walks through a little market, helps himself to handfuls of cherry tomatoes, five or six different colours in boxes all lined up. He steers well clear of the tourists in linen suits and white hats, pervs off the slim, elegant Frenchwomen.

It's midnight when Dylan reaches the hilltop village of Lacoste. Silence. The old buildings silhouetted tall and black against the dark-blue sky. He can hear his shoes chafing quietly on the calade stone as he walks.

He's dusty after a day on the road and sweaty after the climb up the hill, cold droplets running down the bond-melted inner seams of his Peter Storm. He stops for a rest by the fountain, the bubbling noise breaking the silence, the spray twinkling under the stars and moonlight. He sits down in the shadows, breathes slowly, satisfied with the dust on his boots and glad to have the rucksack off his back.

He doesn't have any soap but he's bought a Grolsch bottle full of smelly stuff for a tenner from an old farmer woman in a battered red pick-up truck at the side of the road. Turns out it's lavender oil. He dips his head in the fountain, shuddering as he cups the cool liquid to his armpits. He rubs the oil in his hair to give it half a wash, rinses his head under the faint stream of water, feeling better.

It's too late for a café or a hotel now. He finishes the last of his coffee off, then creeps down a narrow street towards some lights. Something brushes across his face. Instinctively, he falls back out of the way, scared in the darkness. Then, again, something brushes delicately over his cheek. He stands still, letting his eyes adjust, trying to catch the moonlight. He realises there are washing lines across the street with squares of coloured gauze and bits of lace hanging from them. He lets them tingle across his face while he susses out the scene.

Along one side of the street, a handful of grottos, like dungeons or caves dug into the ancient walls, are brightly lit up from the inside. The first one is completely lined with futuristic plastic sheeting, cream with a pearly sheen. The word 'Afterglow' is written on a wall and there's a little golden globe glowing in the dark. Coming through sunken speakers, Dylan can hear waves, then people speaking randomly: words, colours, shouting. It's on a loop. It reminds Dylan of *The Dark Side of the Moon*.

GANG WAR

The second grotto is refrigerated. Clear ice blocks line the walls. It's like a crystal igloo. There are ice sculptures of a living room, with two smooth ice mannequins watching an ice flat-screen telly. There's an ice ready meal in the ice micro, and ice iPod in the ice woman's ear. Dylan reads the display card. Everything in the room's made of ice except for the ice cubes in the ice man's highball glass. The ice cubes are made of human shit. From the person who made the room. Frozen cubes of it. Dylan laughs out loud.

The next one's called 'Sleeping Beauty'. The grotto's lit up with fairy lights. It smells musty and damp. The old walls are exposed and cobwebbed. There's a pink fairy tale-style bed to one side, with a heart shape carved out of the headboard and a patchwork quilt. A wooden Pinocchio is crashed on a rug, chasing with the foil off a Kit Kat and a two-quid throw-away lighter. On the other side, there's a shelf with a row of dildos on it, some with peabs still stuck to them. Dylan gets into the bed and crashes.

The sense that someone's there wakes him. It's daylight now, morning. He must have been asleep for hours. All he can see is the black outline of a girl, in pin-sharp definition, silhouetted against the strong light beaming through the low archway. A tumble of curls corkscrewing over her shoulder, looking black in the backlight, a few stray strands swaying from the outline. A top that puffs out slightly at the waist. As his eyes adjust, Dylan can make out the crinkles in the stiff material around her sides and a slightly reflective ribbon. Her jeans are skinny, tight around the crotch. There's a perfect arch of light between her legs, the silhouette so sharp he can even make out the seam of the denim.

'Elizabeth? That you?'

No reply.

'Is that you? Elizabeth?'

The dark figure turns around and is gone.

The air inside the grotto is heavy and hot now, like a tent. Dylan can smell his breath reflecting back off the heavy quilt. Cheese, coffee and sweat. He gets out of the bed and runs outside, trying to get his trainers on fast. A Japanese tourist steps back shocked. A middle-aged American woman wearing a green golf visor thinks he's part of the installation.

For half an hour he tries to find her. He looks out of place, scares the students eating their breakfast in the café. 'Do you know an English girl? Her name's Elizabeth.' But they fuck him off. He tails off as they look away, embarrassed and awkward. They're startled by his scruffiness and his urgency. He's unwashed, with his laces half undone. Then he goes into the college and looks around an exhibition room. No one. Nowhere. Not her.

Can't do nothing until he's got himself together. He gets a room in a hotel, cleans his teeth, takes a shower, puts some new gear on. His impatience overtakes him. He's still wet when he pulls on his last pair of fresh kecks.

Then, carefully, he digs it out from the bottom of the rucksack. The thing he's been keeping all this time, waiting until he met her once again. He scoops out the green Lacoste top, brushes it down, inspects the row of pinhole burns. Other than them, it's pristine.

He shoots off into the slopey streets, heads through the ancient fortified gates. He plots up outside a bar called the Café de Sade. Her kind of place, he's half thinking: faint pink walls, ivy falling over the crumbling plaster. But no show. After four hours, he's seen no sign of her, and Lacoste is a small place. There's not that many places to go. His stomach begins to turn over. She's got off. For sure. He just knows it. He goes over it in his head. She ran away to here to get away from everything. Then a blast from the past turns up out of the blue. No wonder she's fucked off. Who wouldn't?

Would she want to see the lad who'd got her shagged up the arse by four rapists, who'd been responsible for fucking her life up completely? Dylan shakes his head. How could he have been so fucking stupid? Coming here, just like that, thinking it would all be back on, like the soft cunt that he is.

This is a nightmare. He'll have to get off fast or he'll cause her even more grief. Then he spots it. The library. Savannah School of Art and Design Library, says the sign. It's an old shop that's been converted. He opens the low door quietly. No bell goes off. It's a small room with two red leather armchairs in the middle and a big silver '60s lamp arching over. On the table are some massive books of photographs. And there she is. Alone, her back turned to him, putting some books on a shelf. Just like she was the first time he saw her, at The Place.

Fear and love rise within him at the same time. Without turning around she knows he's there. But she refuses to face him. Embarrassment and humiliation, Dylan guesses. Maybe, but what the fuck does he know about getting raped and all the shit that goes with it? She deffo isn't playing the victim, however. Her back's straight, her stance confident.

Without turning, she suddenly speaks. 'What did you come here for?'

'Cos I had to see you.'

Elizabeth says nothing at first, picks up a book and slots it into place. 'Why do you want to see me?'

'Because I have to. I don't know why.'

'But we hardly know each other.'

For a moment, Dylan's thrown off. Has he read it wrong? He feels awkward, like he's been caught stalking her. She's right, after all – they don't know each other. A few nights together, a long time ago. Then he'd got her raped. *Hardly the fucking big romance, was it?*

It's a good move by her, the 'we don't know each other' line. *A fucking pearler, to be fair.* Leaves him nowhere to go, lost for words. But she moves slightly, almost nervously. *Is she blagging it?* Does she want him to continue?

He carries on, fronts it out. 'I needed to see you. That's all.'

'Why?'

'Cos I fucking love you. Is that e-fucking-nough?'

Elizabeth turns around. She's still beautiful. No one could deny it. Dylan feels ashamed. He'd half-expected her to be disfigured, defiled in some way. But she hasn't changed. In fact, she looks better. Strength shines out of her eyes. But still she's not having any of it. 'It's not enough, Dylan, I'm afraid.' She pushes past him and gets off, saying over her shoulder, 'I want you to leave, Dylan. I don't want you here.'

He starts to tramp back towards his hotel. A first rumble of thunder snaps loudly, racing in from nowhere. Dylan's on edge and angry, and it startles him. Within seconds, the rain is heavy. He can see lightning breaking in the distance, like a faraway battle. Suddenly, he turns around and runs back after Elizabeth.

When he catches up with her, he grabs her arm and swings her round.

'You can't just leave it like this,' he tells her.

'Why did you stop calling me?'

'Because it was my fault they raped you. That's why.'

She looks blankly at him. Dylan knows that she already knew but she wanted to hear it from him. Her hair's drenched flat now, the stiff cotton of her top wilted.

'I felt ashamed. I was as good as guilty of it. They raped you to get at me.'

'If you knew that, why didn't you come to tell me? Anything would have been better than nothing.' Dylan has fuck all to say. 'I knew it wasn't you who raped me, Dylan. Of course I did. But when I didn't see you, it felt like that. It felt like you were standing by whoever it was. By them rather than me.' The skies blackened now, except for a bruised sun tussling with clouds and lightning on the horizon.

'Do you know how that felt Dylan? Not only had I been raped but I thought I'd been betrayed as well. As good as raped again. By the person I'd just fallen in love with. Dylan?'

Dylan rolls with the blows, taking hope from her admission of love. But then she turns on him, furious. 'You destroyed my life, Dylan. You fucked it up completely. Like the way you . . . you *people* fuck up everything you touch. I played with fire getting involved with you, Dylan. Thought I was being some kind of . . .'

She turns to one side, then looks back at him again. 'Do you know how much you fucked me up, Dylan? D'you really want to know how much damage you did? I'll fucking tell you anyway. For a year, I couldn't even go near a man. And then when I finally did, only when I was blind drunk, d'you know the only thing that turned me on, Dylan?' Her voice tails off. She doesn't bother telling him the rest.

It's like a bad trip. He has his head in his hands by now.

'What? Don't you like it, Dylan? Your perfect vision spoiled, your little posh girl fucked up. Thought you could come here . . . Fuck you, Dylan.'

* * *

When Dylan gets back to his digs, his head's wrecked and his stomach's knotted up. He spews all over the fresh white sink, his head spinning. He can't get over the way she spoke. His head's burnt out by it.

He packs his gear, pays the bill in advance, telling the woman that he's leaving early doors to catch a train. But the next day, she's waiting outside for him when he leaves.

'Listen,' Elizabeth says, 'what I said last night was true. Every single word of it. But it's how I felt at the time, Dylan. It's not how I feel now. Or rather it's not how I think. It all came out again. Because I've been waiting since the day it happened to see you, Dylan. There's not a day that's gone by, not a fucking hour, when I haven't thought of you. Of hating you. And loving you.'

Elizabeth tells him that a few months after the rape she vowed to herself that she wasn't going to be a victim, that it wasn't going to make her bitter or hard either. She was living back with her mum and dad. 'For a few months, I lost all my confidence. I lost all trust with people. I was a wreck, Dylan. Defeated.'

'Not surprised, girl,' says Dylan, trying to make her feel better. Anger's welling up inside him now. He wants to torture Nogger.

'But slowly I got a bit better. I just accepted that I'd been raped. I kept thinking that it was just fate or something. That it wasn't my fault. And that helped. I told myself that it only affected my body, not my mind. I let it go, Dylan. I let it go.'

CHAPTER 34

PLANS

He stays in Lacoste. He wants to get to know her properly this time. They're settling in to the good life now, a touch of healthy living, spending their weekends at the beach. He's stopped answering his mobile from back home, turned it off a few weeks ago. A few messages still come through from Holland now and again, saying Dean is asking about him, asking him to come back to work, promising him all kinds of dough. But even they drop off as the summer draws to a close.

Dylan's getting addicted to swimming in the sea, charging off the cold, the shock, the saltwater each time. For a moment, he's cleansed. He even manages to forget about Chalina in the water. As things have settled down, Chalina's drifted back into his mind more and more. Hours of tossing and turning, the hollow feeling in his stomach growing sicker. He tells himself over and over again that it was an accident, that it wasn't his bullet, that it was Nogger or Jay, those mad cunts. But no matter how many times he tells himself it was nothing to do with him, the shadow of Chalina is still there.

* * *

Dylan catches his breath in the waves, the shadows of the mountains darkening the water. Elizabeth's sitting on the beach in shorts and a T-shirt, reading her book, a cold bottle of beer on the go. He swims back to join her and she makes him a cheese sandwich as he gets dry.

'I've got some good news, Dylan,' she says. 'That job I applied for in Italy . . . I got it.' She's smiling and laughing, but Dylan tenses up. 'It's in Milan, a teaching job at the university.' Dylan looks down between his wet, sandy legs, not knowing what to say. 'You could come with me,' she says finally, giving it her boss smile.

'What? You want me to go with you?'

'Yes. We could spend the year there. Or just see out the winter, if you like. Get a flat. It'll be amazing. Once I've finished my studies, the world's our oyster. We could go travelling, anything you want. I want you to come with me, Dylan. Just me and you.'

'But what could I do?' asks Dylan, playing along, not letting her know that the shadow of Chalina is hanging over him, even there on the beach, scraping out his insides, gnawing at his conscience.

'Chill out. Get a job,' answers Elizabeth. 'Whatever takes your fancy. Learn the language. I've got a friend who works in photography over there. You could help him. Money's no good, but it's about time you learned a trade.' She smiles.

'Wow. Yeah. Never really thought of that, but it sounds good.'

'We could even stay there. Italy's a great place to bring up kids,' she says, laughing her mischievous laugh now. Dylan smiles but freezes up again. Thinking of kids just brings up the spectre of Chalina. He feels chilled by the late-summer breeze rushing in off the Camargue across the wide flat beach. He pulls his hoodie down over Elizabeth, hugs her from behind, goes to take a trackie top out of his bag for himself.

Then she calls to him, 'Wait here,' running off behind the dunes on her own, buzzing. 'OK, I'm ready now!' Dylan wallows up the dune. At the top, he sees her lying on the other side, wearing the white bikini she put on that first night. She's more gorgeous than ever. Slowly, she pulls him to the ground.

'I think we've got to celebrate the good news,' she tells him.

'I haven't got a condom.'

She smiles.

Afterwards Dylan lies gazing up into the sky, the clouds moving fast and moody now. He's half thinking of just telling her about Chalina, here and now, like he meant to do when he first found her. He'd lost his bottle. She was still a touch fragile on him, and it was still his baggage, after all. How could you unload that on anyone? Especially her, after he'd already fucked her up once with his shit. She wouldn't wear it again. And who the fuck would? A baby killer? Even Elizabeth wouldn't forgive him for that.

He's para about it, though, in case she finds out by accident. Luckily, she didn't have a TV when the story broke – she only got one after Dylan arrived and doesn't watch it much – and she avoids the papers. Says she doesn't want to know what's going on back home. Of course, she's heard about the troubles on the streets, but she's never said anything much about it to him, so he's sure she doesn't know he was involved.

Dylan switches on the news channels when she's at work. He sits off with a smoke, catches up. He likes BBC World. Better than Sky and BBC News 24 put together, he thinks. Sometimes he watches it when she's gone to bed, sits in the other room with the sound turned down. There's less and less about it on the news. The Chalina investigation has wound down. The CPA is still in there, the army still on the streets of Liverpool, as well as Salford, Moss Side, Glasgow, Nottingham, Newcastle and south-east London. The PMCs had been booted out and the torture stopped, the news said. The focus was on regeneration now. The Imperator had been right. Nogzy was going to be the next Canary Wharf or Cheshire Oaks or Trafford Centre. Whatever it was going to be, it was going to be the Imperator's finest piece of graft to date. No back answers. Dylan and the lads are dinosaurs now, and now they're gone, the Jez is wide open. It's the turn of businessmen and bankers to reap the rewards.

* * *

He knows something's very wrong the moment he walks in, the second he opens the front door, from the sullen silence of the house. Her trainies are strewn across the floor untidily, which is unusual for her. She's been sick the past few mornings and a bit moody, not wanting to get out of bed, but as he steps inside this already feels like something deeper. The whole house is silent. No scran on the go. She's usually busy making them their tea by now. But it's dead. No scent of fresh cucumber and big tomatoes, which Dylan has got used to. No chopping sound of her making a salad. No Elizabeth humming along to the mad French indie station she listens to. The house is gloomy. Dylan's abdomen turns like a cold sea. He knows she knows.

He goes up the stairs. When he gets to the top, he can hear muffled sounds of sobbing and gagging and sighs coming from their room. Dylan waits in the corridor for a second, steeling himself to front it out. He thought this day would come. But not so quick. He's flummoxed on how to play it.

He edges the little wooden door open. She's curled up on the bed, foetal-style, no kecks on, just a pair of pale-blue cotton knickers and a white vest. Spread around her on the bed are printouts from the Internet. His mugshot next to Nogger's and Jay's. And pages and pages of text, old stories from the BBC website and a couple from a French newspaper's site. Dylan stares at the pictures of Jay and Nogger. Fucking it up again.

'You never told me, Dylan. You never fucking told me.'

She's white as a sheet, eyes red and painful looking, her face bloated and soft. Dylan tries to front it out. But his head's down. He squeezes out a murmur: 'There's nothing to tell.'

Elizabeth explodes. 'What? You killed a three-year-old girl. You shot a child. And there's nothing to tell. What kind of a . . . What kind of a person are you?'

The question stings Dylan. It's as though she's saying she doesn't know him, like the day he arrived in Lacoste. As though she's cutting him dead again. 'It wasn't me,' he says. 'That there is just pure paper talk. It's an old story . . . means nothing.'

'What? It's just all made up, is it? It's all just written out of thin air, is it? Just another little thing in your past that you forgot to tell me about?'

'It's not like that. It's just . . .' But he's lost for words.

'Well, what is it like, Dylan? Shall I remind you?' She starts to read one of the stories. '"The suspects in the murder of little Chalina Murphy have been named. Dylan Olsen, 17, of Norris Green . . ."' She bursts into tears again.

'Listen, that's just Internet jangle, them throwing names in the hat without anything to back it up. You know what I was about. But I didn't shoot her. I didn't murder no one. That's just fucking shit put out there to fuck us up.'

Elizabeth picks up another piece of A4 at random, taunting him now. 'What about this one? "Chalina was killed, police say, after being shot twice, once fatally in the head. She died in her mother's arms."'

Dylan tries furiously to explain the situation. '"Fatally in the head." That makes it look deliberate. It was an accident, for fuck's sake. That's what it was – an accident. Was not meant to happen, d'you get me? Wrong place, wrong time, that's all. All that shit about being shot in the head makes it sound as though she was dropped on purpose. By an assassin or something. It's just the bizzies chatting shit.'

Elizabeth guffaws in horror. 'An accident? An . . . accident?'

'Yeah, an accident. Jay or whoever shot her by mistake.' He points at Jay's mugshot on the bed. 'Yeah, I was there. Granted. But it wasn't me who shot at her. I didn't kill her.'

PLANS

'Well, if you've got nothing to be ashamed of, then why didn't you tell me?'

'I didn't think it mattered. You weren't around then. It had nothing to do with you.'

'What?'

'I just wanted to forget about it. I was gonna tell you but . . . I forgot. I mean, I didn't know how.'

'Forgot? Oh, forgot, eh? Like the time one of your friends raped me? And you forgot I ever existed? How many other things have you forgotten to tell me? Have you forgotten which one raped me, Dylan? Which one was it, Dylan?' She holds up the picture of Jay. 'Was it him? No, he looks too young. Was it this ugly bastard?' she asks, holding up Nogger's picture. 'Then again, I suppose it doesn't matter. After all, it could have been a fucking accident.'

Dylan looks away.

'Or was it you, Dylan?' She holds up his mugshot: skinhead, scars, snarly pout. 'Was it you? And you just forgot to tell me?'

Dylan's head's wrecked by now. He doesn't know whether to cough to Nogger raping her. So he just says, 'Come on, listen, this is mad.' But she's sobbing heavily again now. Sobbing in her bedroom. Like he imagined she'd done night after night after the rape. 'If you're saying that I kept quiet about it, then, yeah, I hold my hands up. But I'm hardly going to start telling everyone, am I? Cos it's got nothing to do with me.'

'It's nothing to do with you, you say? For fuck's sake, Dylan. How can you lie to me like that?'

'I never lied to you.'

'You never mentioned it. And that's a lie by fucking omission, in my book. Which is just as fucking bad. It's not as though you crashed a car or had an affair. You went and fucking shot a beautiful little girl.'

'OK, I know I was there, but it doesn't mean it was me.'

'Hold on, Dylan. So you saw a girl shot? By one of your fucking mates? You were there? But you didn't say anything? Why didn't you go to the police?'

'Are you mad? Listen, I didn't shoot her, right. No one has ever said I have. No witnesses. No forensics. No charges. Fuck all. That's why I'm here. If I'd have pulled the trigger, I'd be in jail now.'

Elizabeth has her head in her hands. 'And here's me talking about our future together, wanting us both to go to Italy. "Oh, hello, Signor Vice

Chancellor, may I introduce you to my boyfriend, Mr Olsen. He's wanted for child murder back in our country. But it's OK, there's no forensics on him . . . yet." How stupid have I been?'

'Come on, Elizabeth, behave. You've gone fucking mad.'

Raging now, she is. A rage she wouldn't have known before she was raped. And Dylan's feeling the natural force of it.

'How pathetic am I? Sitting on the beach talking about having babies. But what would it be like, Dylan? Looking over our shoulder all the time. Waiting for the police to come for you. Or maybe you'll just shoot the kids – by fucking accident.'

After a few minutes of silence, she calms down. Dylan takes her by the shoulders, looks her straight in the eye. 'Listen to me. I didn't kill Chalina. I swear on my life that it wasn't me,' he says, using Chalina's name for the first time, for effect. He carries on explaining. She's deffo starting to come round, wanting to believe in Dylan's innocence. But she's sharp. And he knows it won't be long before she starts digging into his explanation again, looking for holes.

Dylan knows the outro he has to take. And he has to take it now, while she's on the cusp of forgiving him. It's a cunt's trick. But he knows he has to do it.

'I've got to get this off my chest,' he says, reaching over to pick up one of the pictures off the bed. She braces herself. Here it goes, she thinks, expecting the worst, that he's going to confess to killing the little girl.

Dylan hands her the mugshot of Nogger: 'You were right,' he says. 'This is the feller who raped you.'

Elizabeth falls to the floor, into a pile of dirty washing, holding up the shirts to hide her howls, soaking up the tears in a sandy beach towel.

Dylan looks on. Hurting the thing that he loves most. Hurting it in order to keep hold of it. Hurting her to save himself. 'He raped you. But I never killed the girl. OK?'

* * *

Chalina's never mentioned between them again. The worst thing is when she thanks him for telling her that it was Nogger who raped her. She says that the knowledge has finally laid it to rest.

Dylan goes skinny over the next few weeks. He stops eating for a bit. He feels all his muscles are tensed up, even starts panicking a bit, having attacks over little things. He thinks he's getting followed, starts phoning the lads back home, Pacer, Clone, New Loon, asking about Chalina, if there's still any heat from it, if the bizzies or the army have been round to his ma's asking about it.

The lads can't believe it. New Loon's like that: 'Fuck off, Dylan, it's safe. Calm down. You're home and dry.' He asks Dylan where he is but Dylan's too para to tell him. He asks Pacer about stupid things they did years ago. Robberies. Aggravated burglaries. Assaults. Asking him whether anyone has been asking about them, throwing him in for them. Pacer tells him he sounds as if he's been snorting too much. He shakes his head. 'Dylan's lost it, la. Properly gone mad. Can you believe that? Dylan Olsen?'

CHAPTER 35

REPRISE

A few weeks after Elizabeth finds out about the accident, Dylan's watching BBC World and Sky, the sunset shining through the massive open windows. It's getting cooler now, the gusts of wind outside getting longer and louder.

Suddenly pictures of the hotel flash up. Paul's hotel back home. *The Imperator's Palace*. All the front has been blown up and mangled. There's a red car half inside the lobby roaring with fire. The white marble is charred and crumbled, the girders underneath exposed and twisted. The heavy curtains are tattered, blowing out of the windows, drenched in water from the fire hoses.

Dylan turns up the sound. A reporter's stood halfway down the street, the other half of the screen showing CCTV images and shots taken earlier.

The reporter says, 'Military police have confirmed that a car bomb was driven into the front of the hotel behind me at around one o'clock today. Bomb-disposal experts believe the car was armed with an improvised explosive device and detonated inside the lobby to cause maximum loss of life.

'One source has told Sky News that a cocktail of industrial fireworks, petrol and gas canisters may have been used. Six people are so far reported to have been killed, including three members of the security forces.

'As we know, this hotel, one of the higher-end venues in the region, was popular with officers deployed on anti-TerrorCrime operations in the city's North End.'

Dylan fucks this off. He knows what this is about straight away, and it certainly isn't insurgency against the army or the CPA. Dylan turns the telly down for a second, walks around the room in his boxies, half shocked, half trying to work it out. He notices that Elizabeth has left a note on the table:

> Good afternoon, Gorgeous – you lazy git.
> Felt sick again this morning. But now I think I know why!!!!????
> Got something to tell you, I think!!!!! Start packing for next
> week if you can. See you tonight.

Dylan puts it down, his head too wrecked to give it the time of day. He turns the telly back up, and the fat-faced local-radio phone-in host he saw visiting the scene of Chalina's murder is punditing-up the tragedy, saying that the city is pulling together in mourning, that the members of the security forces who were blown up were heroes. But Dylan knows they weren't the targets, that they were just collateral damage.

He turns over to BBC World.

A blonde reporter is positioned outside the police cordon. 'More casualties have been confirmed, including a forty-seven-year-old man and a second man aged fifty-two.' Dylan nods, working out how old Paul was. 'One of the men is believed to be an international businessman.' The banks in the Far East and the mines in the Baltic. 'Local sources describe the men as well-known community leaders.' Journo shorthand for 'gangsters'. 'Merseyside Police have confirmed that both men were known to them.' Dylan laughs at the understatement.

He rags his mobile out from his rucksack underneath the bed, switches it on and listens as dozens of unread texts and unlistened-to messages bleep their arrival. Dylan bells Nogger, keying in the Dutch mobile number from memory.

'Was that you?' he asks straight off.

Nogger doesn't answer, just tells him to call him back on a safe sat phone, texts him the number a few minutes later. Dylan's going mad with impatience now. But he knows from Nogger's silence and the sat phone behaviour what the answer will be.

'Fuck's sake, lad,' he says when he gets Nogger again. 'Why the fuck did you blow up Paul?' He's not bothering with his usual careful handling of Nogger. This is too huge.

'He had to go, lad. He was saying all kinds, lad.'

'But it was Paul. Our mate. Our sponsor. Our fucking boss.'

'Not my boss, lad,' Nogger retorts, a bit stung. 'Anyway, lad, now he's out the way, it makes life a lot easier, graft-wise. Cos it's wide open now, d'you get me? Anyone's business, innit?'

'What? What? Anyone's business? Do you mean your business? That you're going to take over Paul's graft? You've gone mad, lad. Can't believe you're speaking like that.'

'Like what?' asks Nogger, a touch embarrassed by his boasting, a touch enraged by Dylan buzzing off him for it.

'This is not the filmies, lad. No one's Tony Montana here, lad. No one can front this.' Nogger's humiliated by Dylan's *Scarface* put-down. Dylan carries on, even though he knows he's risking it here. Doesn't matter that Nogger's 500 miles away. 'Paul's firm'll be on your case big time, lad. D'you get me? No one's going to let this go. They'll be on my case, Jay's case . . . every one of us. We'll all have to get on our toes, for ever.'

'Not arsed about all that. As you say, it's not the filmies, is it? Not going to be a big mad settling of scores at the end, either. It's just business as usual.'

'Business as usual? What about Dean and Richard? They're not going to be happy, are they? That you've dropped their impresario, their mate of 30 years, their main backer, their fucking protector.'

'Don't be worrying about them pair.'

'Why not?'

'They're gone.'

'What do you mean gone?'

'Gone. I mean just that they're gone.'

'Gone?'

'Yeah, gone. How many times do I have to say it?'

'D'you mean just gone away? Or proper gone?'

'Just gone. Gone. Gone. Gone.'

Nogger hands the phone over to Jay and tells him to tell Dylan what's happened to Dean and Richard. Dylan hears a bit of rustling of pockets and hoods as Jay takes the phone, the tunes from his DS tinkering away. Then he comes on the phone and says, 'Gone,' while he's still playing. Then he hands the phone back to Nogger.

'D'you understand now?'

'I can't believe it. Not only Paul but them two as well?' asks Dylan. But he refrains from any further insults.

'Listen, I did it for fucking you, right. For us. You don't understand what's going on now. You're living wherever you are, doing what you're doing. Meanwhile, back in the real world, it's coming on top badly.'

Dylan goes quiet, taking the slight, waiting for the explanation. 'Paul was getting out of order. He was saying bad things about you and me. The cunt was planning to have us ironed.'

'No fucking way,' says Dylan, like he just heard a bit of too-much gossip.

'Yes way, lad.'

'You're fucking joking, aren't you?'

Nogger switches the chat away from Paul, deftly showing off his new business skills. 'But he was only half the fucking problem. It's Chalina's ma. She's behind it all. She's kicking off all over the place.'

'Hold on, you've lost me here. Paul. Dean. Richard. Gone. Gone. Gone. But the problem itself has not gone. And it's Chalina's ma?'

'She's planning to stir all the shit up again. All the shit about us, me, you and Jay, on the anniversary of Chalina's death next week.'

'What?' Dylan's head's burnt out now.

'She's going to go on telly to call for us to be nicked by SOCA and Interpol. I've had fucking *Panorama* following me about all week. The police and the army say they can't arrest us cos there's still no evidence against us. No murder weapon. No witnesses. But she's threatening to go on telly and cause loads of shit about it. Blame us, the bizzies, everyone.'

'Someone's chatting shit to you, mate. Winding you up.'

'Dylan, lad. It's 100 per cent. We've had it checked out back home. The Devil's on it and everything. Next week, she's going to Parliament, she's saying she's going to see the fucking Queen and everything. She's going to go on the telly saying that we shot her daughter and we're laughing in the face of the law and dancing on Chalina's grave.'

'So what? It'll die down afterwards. And what the fuck does that have to do with Paul?'

'He lined himself up with her, gave her all kinds of info on us to make himself sweet with the bizzies. Making himself look like a nice feller with all his new mates. The fucking business people. Straight-goers. Even the CPA and all that crowd. You wouldn't believe it, mate, what he was getting up to.'

'You're saying Paul was a grass?'

'Not saying. I know. Even better, I can prove it, lad. I've seen *the paperwork*.' He's super-showing off now.

Dylan's shocked at this. Before anyone can be called a grass, especially someone as high up as Paul, as staunch as him, there has to be paperwork. To prove to the lads that it's not just jangle or jealousy or sour grapes. Deps. Contact sheets. Undercover police reports. Anything. But it has to be in black and white before anyone will believe it, never mind act on it.

'Chalina's ma went to see him, asking him to use his sway with the lads to get the Chalina thing cleared up. He said that he would. Said that he'd help break the wall of silence and all that bollocks, find out where we stashed the evidence, the weapons, all that.'

'No way, Nogger. Paul? A midnight mass? Fuck off.'

'Telling you, lad. Paul was telling all the lads back home that we were little cunts and he was gonna serve us up to the bizzies, with fucking witnesses and everything.'

'Fuck off. You must have it wrong. You're talking about the staunchest feller on the planet.'

Nogger is bored of Paul now. Ancient history. 'I need you here, Dylan. There's graft to be done. Chalina's ma has to be *spoken to*.'

Dylan knows what that means. He drops the phone, head blown, gone. Nogger wants the mother killed. He has to get to The Dam now, to speak to Nogger, to talk some sense into him. If not, he has to be stopped. Dylan thinks of Chalina's death hanging over him. His conscience can't cope with another one.

He gets dressed, fishes out four grand's worth of euros from his stash. Grabs his phone charger and a couple of IMED-scrubbed pay-as-you-go SIM cards, pockets them. He finds two jarg passports he's hidden, puts one down his bollocks, the other with his moody IDs in his arse pocket. Then he tips the rest of his worldly possessions onto the bed. His old bottle-green Lacoste, some paperwork and bank cards, a few other bits and pieces. Other than the clothes he's standing up in, that's everything there is to prove that he was ever there.

None of his three bank accounts is in his name. They're all numbered accounts, Internet password accessible, with debit cards he's activated but never used. He takes out a pen and slowly writes down instructions and passwords on the back of an old statement.

Then he picks up the postcard of Cerne Abbas that Elizabeth gave him on their first night together. The fertility symbol.

Elizabeth,
I've got to go away a while. Know you don't want me to but
it's something I can't run away from. Someone I know needs a

bit of help. So I've got to go and get something sorted. Know we're off to Italy next week but if I'm not back take my gear. And I'll be there one way or another, don't you worry. Got some dough there. Look at the note on the statement. Use it to get us set up. Do what you want with it. It's ours.

And don't worry – I'll do the right thing and get back to you as soon as.

Lots of luv,
Dylan

CHAPTER 36

REDEMPTION

Dylan jumps a taxi to Marseilles and a shuttle flight to Schiphol. Jay phones him with the address of their new graft pad. Dylan switches taxis three times, just to make sure, first going through the old town, getting lost in the busy streets, in the shadows of the old buildings, checking reflections in their windows. Then he cruises through a neighbourhood of big, detached houses, footballer-style, with high walls, pillars and private security.

Nogger's new pad is massive, a mish-mash of Renaissance style and Spanish haçienda. Dylan buzzes the intercom. A familiar voice answers and Dylan's blood freezes. Through the gates, up the path. The glossy white double doors open and there she is. Stood there in a goldy-beige backless silk dress, split right up the side. 'For fuck's sake,' says Casey. 'Look what the cat dragged in.'

Dylan pushes past her. Jay's stood there in a black Paul Smith shirt and a pair of dress kecks, a baggy black Helly Hansen draped over him. 'Dylan, mate. Made up to see you.'

'What's she doing here?'

'Casey's been over here for a while now, lad. Her and Nogger, you know . . .'

'Fuck's sake. Should have known. People getting dropped, left, right and centre. Should have known that she'd be at the centre of it all, putting him up to all kinds.'

Casey laughs. 'You know me, Dylan. Always found success a turn-on. How you doing anyway, hun?' she asks, looking him up and down, taking in his old green kagoul, his grown-out skinhead, his hair about an inch long now.

Dylan carries on walking, asks Jay, 'Where's Nogger?'

''Ere y'are, I'll show you through. He's in the bath.'

The main entrance is protected by a walk-through metal detector and a ThruVision scanner. A sign on the arch reads 'To protect against person-borne suicide attacks'. Jay looks a bit sheepish. 'Mad, innit? But Nogger's gone pure para. Thinks everyone's on his case.'

Dylan walks with Jay through the marble corridors, past gold statues and fountains. 'Where d'us get the pad?'

'Richard's, wannit? Took it off him after he went. Threw his wife and kids out.'

Jay opens the double doors into the brown marble bathroom. Nogger's in a sunken hot tub with gold taps in the shape of eagles, watching a bluey on a giant home-cinema system. He's trying to stop the bubbles wetting the remote, cursing the mini-mountains of foam. He swims over to the other side when Dylan comes in. 'Made up to see you, mate,' he says as he gets out, long Everton shorts sticking to his legs. ''Ere y'are, let's have a chat.'

He sits down on one of the sunbeds, asks Dylan, 'You OK?'

'Sound.'

'Listen, let's get down to business.' He's showing off again now, playing the time-poor higher-up with a lot of graft on the go. 'Chalina's ma has got to go. Proper. And I want you to do it.'

Dylan says nothing, just looks down at the puddles Nogger's dripping shorts are making on the floor.

'The other problem is the bits. The two Mac-10s and the .455 that did Chalina. They're the only thing in the world that connects us to her. I've had them buried on a field in The Boot, but they need to be fetched and slung for good.'

'So what are you saying?'

'Take the bits out the ground. Bin two of them. And use the other one to do Chalina's ma.'

'You want me to shoot the girl's ma? With the same fucking guns that shot her daughter? You're one sick puppy, you, lad.'

'Listen, lad, if we don't fucking get rid of her, we'll all be getting nicked. It'll be thirties and forties for all of us. By the time we get out of the shovel, we'll be auld men.'

Dylan thinks of Elizabeth. Of setting up a new life in Italy. Of doing one last piece of graft. Graft that will free him up for the rest of his life. No evidence. No case. No worries. Dylan thinks about what Elizabeth said when they first met, about freedom making you happy. This would release him for ever. He reasons it up in his mind.

'Why me?' he asks. 'Why not you or Jay?'

'I'm too on top. And he can't do it on his own. Only you can think through a bit of graft like this.' Nogger pushes on, seeing that Dylan's on a wobble, that he isn't that arsed about doing it: 'We might never fucking get out of jail. Remember, we're kiddie killers. We're as good as nonces in the jug. Everyone'll fucking hate us.'

Dylan looks up, watches Casey coming down in the glass lift, wearing a white bikini, showing off her new F-cups. She's had all the fat sliced off her arse. The semi-cylindrical doors open and she steps out and into the pool, looking daggers at Dylan. 'You coming in, hun?' she asks Nogger.

He ignores her and pulls Dylan in close to whisper in his ear, not wanting to speak about weakness out loud. 'Remember, you can't get a gun into jail. Remember, at the end of the day what are we without our bits and bobs? Nothing. Just skinny, white young ones. What are we gonna do when a six-foot-wide nigger growls at us. All the people we've terrored over the years. All the smackheads we've told off.' Nogger's thinking of the baghead he mugged outside the chemist and the hundreds like him who'll march on them like zombies, who'll have their day, who'll want their revenge. 'In the jug, Dylan, them people clean up. We'll be annihilated. Think about that, lad.'

Nogger keeps up the hard sell, showing off his negotiating skills, going in for the close: 'Listen, once you've done it, I'll give you half of what I've made so far in The Dam. That's five or six million euros, Dylan. I've been grafting for both of us over here, Dylan. I've had your back ever since we've been here. You can go anywhere with that kind of dough. *With whoever you like.* Sit off in luxury for the rest of your life.' Casey switches the bluey back on and starts lathering herself up, closing her eyes and then looking over at Dylan. 'D'you get me?' Nogger asks.

Dylan thought about Elizabeth. It's true. With that kind of dough, he could go anywhere. They could go anywhere. Be anyone.

'And with Chalina's ma gone, we've got no more Chalina case hanging over us. The bizzies and the army *want* to drop the case, Dylan. They want to fucking bin it for ever. They've got what they wanted: total control of the streets, armed police, the estates crushed. The breadheads have got what they wanted: prime real estate, new shopping centre, nice new skyscraper, us out the way, not grafting on their patch. It's a win-win. But they can't fucking forget about it while that slag's still dancing up and down about it.'

Dylan doesn't respond. Nogger keeps lovebombing him with reasons. 'The bottom line is this,' he says, talking his new language of international supergraft. 'Everyone hates Chalina's ma anyway. Trying to become famous on the back of her kid being shot – it's fucking disgusting. She deserves to be shot, lad. She's a dog.'

Dylan can see where Nogger's coming from. The Chalina thing's water under the bridge now. Everyone's got on with their lives. The bizzies. The businessmen. Nogger. Even him. Even Elizabeth.

'If Chalina's ma goes on telly crying again,' says Nogger, 'it'll bring it on top for everybody. And at the end of the day, nothing she does is gonna bring back Chalina anyway. It's just going to ruin all their lives. And after all, it was a fucking accident. Why should we pay the fucking price? It wasn't our fucking fault.

'There's only one way out of this nightmare, and she's blocking the door. No one wants to do it. But sometimes . . . listen, where would you rather be: sat on a beach in Thailand or fuck knows where, eating prawns the size of bananas, or sat in Walton jail getting shagged by a six-foot nigger?'

Dylan thinks of Elizabeth again. She's taken him back twice, against the odds each time, when she was totally within her rights to fuck him off. She won't do it a third time if he fucks her life up again, if all of this Chalina shit comes flying back. She'll cast him adrift. 'OK,' he says. 'I'll go.'

'That's the spirit, lad. Knew you wouldn't let the lads down.'

※ ※ ※

Early doors the next day, Dylan's moving through Schiphol, through the cathedral of light, sure and slow. Through the colours and shapes. He's totally hooded up. Silvery grey light floods in through the angled glass ceiling, glinting off the moving walkways, washing over tired eyes.

He glides past the coffee stands, past the Dutch breakfast bars, past the duty-free cabinets. Onto the plane, business class, the hood pulled down tightly over his head. He stares straight ahead. An air hostess leans in trippily. Her lips move but he can't hear what she's saying. He leaves the coffee and croissant untouched. Suits eye him up nervously from behind their laptops.

GANG WAR

Through the smudgy porthole, dawn breaks above the clouds, a spray of gold light fanning up on the horizon, shining off the brilliant white and glinting on the brushed steel of the wing. All the way, Dylan hears a strange ringing in his ears.

He's the first off at John Lennon, bails through baggage reclaim, travelling light. Shows his moody passport at the Borders Agency. The police spotters miss him, a black shadow moving too fast past the two-way mirrors.

Cold blue light. The city's waking up. A biting breeze sweeps across it, fresh off the Approaches. Dylan jogs on, cross country, over the backs, through the fields and factories, down the backstreets. It won't be long before the bizzies lock on. They'll be scanning the images from the CCTV at arrivals through the visual recognition system. He slips through the concrete and weeds, through the wide open spaces, the only sound his own breathing. He heads down the railway tracks, up the embankments, mask on, flaps open, Velcroed-up. Sweat filters out through the Gore-tex of his jacket, air streaming in through the micropores.

He's onto the estate, ready to go, taking it easy through the streets. His old neighbours spot him, exchanging glances and whispers. Curtains are twitching. Word's going round already, that he's home, that he's returned. Women look out of their windows, peek round doors and through spyholes, get on their phones and computers. Kids are told to come inside. The shutters are going down. An old docker-type, hobbling past with his paper, clocks Dylan and shakes his head. He can see what's coming. 'Do what's right, lad,' he says.

Dylan heads for the field Nogger told him about, digs up the parcel. Kids and mas are hanging off the railings now. Shouts of 'Go on', 'You can do it, lad', 'Put her out of her misery'. Word's going round fast now. He leaves the square of oilcloth next to the hole. He picks up the pieces, lashes the .455 in his side pocket, de-clips one of the Mac-10s. He puts the barrel and stock in the other pocket, the second Mac-10 down his jacket, held close to his belly by the toggle.

He marches on. More people are coming out now, braving it, on their doorsteps, at their gates, on their garden walls. They're staring, shouting, smiling.

He heads through the gated community and onto the estate. Saloons are in the driveways, engines on, ready to go to work. Men are kissing their wives goodbye, wiping frost off their windscreens. Dylan stands in front of Chalina's gate, clips up the Mac-10 and slings it over his shoulder, IDF-style on a short strap. He has the second Mac-10 in one hand, the .455 in the other.

He boots the black and gold gate open. The white front door opens and Lynda's stood there in a pink nightgown. Her husband's behind her in a white short-sleeved shirt and a tie. He's trying to get her back inside, putting pressure on her shoulder. He tries to kick the door shut but it falls off at the lower hinge.

Blue light sparkles in the double glazing. White UPVC surrounds shuddering. The gate bangs shut, the wind blowing her hair. She breaks free of her husband, makes a run for it down the path. Dylan brings up the guns, spying the reflection of the red dots on his skin, glinting off the brass fittings of the door.

Bang! The first bullet cracks the back of his skull away, lifting a chunk of hair and bone. The second round goes through his cheek. The hovering OH6 above sways mildly with the recoil. The marksman hanging off the side steadies himself for the third, but the ARV on the ground opens up, firing rounds from a Heckler into Dylan's shoulder and back.

Dylan falls forward, his body straight. He falls into her arms. She strokes his face. It's laid to rest, the evidence in her hands.

GLOSSARY

baba	the Turkish term for 'godfather', used to refer to an older, senior Turkish heroin trafficker
back-door	betray or rip off
baghead	heroin or crack addict
bar	£1 million (derived from trading-floor slang for a unit on a bar graph on a computer screen)
base	riot van
beak	cocaine
beaut	general term of abuse
beno	benzocaine, a painkiller used to cut street cocaine
bin lid	kid (rhyming slang)
brown	heroin
bug	yellow police van, usually a StreetSafe.
buck	bullets (abbreviation of 'buckshot')
buff	pounds, quid
bukakke	to cover something in a liquid or powder by spraying it or squirting it liberally (derived from pornographic film slang for a particularly over-the-top final scene)
burg	burglary
cone	fat, conical-shaped joint
contact sheets	police documents logging meetings with informants and information supplied
cop for	ambush or accost; steal in a smash-and-grab raid
corner	a quarter kilo of heroin or cocaine
dark	heroin
deps	court depositions
diesel Mercs	Turks (rhyming slang)

GLOSSARY

dollars	money in general
fairsensabough	fair enough (backslang)
feds	police
the Flat Place	Holland
GPMG	General Purpose Machine Gun
gorping	stoned state in which the smoker stares aimlessly, often characterised by a smirking, gormless expression
green	home-grown skunk cannabis
grid	face, mouth, teeth or smile
jack	undercover CID officer
jarg	illegal, stolen, counterfeit
John Gotti	shotgun (rhyming slang for 'shottie')
John Waynies	trainers (rhyming slang for 'trainies')
ken/kennel	home
ki	kilo
let-on	greeting, acknowledgement to an associate, usually understated
long feller	full-length shotgun
Lowies	black, hooded-up mountain gear, including brands such as Lowe Alpine, Berghaus, Northface
LZ	landing zone
militai	working on drug deals abroad
mouthpiece	bragger, talker
naked	not carrying a gun
nine	9-mm pistol
ocifer	policeman
OT	out of town
quid	£1 million
scraigs	knickers or boxer shorts
ship	police riot van
sick	good, dangerous or lethal
side-by-side	double-barrelled shotgun
slipping	moving through a rival gang's area, usually covertly
snide	sneaky person
The Snow	North Liverpool, so nicknamed because it is a predominantly white area
spark	knock out
steds	steroids

stoley	stolen car
stripes	(lines of) cocaine
Subutex	heroin substitute; alternative to methadone
sussies	suspenders
twenty bag	a £20 bag of drugs
wagar	war (backslang)
whisky	cocaine (W in the phonetic alphabet, referring to 'white')
white	cocaine
winnet	general term of abuse
wool	from the country or out of town